Dear Reader,

The Red Hat Society®, an international "disorganization" of women, came into being as the result of a happy accident. One woman gave another a gift of a red hat and a copy of a famous poem that suggested that one can grow older without losing one's playful spirit!

There is an inherent excitement in this view of life. Red Hatters refuse to passively sit back and allow life to slowly lose its fizz. We prop open the doors to our minds, determined to explore, learn, and find ways to infuse play into our lives.

Within a few short years, more than one million women all over the world have rushed to join this playgroup. Wearing the highly symbolic red hats on our (graying) heads, we search out and embrace opportunities to enrich our lives. The Red Hat Society philosophy of life suggests that one is never too old to make new friends, try new things, or have adventures. One of our favorite catchphrases is, "We aren't *done* yet!"

So it is with great excitement that I introduce you to this *official* new line of Red Hat Society romance novels. Featuring stories of men and women finding romance in midlife, and women of "red hat age" making new friends and meeting new challenges, these novels were written to touch your heart and inspire you. You'll also meet some wonderful younger characters, like runaway teen Rachel in this first book, who changes the lives of the three women who shelter her.

I hope you enjoy ACTING THEIR AGE and the forthcoming Red Hat romances. The heroines will be women like you, women who look into the future knowing that it can still test them, surprise them, and take them places they never expected to go.

In friendship,

Sue Ellen Cooper

ATTENTION CORPORATIONS AND ORGANIZATIONS:
Most WARNER books are available at quantity discounts
with bulk purchase for educational, business, or sales
promotional use. For information, please call or write:

Special Markets Department, Warner Books, Inc.,
1271 Avenue of the Americas, New York, NY 10020-1393
Telephone: 1-800-222-6747 Fax: 1-800-477-5925

The Red Hat Society's

Acting Their Age

∞

Regina Hale Sutherland

WARNER
VISION
BOOKS

NEW YORK   BOSTON

If you purchase this book without a cover you should be aware that this book may have been stolen property and reported as "unsold and destroyed" to the publisher. In such case neither the author nor the publisher has received any payment for this "stripped book."

Copyright © 2005 by The Red Hat Society, Inc.
All rights reserved. No part of this book may be reproduced in any form or by any electronic or mechanical means, including information, storage and retrieval systems, without permission in writing from the publisher, except by a reviewer who may quote brief passages in a review.

Warner Vision is a registered trademark of Warner Books.

Book design and text composition by L&G McRee

Warner Books

Time Warner Book Group
1271 Avenue of the Americas
New York, NY 10020
Visit our Web site at www.twbookmark.com

Printed in the United States of America

First Printing: December 2005

10 9 8 7 6 5 4 3 2 1

The Red Hat Society's

Acting Their Age

Chapter 1

Muddy Creek, Texas, January 7

Mia MacAfee hated mornings, but at five A.M. on Friday, hers were the first bootprints in the two inches of sugar-soft snow that had fallen during the night.

It's the best part of the day, Mia, she imagined Dan whispering in her ear. *Why would you want to snooze it away?*

Mia glanced over her shoulder, half expecting to see her husband behind her, a wink from his flashing green eyes, his lopsided smile and crooked front tooth. Instead, she saw only the curved pathway she had carved through the sleeping streets of Muddy Creek. In her mind, she whispered back to him, *Okay, Dan MacAfee, you win. It is beautiful. Peaceful, too. And cozy, in a weird sort of way. But the quilt on our bed is also all those things and it's* warm.

They had these conversations from time to time,

Mia and her dead husband, the same intimate banter they'd indulged in when he was alive. The talks kept Mia sane, though she suspected if she told anyone, they might disagree with that assessment of her mental state.

Like every morning, Mia made her way to the Brewed Awakening, the coffee shop she'd opened four years ago with Leanne Chilton, her most unlikely friend, as Dan used to call her. A year ago September, only a couple of weeks before Dan died, she recalled sitting with him in the stands at a football game in Brister where their son coached. When the band marched onto the field, the brass section drowning out everything else, Dan laughed and said that if women were instruments, Leanne would be a trumpet. All brassy and full of sass. "Now *you*, on the other hand," he started, then some kid had dumped a Coke in his lap, ending the conversation. It was one of many talks left incomplete between them, little discussions they probably would've continued at some point, had he lived.

While Mia had no clue what instrument she'd be, her friend Aggie Cobb was another story. Dan hadn't gotten around to Aggie, either, but Mia saw the older woman as a flute. Upbeat, fluttery, happy. Or a bass drum. Steady as a heartbeat, predictable, reliable.

Unlike her friendship with Leanne, Dan understood her friendship with Aggie. So did Mia. Which was why she was up and out this morning so much earlier than usual. Some things in life are more important than an extra hour beneath the covers, Mia thought. Some things can't wait. Some things are so troublesome they have the power to jar even a morning-hater awake before the alarm.

Please, God, please let her be in the kitchen like always, kneading the sweet roll dough, humming along to Patsy Cline.

Mia shoved her fallen purse strap up to her shoulder then settled one mitten-covered hand atop the stack of clean, folded tablecloths she carried. How old was Aggie's mother when her mind started slipping? Older than Aggie, surely. Much older. Seventy, at least.

Seventy.

A sigh slipped past her lips in a puff of smoky white as Mia remembered that Aggie wasn't much younger than seventy. It didn't seem possible her friend had turned sixty-eight last month. She remembered Aggie's mom, Sally, at seventy as a fragile, defeated old woman. But Aggie sparkled with life and enthusiasm. She had the most positive attitude of anyone Mia knew. Up until last week she had, anyway. Or was it the week before?

Mia couldn't pinpoint the moment the changes started. At first only little things caught her attention. No smiles for the customers. No corny jokes. Long stretches of time unpunctuated by Aggie's usual cheerful chatter. Then, on Tuesday, she burned three batches of sweet rolls, one right after the other. On Wednesday, she forgot to add baking soda to the blueberry muffin batter and the muffins came out rock hard. Aggie blamed the oven for both incidents, complaining that Leanne and Mia bought "cheap" merchandise. Yesterday, Aggie burst into tears when Old Man Miller wished her a Happy New Year. Then she missed a curve in the road on the way home from work and mowed down the decorated spruce tree in Joe and Missy Potter's front yard.

A heartbreaking air of sadness surrounded Aggie lately. Most of the time, she seemed only physically present, her mind a million miles away. At fifty, both Mia and Leanne were eighteen years younger, but they had always had to stay on their toes to outrun, outsmart, or outwit Aggie. As the only morning person of the three, Aggie volunteered to open the shop every day when they'd hired her to work part-time. Each morning, she arrived by four-thirty to start the baking. Mia normally dragged herself out of bed and joined her an hour and a half later. They unlocked the door for customers at seven. Then, by eight-thirty or nine, Leanne, who was dangerous to talk to before noon, showed up, cranky and grumbling, and Aggie left for home at ten.

Drawing crisp, cold air into her lungs, Mia tried to divert her mind to other, happier things. Cold or not, she loved the snow, as long as the wind didn't blow, which was as rare in Muddy Creek as rain in the Sahara. This particular morning settled around her like a sleeping baby's sigh. The air seemed reluctant to disturb the silence; even the naked trees refused to shiver.

Though already a week into the New Year, a few houses on the side streets off Main still twinkled with Christmas lights. Mia gave thanks that the holidays had ended. This Christmas without Dan hadn't been any easier than last year's. That man did love the season! He used to plunge headfirst into the festivities: the kids singing carols at the school play, the baking, the decorating, the rattling of bright, shiny boxes. Dan's enthusiasm for the holiday had been contagious, and Mia had caught it early in their marriage. But that all ended with his sudden heart attack. Now *Silent Night* and colored lights only made her ache.

As she neared the shop, Mia spied a huddled form at the door, stomping snow from a pair of cowboy boots on the welcome mat and muttering something inaudible.

"Leanne?" she called out.

"You're early." Leanne's groggy voice came from beneath the faux leopard fur-trimmed hood of a fitted coat.

"*I'm* early? This is what time you usually *go* to bed, isn't it? Not get up."

Leanne pulled a ring of keys from her coat pocket. "I couldn't sleep."

"Me either." She glanced into the softly glowing shop window, the only one lit up along Main. "Aggie?"

"Yeah." Fatalism darkened Leanne's quick look, a helplessness at odds with her usual brisk self-assurance. "I'm worried about her."

"Me, too. I've never seen her so down. Or so scatterbrained."

"She chewed me out good yesterday for making a mess and leaving it for her to clean up. Said I reminded her of Jimmy when he was a kid, expecting her to be his maid. I think those are the only harsh words I've ever heard come out of that woman's mouth."

"Other than her comment about our cheap oven, you mean?"

A short, sharp laugh, then, "I forgot about that." Her keys jingled as Leanne searched for the right one. "With Aggie's family history, I can't help wondering if—"

"Don't even think it. We're jumping the gun, worrying about that."

"So, you admit it's crossed your mind, too?"

"Sure it has. But it's an overreaction. Something's bothering her, that's all."

"I hope you're right." Leanne slipped the key into the doorknob and turned it.

The shop's bell tinkled as Leanne opened the door. A swirl of warm, scented air rushed to greet Mia. Cinnamon and yeast. Comfort. Memories. Aggie provided most of the baked-good recipes served at the coffee shop, but the sweet rolls belonged to Mia. She had perfected them through years of cooking for Dan and their three kids, all grown now and gone.

Mia's oldest, Brent, currently lived more than an hour and a half away in Brister with his wife, Sherry, and their two children. Brent had followed Dan's example by becoming a smalltown high school football coach. Trey, Mia's middle child, lived the single life in Dallas, where he worked as some kind of business consultant; she never had figured out exactly what the job entailed.

Then there was Mia's daughter Christy. Twenty-seven and twice divorced, Christy lived in New York City where she waited tables. At least, the last time they'd talked she did. How long had it been? Over six months, at least. And ten long years since they'd seen each other. Mia had tried to reach Christy at Christmas, but her home phone had been disconnected, and she didn't answer her cell or return messages.

And Christy didn't send a card.

"Aggie?" Mia shouted. No response came from the kitchen, and Mia caught Leanne's frown. No country music played on the sound system, no off-key voice sang along, no pans clattered. Something wasn't right. Tension hung in the air, as thick as the yeasty scent of baking dough.

Mia didn't bother taking off her coat or wiping the soles of her snow boots on the entry rug. Nor did Leanne. They hurried through the small dining room, past a hodgepodge collection of wooden chairs and scarred oak tables, around a glass-front counter soon to be filled with rolls, muffins, and pies. Mia placed the stack of tablecloths on it and, with Leanne on her heels, pushed through the swinging doors leading into the kitchen.

They froze.

Five-foot-tall Aggie stood with feet apart, clutching an icing tube in one hand and aiming it toward the closed storage room door. Flour smudged her cheek and dusted the red baker's apron she wore over a loose beige sweater and stretchy double knit black pants. The tube shook like a tambourine.

Mia took a cautious step toward her. "Aggie . . . what—"

"Shhh!" Her gaze intent on the storage room door, Aggie whispered, "Something's in there. Hear it?"

Leaning forward, Mia strained to listen. Paper rustled faintly on the other side of the door. Relief rushed from her lungs.

"Lower your weapon, Annie Oakley," Leanne said with wry sarcasm. "Sounds like we've got ourselves a mouse, that's all." She shrugged out of her coat, revealing a skintight sweater and a tall body still shapely enough to turn the heads of men less than half her age. "I'll have Dale Roby come by later to get rid of it."

"It's too big for a mouse." Aggie's voice wavered, sounding more like a piccolo than a flute or a drum.

Leanne groaned. "Okay, *mice*."

Reddening, Aggie thrust out her jaw. "Tell me this, smarty pants. How many mice would it take to move a step ladder? I swear I heard it scrape across the floor a minute ago."

"Rats, then." Leanne shook out her long mane of bottle-blonde hair, then went to hang her coat next to Aggie's on the rack beside the back door. "Or even a possum."

Mia put her purse aside, took off her mittens and stuffed them into her coat pocket before handing it to Leanne to hang. "It's okay, Aggie. We'll call Dale, like Leanne said."

The tube shook harder. Aggie shuddered, her face as pale as a winter sun. "You know how I hate rodents."

Shaking her head, Leanne asked, "What're you plannin' to do? Shoot it with icing and send it into a sugar coma?"

Mia walked past Aggie and reached for the storage room door handle. "Come on, let's take a look."

"Oh, Lord." Whimpering, Aggie kept the tube poised to squirt.

"No one would ever believe you live on a farm, Ag," Leanne said with a sigh.

The hinges squeaked as Mia pushed the door wide, letting the light from behind seep into the storage room. Blinking, she scanned the small, crowded area stacked high with supplies. As she stepped in, she heard a gasp in the far right corner, a sharp intake of breath.

"Turn on the light, Leanne," Mia whispered. Her heart ticked like an over-wound clock as she peered toward the shadowy corner from where the sound had come. The bare bulb overhead flared, illuminating a pale, frightened face with dark, hollow smudges for eyes. The eyes stared back at Mia.

Aggie screeched, and Mia felt something hit her back. *Icing*.

"Sorry," Aggie murmured. "My finger hit the trigger."

Ignoring the ooze beneath her left shoulder blade, Mia concentrated on the girl crouched on the floor in the corner, hugging dirty, torn, blue-jean–covered knees to her chest. "Hello, there." Mia reached out a hand.

Cringing, the girl scrambled to her feet, her eyeliner-smeared, sleepy brown eyes too big for her face; her short, dark-rooted, white-blonde hair flattened to her head on one side and stuck out in spikes on the other. She appeared too young for makeup and bleached hair. Twelve, maybe. Thirteen at the most. A kaleidoscope of emotions flashed across her face then quickly disappeared behind a stony mask.

"Heavens," Aggie whispered.

Leanne moved up beside Mia as the skinny, shivering girl pressed closer to the wall. "We have a rat, all right. A packrat." She pointed to the nest at the girl's feet: a man's down jacket, a well-worn backpack, two tablecloths bunched into a makeshift bed. A scatter of crumpled paper muffin cups surrounded an empty Brewed Awakening mug. "A packrat with an appetite."

Mia detected a hint of concern in Leanne's tone.

The girl's chin lifted as she blinked the sleep from her eyes then narrowed them into defiance. Mia took another step toward her. "What's your name?"

No answer.

"How'd you get in here?" Leanne crossed her arms, one cowboy boot tapping out her impatience. "You better check the safe, Aggie. Make sure our little packrat isn't a thief, too."

"No one could crack that thing," Aggie scoffed.

"Are you okay?" Mia asked the girl in a careful voice. No use frightening her more than she was already.

"You would'a been smarter to break in to the beauty shop down the street," Leanne said. "Betty hates a cold shop in the mornings. She leaves the heater running full blast all night."

Aggie squeezed in on Mia's other side. "Talk to us, sugar. We don't want to hurt you. But we can't help you, either, if you won't tell us who you are."

When the front bell jingled, the girl jumped, her gaze darting toward the door.

"Well, damn," Leanne huffed. "Don't people know by now we're not open this early?" She called, "Just a sec!" then backed out of the storage room for a moment before poking her head back in. "It's the sheriff. I swear, Mia, the man gets earlier every day." Her half-grin brimmed with insinuation. "Guess he can't stand not seeing your smiling face first thing in the morning."

For once, Mia welcomed Sheriff Cade Sloan's daily visit, instead of dreading it. She'd known him most of her life, did the sports booster club thing and PTA with him and his ex-wife, Jill, before they divorced. Years back, she and Dan had even socialized with them some. Then, a couple of months ago, Cade started flirting. Now, just the sight of him made her as nervous and self-conscious as a girl at her first school dance. Especially since Leanne and Aggie insisted he had a "thing" for her.

Mia wasn't convinced of that. Like Leanne, Cade was a tease and always had been. At one time or another, every woman in town had been the recipient of his playful joking. Now it was her turn, that was all.

But the looks he gave her lately still made her heart skip a beat. Though she'd never admit it to Leanne or

Aggie, Mia feared *she* was the one with a "thing" for *Cade*, not the other way around. "Tell him to come back here," she said.

"No!" The girl stepped toward the three women, one arm thrust out, trembling. "Don't tell him I'm here."

Mia's heart beat too fast. Why did this child seem so familiar?

"Please," the girl whispered. "Just give me a chance."

And then, at once, Mia knew. Her eyes had a different shape. The color was wrong, too; brown rather than blue. But the flash of desperation, the lost look in them, was identical to what she'd glimpsed briefly in her own daughter's eyes before Christy ran away.

Chapter 2

$\mathcal{M}$ia walked into the main dining area, followed by Leanne and Aggie.

Sheriff Cade Sloan stood just inside the front door. "Morning, ladies." When he tipped his Stetson, Mia's heart tipped, too. Although he addressed the three of them, his gaze stayed on her. His eyes were the hazy gray of a rainy afternoon and, as usual, spilling mischief. When Mia looked into them, she couldn't look away; it was as if he wouldn't allow it. She wanted to, though. Wanted to turn her back on the feelings Cade resurrected in her. Mia didn't want to admit to herself that she could have such a strong attraction to anyone other than her husband. Dan still lived in her heart; any interest in another man felt like a betrayal.

Besides all that, Cade seemed to be smiling to himself, and she couldn't imagine what he thought was so funny. Maybe to him a fifty-year-old woman looked silly in overalls. Or maybe, in his mind, a woman her age was pushing it by wearing her hair in a loose braid over one shoulder. Or maybe a piece of last night's broccoli was wedged between her front teeth. Who knew?

No maybe about it, though, it was high time she stopped second-guessing herself whenever Cade looked at her. Especially on this particular morning when she had more important issues on *her* mind than what was going on in *his*.

"Good morning, Sheriff." Mia struggled to sound normal.

Aggie echoed the greeting.

"Cade Sloan, you're sure on the ball this morning," Leanne cooed in the honey-coated voice she used whenever she spoke to men. Young, old, good-looking or homely; it didn't matter to Leanne. They all received the same treatment. Pushing hair away from her face, she said, "We—"

"—don't open for another hour and a half," Mia cut in. "The coffee's not even on yet."

A look of uncertainty crossed Leanne's face. She stared at Mia with raised brows. "But, we do have *something* in back that might interest him, don't we, Mia?"

Mia sent her friend a quick, barbed glance. "The sweet rolls aren't quite ready, Leanne." She turned her brightest smile on Cade. "If you come back in a little while we'll have a hot one waiting for you with plenty of icing. Just the way you like it." With a scolding look, she added, "You know better than to show up so early, anyway."

Humming a nervous tune, Aggie lifted the top

tablecloth from the stack on the counter and unfolded it as she moved around to the nearest table.

Cade removed his hat, revealing short, dark hair, salted at the temples. He stepped further into the dining room with an easy, self-assured grace that might've seemed arrogant on any other man. "Ordinarily, I wouldn't bother you at this hour, but I've got myself a problem."

"A problem?" Mia crossed her arms.

Cade walked to the counter, but didn't sit. He leaned back against it, elbows propped up, his hat beside him.

"Late yesterday afternoon, Mack Holden caught a young girl lifting merchandise from his grocery store. The kid had stuffed her backpack with stolen food. A pair of pink suede boots are missing from Jesse's Boutique, too."

"Little packrat," Leanne murmured, generating a curious stare from Cade and sinking Mia's heart.

Aggie's gaze darted toward the swinging doors that led to the back room then over to Leanne. "Would you help me with this?" she asked in a jittery voice. Her hands visibly shook as she smoothed the first cloth into place on a tabletop then grabbed another one from the stack. "I'll get the centerpieces."

"I've been eyeing those pink boots at Jesse's myself," Leanne said as she moved around the counter to take the tablecloth Aggie handed her. "The girl has good taste."

Cade studied Leanne a moment longer before shifting his attention back to Mia. "Right as I pulled up at Mack's, she got away and took off running. I recognized her from a photo the Amarillo PD posted. They've been looking for her a couple of days now. She's a runaway. A fourteen-year-old foster kid name of Rachel Nye. The foster parents reported that she was missing when they woke up Wednesday morning." He heaved a tired sigh, and Mia wondered if he had slept last night. "I thought I had her cornered, but she slipped right past me and disappeared."

Aggie pulled vases of dried flowers from beneath the inside counter. "That poor, poor, girl," she said. "Her family's probably worried sick about her."

"There are only the foster parents, and she hasn't been with them more than a few months." Cade pushed away from the counter and walked to the small fireplace at the side of the room. He glanced back at Mia. "You want me to get this going?"

When she nodded, he slid aside the screen and rearranged the logs. He took a match from the mantel and lit it. Flames leaped, danced, and crackled as he tossed it in and turned on the gas beneath the logs. "Stupid kids," he rumbled. "They just don't think."

"Same as when we were young," Leanne said, a frustrated edge to her tone. She fanned the checkered cloth she held, flapping it until it billowed.

Cade watched the fire until the logs took hold of the flame. Then he turned off the gas and replaced the screen. "Anyway," he continued, standing, "You ladies are my first stop this morning. I plan on dropping by all the local businesses to give them a heads-up. I'd appreciate a call if you see any sign of her. She has a history of stealing. Nothing seemed out of place in here this morning, did it?"

Leanne glanced up from her work. She blinked at Mia then said, "Nothing except the fact that in our storage closet we found—"

"—a mouse," Mia blurted just as Aggie made a quick turn and knocked a vase from the table behind her. The vase didn't break, but dried flowers scattered across the floor.

"For heaven's sake!" Aggie's voice fluttered along with her hands as she stooped to clean up the mess.

Leanne, Cade, and Mia converged to help.

Cade chuckled. "What's got you so jumpy this morning, Aggie?"

Aggie blinked worriedly. Leanne started to answer him, but Mia cut her off. "Post holiday jitters, most likely. I know *I* have them. Too many Christmas goodies."

When the flowers were all back in the vase, everyone stood. Cade went to the counter for his hat, tugged it on then started for the door.

Suddenly, the phone on the wall behind the counter rang. Aggie gasped, jumped, and stumbled backward against a table.

Cade crossed to her quickly. "You okay?"

She pressed a palm to her chest. "Just startled." Her face turned as splotchy red as the checks on the table-cloths. "Who would be calling at this hour?"

"You did eat too much sugar." He smiled as she hurried past him, rounding the counter to answer the phone. "I thought maybe you saw that mouse."

"Oh, hello, Roy," Aggie said after picking up. She paused. "Clean socks? They're in the dryer. I didn't get around to folding them." Another pause. "There's no such thing as a left sock and a right. Just take out two and put them on."

Listening to the phone conversation, Mia smiled at Leanne, who continued dressing the tables. Leanne didn't smile back. She looked up at Mia with pursed lips, then said, "We don't have a mouse, we have a packrat." Her scowl left no question that she disagreed with Mia's decision to cover for the runaway girl.

"A packrat?" Cade looked back and forth between the two women. "If I'm not mistaken, that's how you referred to Rachel Nye a minute ago."

Before Leanne could respond, Aggie hung up the phone and said, "That husband of mine . . . I swear I don't know how he'd take care of himself if I wasn't around." She tightened her apron sash.

Mia bit her lip as she locked gazes with Leanne. She wished she'd had a chance to talk with her before Cade arrived. She wanted more time with the girl, wanted to hear her side of the story. What harm could come of another hour or two? Mia guessed her eyes conveyed that message because Leanne's expression suddenly shifted. She looked torn, undecided. Still irritated, yes, but Mia couldn't blame her for that.

Leanne finished with the tables then walked to the cash register, unlocked it and pulled the empty money tray out. "What happened to the girl's real folks?"

"From what I could gather from her caseworker, she's been in the system since she was four," Cade answered. "Her mother was a crackhead. No father in the picture."

"Mack and Jesse plan to press charges?" Mia asked, sympathy squeezing her heart.

"Afraid so. But first I've got to catch her."

Cade rubbed his fingers across his jaw, and Mia noticed he'd failed to shave. A mixture of silver and dark brown stubble covered his face. A tough, weathered face that, at the moment, looked tired and vulnerable, but as strong as always. The lines beside his eyes seemed more deeply etched than she remembered them being before. But the eyes themselves were clear. Alert.

"Well, I hope her foster parents get good news soon," Aggie said, placing another centerpiece on a table.

"I'm afraid she's not their worry now. Seems this thing with Mack and Jesse makes for the kid's third strike. Strike one was also shoplifting. Strike two was an MIP."

Aggie frowned. "MIP?"

"Minor in possession of alcohol," Leanne answered before Cade had a chance, and Mia noticed that she suddenly looked pale.

"Heavens." Alarm rang in Aggie's voice. "And the girl's only fourteen?"

Cade nodded. "Once I catch her and haul her back to Amarillo, she'll most likely be looking at time in a juvenile placement facility."

He sounded as disturbed over the girl's situation as Mia felt. The child had no real family to lean on, to offer guidance and love and unconditional acceptance. *Fourteen*. The girl's future should hold limitless possibilities, and yet, right now, what were her choices? A prison for kids, or making it on the streets. Alone.

Give me a chance.

"I hate to hear that," Mia said, meeting Leanne's gaze. Leanne's nod was so slight, Mia knew she was the only one who saw it.

To avoid Cade's scrutiny, she went to a cabinet for a box of sugar packets. "Good luck finding her, Cade. We'll call you first thing if we see anything."

Cade started to leave when a rustling noise drifted from the back room. Everyone looked toward the swinging doors and Mia held her breath.

"Why don't you let me see if I can catch that mouse for you?" he asked, pausing at the door.

Mia shook her head. "That's okay. We already took care of her."

"Her? You mean to tell me you know the mouse was a female?"

"The little Prada handbag was a dead giveaway," Aggie quipped, her expression deadpan serious.

"Not to mention the tiny slingback pumps," Leanne joined in. "Four of them. Hot pink with pointed toes and polka dot bows."

Aggie's cheek twitched as she started around the counter. "Cute as pigs' feet, those shoes."

Despite the awkwardness of the silly conversation, Mia was glad to hear Aggie sounding more like her fun-loving self again. And glad to know that Leanne had relented and was going to help them buy the girl some time. "The rolls, Aggie," she said, with a nod toward the kitchen when the oven timer sounded.

Leanne looked from Cade to Mia and said, "I'll help you, Ag."

When the two women left, Mia met Cade's gaze straight-on and steady, despite the fact her insides flip-flopped like a beached fish. She wasn't used to lying and hated doing so now. But she kept hearing the young girl's plea, kept seeing all those troubled emotions in her eyes. Emotions she'd failed to take seriously enough when her own daughter had displayed them.

The silence stretched on too long. Mia glanced down at Cade's boots and the melted puddle of snow around them. "Look at my clean floor," she scolded, just to make noise. "I know good and well your mother taught you to wipe your feet before you come into a room."

He lifted one foot, then the other, using the soles of his boots to swipe unproductively at the dirty water. "Sorry about that. Show me to a mop and I'll clean it up."

"I'm teasing you. No use fighting puddles on a day like today."

Cade shot her an arrow-straight stare from beneath the brim of his Stetson. "You'll tell me if anything out of the ordinary comes up, right, Mia?"

The question seemed a command rather than a request. For once, Mia saw more in his expression than flirtation; she saw suspicion. She drew a silent breath, released it, smiled. "Of course I will, Sheriff. You'll be the first to know."

Nodding once, he turned toward the door then looked back at her, his eyes sparkling with sudden amusement. "How long have we known each other?"

"I'm not sure." Mia shrugged. "When did you move here? Junior High?"

"Seventh grade. Sat behind you in Miss Goforth's history class, remember?" One corner of his mouth curved up. "I do. Every day for the better part of nine months I wished I could get up the nerve to call you."

Heat crept into her cheeks. "You never told me that."

"Now you know." He grinned.

"Well if you're trying to make me feel sorry for you, forget it. You got over me. By the time we got to high school, anyway. Sophomore year, I remember you asking to borrow my Carole King "Tapestry" eight-track right after you got your driver's license. You wanted to take Lynnette Byers to Cooper Lake and make out."

"I did?"

"If you want to play innocent, do it with someone who didn't know you back then." She tilted her head. "As I recall, somebody told you that Carole King's music really put girls in the mood."

His grin broadened. "Now that you mention it, I do remember. You loaned that tape to me, too."

"And you never gave it back. So, I'm guessing it must've worked."

"I don't kiss and tell."

"I'll take that as a yes."

"No comment." Cade laughed again, assessing her.

"See? That's my point. We share a lot of memories. By my count, we've known each other thirty-eight years, give or take."

"That sounds right to me."

"So, since when did you stop calling me Cade and start calling me Sheriff?"

Something fluttered at the base of Mia's throat. "Since you were first elected, I guess."

He shook his head. "That was more than five years ago. It's only been in the last few months you started being so formal."

"Have I? I guess I didn't notice."

Cade opened the door then closed it and returned to where she stood, reaching an arm around her.

Startled, she stiffened. He had never touched her before. No man had since Dan.

Cade's hand brushed her back, just beneath her shoulder blade, then came away quickly. He lifted his hand. Icing covered his forefinger. He brought it to his mouth, his smiling eyes on hers. "Lots of icing," he said in a low voice. "Just the way I like it." Then he left the shop.

And left Mia breathless.

She locked the door.

When Mia returned to the kitchen, the back door stood open and Leanne was nowhere in sight. The runaway sat on a stool in front of the center island work counter. Aggie served her a coffee mug full of milk and a warm sweet roll fresh off the first pan pulled from the oven.

"Mia, meet Rachel," Aggie crooned, smiling at

their uninvited guest. "She's starved to death, poor thing."

"Hi, Rachel."

Rachel took a huge bite of the roll. With a full mouth, she mumbled, "Hey." She didn't look up from the plate.

"Where's Leanne?" Mia asked.

Shaking her head and looking frustrated, Aggie answered, "Outside smoking."

"I thought she quit?"

"I did." Leanne entered through the back door, shut it then lifted the cigarette pack for Mia to see. "I took this away from our new friend. Little thief stole it from my coat pocket. Anyway, New Year's resolutions are meant to be broken." Leanne walked to where her coat hung and returned the pack to her pocket. "Anyway, that was last week. Before our little packrat showed up and you turned me into an aider and abettor of fugitives."

Rachel glanced back at her. "I really like your coat."

"And my cigarettes, too, apparently." Leanne shifted her scowl from Rachel to Mia. "What in the *hell* do you think you're doing?"

"*Leanne*." With widened eyes, Aggie tilted her head toward the girl and hissed, "Your language."

Smirking, Leanne said, "Look at her." She walked toward the others and nodded at Rachel. "Doesn't impress me as the type to be shocked by an off-color word. You shocked, packrat?"

Chewing, Rachel pointed at Leanne's coat. "If I say 'yes,' will you let me borrow that?"

" 'Fraid not, but nice try." Leanne looked pointedly at Mia. "So?"

Dragging another stool up to the island, Mia sat across from Rachel. "I'd like to hear what she has to say."

The girl took another bite and met Mia's gaze before averting her eyes.

"So, what do you have to say, Rachel? Why should we give you a chance?"

Rachel gulped her milk then lowered the mug. "If I go back, they'll lock me up."

"Do you deserve to be locked up?"

In answer, she crossed her arms, leaned her messy head back, and stared at the ceiling.

"Sheriff Sloan said you steal things. Is that true?"

"I just told you she swiped my cigarettes," Leanne scoffed. "And I looked in her backpack. Everything Cade mentioned is there. The food. The boots. And she broke into here. What more answer do you need?"

Defiance flared in Rachel's eyes. A crumb clung to one corner of her lower lip. Two bright pink dots of color bloomed high on her cheeks. "I didn't break in. You don't lock the back door during the day."

Aggie smiled smugly at Leanne.

Looking defensive, Leanne headed for the back door she'd failed to lock after her smoke.

"You got in here yesterday before we closed?" Mia asked Rachel.

"I hid in the storage room."

"How did you slip past us?"

"It was easy," Rachel said to the ceiling. "Y'all aren't very observant."

When Leanne returned from locking the door, Rachel blinked complacent eyes at her and added, "And I only *borrowed* a cigarette. So what?"

"It's wrong, sugar." Aggie placed another roll on the plate in front of the girl. "Thou shalt not steal."

Leanne groaned.

"*Well.*" Aggie tossed back her short steel-gray hair and planted a fist on one rounded hip. "Maybe no one ever taught her the Ten Commandments."

"Or maybe she snubs her nose at authority to get attention. Am I right, packrat?"

Ignoring both of them, Mia asked, "Why did you run away, Rachel?"

"I don't know. Just because."

"You'll have to do better than that."

"I hate my school." With a sniff, Rachel met Mia's gaze briefly. "I hate my stupid foster parents. I told them I wanted to transfer to a different school this semester. But my foster dad was like, '*No, we are NOT getting you a transfer, young lady. And you will NOT skip ONE SINGLE CLASS this semester OR ELSE. DO YOU UNDERSTAND?*'" Rachel's head jerked left to right, emphasizing each word as she imitated her foster dad's voice. "And I'm like, '*Or else WHAT?*' And he was all, '*Or else you're not living under my roof anymore. Got it?*' So, I'm like, '*Whatever.*'" She shrugged dramatically. "Then my foster mom jumped all over me for getting smart with the butthead, so I left."

"Sugar," Aggie scolded, pouring batter into a muffin tin, "That's no way to speak about your father."

Rachel huffed. "Ricky Underhill's not my father."

"So when you left, you headed here?" Leanne asked.

"Not right away." The girl pushed her plate to the center of the island then rounded a fist and popped her knuckles. "I didn't know where to go, so I went back to the house to get my books and go to my stupid school, but they'd locked me out and nobody would answer the door."

Aggie placed two muffin tins into the top oven then returned to the counter to stir another batch of batter. "Maybe no one was home."

"I'd only been gone something like ten minutes. I sat on the curb at the end of the block. If they'd left, I would've seen them. I knew they kept twenty bucks in the car glove compartment for emergencies, so I took it. Then I grabbed Ricky's coat from the backseat and left again. For good, this time. I'm through with foster homes. I won't be someone's charity case or help them pocket a few extra bucks anymore."

An image of Rachel knocking at the door of her house while the foster parents sat inside ignoring her stuck in Mia's mind like a thorn. Cade said the couple reported waking up and discovering Rachel gone. Why would they lie about that? *To avoid admitting the argument they'd had with Rachel and the bad way they handled it, that's why.*

"What do you mean about helping them make a few extra bucks?" she asked Rachel.

"The Underhills? They only wanted a foster kid for the money the state pays." Rachel's voice tightened with anger. "They're the same as the last family I got dumped with. And the one before that."

"The other families you've lived with only wanted the money, too?" Aggie asked softly.

"Some of them did. Some of them wanted to make themselves feel better by taking in a stray. You know . . . I was their good deed or whatever."

Mia tilted her head. "Did you ever run away before?"

Rachel shook her head.

"Why this time?"

"No one ever hit me before."

Aggie gasped and stopped stirring, her wooden spoon poised above the bowl and dripping batter.

Mia's stomach knotted.

Leanne stepped toward Rachel. "Who hit you?"

"Pam. My foster mom. She was mad at me for talking back to Ricky, so she slapped me."

Tense silence fell over the room. The girl mentioned the abuse so matter-of-factly. Not a hitch in her voice. Not a blink of her big, dark eyes. As if she was relaying a story about being sent to her room.

Leanne crossed to the island. Then Aggie left her spoon in the bowl and joined them, too. The three women exchanged looks, and Mia noted that Leanne's tough façade had slipped, revealing the softness she only shared with those closest to her.

"Where were you headed next?" Leanne asked Rachel in a much gentler voice.

"No place." Pressing her lips together, her expression still devoid of emotion, Rachel looked up at the ceiling again. "Anywhere but there. It doesn't matter."

Aggie placed a hand on the girl's shoulder. "How'd you get here, sugar? It's fifty miles from Amarillo to Muddy Creek."

"Walked partway. Caught a ride with a trucker the rest."

A memory floated up from the depths of Mia's mind. A frantic middle-of-the-night phone conversation from almost ten years ago. Christy insisting she was okay, but she wasn't coming home, the clipped abruptness of her voice not quite hiding her fear.

Blinking away the memory, Mia looked at Leanne and saw that her eyes were also haunted. Leanne glanced away, obviously uncomfortable. Aggie, not as adept at hiding her emotions, peered at Rachel with sad, puppy dog intensity.

"Can I borrow your Blazer, Aggie?" Mia asked her.

Aggie was the only one of the three women who drove into work each day since she and her husband, Roy, lived on a farm outside the city limits. Leanne and her husband, Eddie, owner of the town's newspaper, *The Muddy Creek Chronicle*, had a small house just a couple of blocks from the shop.

"I'll take Rachel to my place so she can shower and get some sleep in a real bed," Mia explained.

Leanne studied her. "Then you'll talk to Cade, right?"

"We'll see."

Frowning, Leanne nodded Mia aside.

Mia met her in the corner.

"What are you planning to do? Go on hiding her?" Leanne asked with quiet intensity. "Cade should be the one to handle this, not you."

"We'll talk about it after she gets some sleep."

Leanne crossed her arms. "I only kept my mouth shut for your sake. This is a mistake, Mia. She's trouble."

"You don't know that." Mia touched her friend's arm. "Don't worry so much. Nothing's decided yet." She returned to the island and said, "Grab your things, Rachel."

Aggie's brows puckered above her big, wire-framed bifocals. "What if somebody sees her?"

"I'll make sure they don't."

"Cade suspects something. Couldn't you tell?" Leanne tapped the counter with a long, French-manicured fingernail. "He might be watching the shop. If he sees you leaving, you can bet he'll follow."

"If he does, I'll think of something." Mia nodded at Rachel. "Wait by the storage room door. Aggie parks out back."

"Packrat?" Leanne called after them as Aggie pulled a set of keys from her coat pocket by the door. "For such a little thing, you sure have caused a big stir."

Chapter 3

Rachel waited inside the Brewed Awakening while Mia drove Aggie's car down the alley. When Mia stopped at the back door, Leanne led the girl out and motioned her toward the rear seat. Tossing her backpack onto the floorboard, Rachel climbed in.

"You'd better lie down." Leanne glanced up the alley and added, "I feel like a criminal, sneaking around like this."

Mia didn't want to admit that she felt the same. "Once Rachel's sleeping, I'll be back."

Frowning, Leanne shut the back door and hurried around to the driver-side window. When Mia rolled it down, she said, "Can we have a word alone?"

"Sure." After rolling up the window again, Mia stepped from the SUV and closed the door. "Make it quick. I don't want Cade driving by and seeing us out here." She shivered. "Besides, I'm freezing."

"Are you crazy?" Leanne hissed. "You can't leave that girl by herself at your house. She's a thief!"

"I won't leave unless I'm sure she's asleep. And I won't stay away long, just to help you and Aggie through the early morning rush. Anyway, I'm not really worried about her taking anything. All she needs is for someone to have a little faith in her."

"How can you say that? You never laid eyes on the kid until this morning."

"There's just something about her." Mia sighed. "Let me see how I feel after we get home and we have some one-on-one time. Then I'll call you."

"Aggie and I can handle things here."

"You saw how Aggie is today. It'll be like you're working alone. Or worse, with a nervous new employee."

Crossing her arms, Leanne shivered. "I can take care of things."

"We'll see." Mia opened the door, climbed in and started off.

She adjusted the rearview mirror so she could see Rachel, who was stretched out across the back seat, nibbling the cuticle of her index finger.

"Why are you helping me?" Rachel asked, studying her hand. "I mean, it's not like you know me or anything."

"Maybe because I have a daughter and if she were in trouble, I'd hope someone would be kind to her. Don't think this means you're off the hook, though, Rachel. I want you to rest up and then we'll talk and figure out what to do next."

Rachel frowned, shifting her position on the seat. "I already know what *I'm* going to do."

"What?"

"*Duh*." She pronounced the word *duh-uh*, in two syllables. "I'm getting as far away from Amarillo as I can. Someplace where they don't grow cows. I hate cows. They stink and they're stupid."

"Like I said, we'll talk. But you need a shower and some sleep first."

Mia didn't like the expression on the girl's face. She wore the same one when they first turned on the storage room light: that of a cornered animal looking for an escape.

As she slowed for a red light, Mia glanced in the mirror again. When the Blazer stopped completely, Rachel reached for the door handle. Mia hit the automatic locks. "Don't even think about it."

Aubrey Ricketts pulled up alongside the Blazer in his rattletrap pickup. The retired bank security guard combed the streets at all hours of the day and night, keeping an eye on other people's business. Everyone in town speculated whether or not he ever slept. Though still dark out, the streetlight shined down on them, and she saw him wave an arthritic hand. Waving back, Mia whispered to Rachel, "Scoot down."

Rachel did, muttering, "Why should I? You're just gonna turn me in, anyway. Why didn't you just do it when that sheriff came by?"

The light changed to green. Mia pulled away slowly, allowing Aubrey to move ahead of her. "Nothing's decided yet," she told Rachel. "You want me to give you a chance? Then you have to give me one, too. Trust me, okay?"

Rachel's sigh sounded dramatic, and Mia imagined the girl rolling her eyes. She heard a sound like knuckles popping, then, "*Whatever.*"

Nearing her house, Mia reached into her purse for the garage door opener, and the door lifted as she turned into the drive. She eased into the garage, parking next to her Tahoe in the spot where Dan's Ford pickup used to sit until six months ago, when she had finally sold her husband's flame red pride and joy.

"Nice house," Rachel said when they entered the kitchen. She dropped her backpack on the tile floor. "I used to live in a house like this with my real mom and dad."

The skin at the nape of Mia's neck prickled as she recalled Cade's words about the girl not knowing her father and losing her mother at the age of four. Setting her purse on the counter, Mia unbuttoned her coat. "Really?"

"Yeah." While she talked, Rachel's gaze scanned the cabinets, the refrigerator, the row of canisters on the counter. "It was white, though, not red. And not brick. We had this awesome front porch with a swing. And a flowerbed. My mom loved flowers." She sneezed, then added, "She and my dad? They died in a car wreck two years ago."

Swimming in the man's down ski coat she wore, Rachel hugged herself as she walked into the living room.

After draping her own coat over a chair, Mia followed.

"Wow. It's really clean in here," Rachel said, running her hand along a couch cushion. "Do you have a maid?"

Mia laughed. "Don't I wish. I'm the only one living here, so there's really no need."

"What about your daughter?"

"Christy? She's grown up and gone. My sons, too."

"You aren't married?"

Mia explained that her husband had passed away, and Rachel said, "Oh," then wandered over to the television. She picked up the remote and turned the TV on then off again. "We had a maid. And a bigscreen TV, too. Bigger than yours, even." She made her way to a photo-covered wall, where images of Mia's kids and grandkids stared back from dozens of frames. Trailing her finger along the edge of a picture of Brent in his high school football uniform, she said, "My dad? He liked football. He played for Texas Tech. He was a quarterback."

"Both of my sons went to Tech," Mia said, watching the girl's movements and feeling strangely apprehensive.

"We used to see all the college and pro games on our big screen. Mom always popped popcorn." She slid Mia a sidelong glance as she passed the fireplace, her fingers touching each item on the mantel: candlesticks, a vase of dried flowers, great-grandmother MacAfee's antique clock. "Sometimes we'd even make a fire and roast marshmallows."

Though the house was warm, Mia felt a bone-deep chill, an ache inside. She understood Rachel's need to pretend. She did it herself. Her mental conversations with Dan, the king-sized pillow she spooned at night while she slept. But she couldn't help wondering if what Rachel had said earlier was also fabrication. About the foster family locking her out. The mother hitting her. Her bad experiences with her previous foster families. What if she really did take off in the night? **What if those** people were sitting at home, crazy **with worry, like she and** Dan had been when Christy disappeared?

She left Rachel alone a moment and went to her bedroom closet where she found an old flannel gown, one she'd worn before Dan died and she lost so much weight. Then she called the girl into the guest bathroom and showed her the washcloths and towels.

While Rachel showered, Mia tossed the girl's dirty clothes into the wash: a pair of jeans, ripped at the knees and beneath the back pockets, frayed at the hem and embedded with grime; a purple pullover sweater nappy from too many washings; a black t-shirt; cotton socks with holes in the toes. The elastic in her panties had lost its stretch. She had no bra and didn't appear to need one. Her green Converse tennis shoes were soaked wet from the snow. Mia threw them into the machine, too.

After Rachel showered and took a nap, Mia would follow Leanne's advice. She'd find Cade and tell him the truth. Trust him to handle the situation in a way that would be in Rachel's best interest. She told herself she had been crazy to ever consider doing anything else.

Mia put linens on Christy's bed then waited on the couch in the living room. She studied the photos on the wall like Rachel had, trying to see her family through the girl's eyes. Her sons dressed for football, track, in prom finery and graduation caps and gowns. Her grandson in Little League and soccer garb. Her granddaughter in tutus and tights.

Christy had no extracurricular activities. Her pictures were all the standard school ones taken at the beginning of each year. First grade, second grade, third, all the way through the senior year she never finished.

Mia zeroed in on eighth grade.

Eighth grade.

Her daughter would've been fourteen. Rachel's age. Was that the year her friends stopped coming over? When Christy started spending so much time in her room alone? When she stopped talking to the family in anything more than one or two word sentences?

"So, you're going back to the coffee shop now?"

The sound of Rachel's voice brought Mia's head around. The girl stood in the doorway to the living room, damp hair slicked down around her face, her body so tiny, so thin, Mia's gown swallowed her.

"I thought I might while you take a nap." Standing, Mia started toward her. "You can sleep in Christy's bedroom."

"Your daughter?"

"Yes."

The girl's gaze darted around the room, left, right, up, down, reminding Mia of the jerky movements of a hummingbird. Her behavior set off a warning alarm in Mia's head.

"Where are my clothes?"

"In the washer. I'll toss them into the dryer before I leave."

Once in Christy's room, Rachel waited at the foot of the bed while Mia fluffed a pillow. The girl's toes peeked out from beneath the gown. Sparkly blue, chipped polish coated her toenails. "I had a canopy bed," she said. "The spread was pink with ruffles. Mom made it for me. And matching curtains. She loved to sew."

Mia pulled the comforter down further, patted the mattress. "Here you go." Rachel climbed in. "You need anything else before I leave?"

"No." She propped up against the whitewashed headboard, looking tense instead of relaxed, like a Jack-in-the-box, ready to spring when the door closed instead of when it opened.

"Okay, then." Mia started from the room, pausing at the door. "I'll check on you in a couple of hours."

Pulling the comforter to her chin, Rachel yawned, her eyes shifting to Mia, then down, then over to the wall. "Sure. Whatever." She yawned again. "I'll probably sleep a really long time."

Mia closed the door and headed for the kitchen phone.

"Brewed Awakening," Leanne answered on the second ring.

"Hi, it's me. You were right. I don't think I should leave her here alone."

"Just a sec." Mia heard the cash register ding, then Leanne say, "Thanks. Sure you don't need a sweet roll with that?"

"I do, but my hips don't," came the customer's reply.

"I'm looking forward to next week's Red Hat meeting, Betty," Aggie called from in the distance, and it crossed Mia's mind that the women would soon be encouraging her to start attending again, too, like they had every month since Dan's death. *Get the widow out of the house. Keep her busy.* The shop bell jingled, and Mia heard Betty Rigdon say goodbye, followed by laughter from The Coots, as Leanne had named the weekday morning regulars.

"Okay." Leanne blew out a breath and said quietly into the phone, "I opened early. Seems nobody can sleep this morning. What's up?"

"Can you talk?"

"For a minute."

"I'm afraid she's going to bolt if I leave."

"Or rob you blind."

"Maybe. She sure is interested in all my things." A door hinge squeaked. Mia glanced up and saw Rachel peek down the hallway then duck out of sight. "In fact, she's already up and checking to see if I'm gone."

Leanne sighed noisily. "Like I said before, this is a mistake. You know that, don't you?"

"You're probably right. I'm having second thoughts. Why'd you go along with it?"

Another sigh. "She reminds me of me at fourteen. I can't imagine what might've become of me if I hadn't had Aggie to see me through those days."

Leanne's mom had died of cancer when she was in third grade. Aggie, Marion Wells' best friend, stepped in as a second mother to Leanne. Her father never got over his grief and had spent the last decade of his life lost in a bottle.

"Ask Aggie to make an excuse to Roy so she can come over here after she leaves the shop. Then I'll come up there and help you close early."

"Then what?"

Mia wavered between telling Cade right away, or giving Rachel some time while they tried to convince Mack and Jesse not to press charges. "Then you'll decide what we should do."

"*I'll* decide," Leanne huffed. "Thanks a lot." Her laugh rang with cynicism. "Aggie'll spoil that girl rotten before the day's over."

"Something tells me Rachel could use a little pampering."

"Don't kid yourself that's all it'll take. Troubled teenagers aren't easy to fix."

"I know."

Silence, then, "Of course you do. I'm sorry, Mia. I didn't mean—"

"I know you didn't." She squinted to see down the shadowed hallway, looking for signs that Rachel hid there, listening.

"I'll call Eddie now and tell him we're having an

impromptu Red Hat meeting after we close. We can go to your place and figure this thing out."

"Eddie won't mind?"

"He'll be glad to have an excuse to go shoot some pool before dinner."

Leanne's sarcastic tone concerned Mia. For weeks, she had sensed tension between Leanne and her husband. "I hate to ask you to keep something from Eddie, but I'd feel better if you didn't tell him about Rachel yet."

"That should be easy enough. Lately, our conversations are few and far between."

Mia hesitated then asked, "You want to talk about it?"

"It's nothing, really. We're just in a slump. We'll pull out of it."

"I'm here if you need me."

"I know you are."

Mia spotted Rachel again, but she backed away when their gazes met. "Well, I wouldn't ask you to keep Rachel a secret from him," Mia said quietly, "but Eddie *is* a newspaper man. He might feel obligated to go to Cade before we're ready."

Leanne sighed. "The truth is, I really *don't* like hiding things from him. We've always had an understanding about that. But I'll keep quiet until we decide what we're going to do with her."

"When you're ready to tell him, warn me first. And you'd better ask Aggie not to say anything to Roy, either."

The sound of the doorbell made Mia's nerves jump. "Someone's here, Leanne. I'll call you later."

She hung up and went to answer the door, expecting to find her neighbor, Amber. Since Dan died, the young mother often checked on Mia. She probably saw Aggie's Blazer drive up at this ungodly hour and was worried.

Pasting on a smile, Mia unlocked the door and opened it wide. A blast of cold air hit her in the face.

Cade grinned at her. "Hello again, Mia."

Chapter 4

$\mathcal{M}$ia's startled expression all but confirmed Cade's suspicion. She, Leanne, and Aggie had more in the making than coffee and pastries. He'd guessed as much back at their shop.

"Hi, Cade. What are you doing here?"

He wasn't surprised that she didn't ask him in. "I just ran into Aubrey Ricketts over at the Fina station. He said he saw you driving away from the coffee shop a while ago in Aggie's Blazer."

"That's right. I borrowed it. I didn't drive my Tahoe to work this morning."

"What's wrong? Forget something?"

"As a matter of fact, I did. Is forgetfulness a crime these days?" she asked in a teasing tone.

Cade smiled and waited for her to offer more information. She didn't. Instead, she stood with her chin lifted and her smile unwavering. A five-foot-four-inch, one-hundred-twenty-pound, green-eyed iceberg.

"So . . ." she finally said. "You need anything else?"

He took off his hat. "I've been sitting in the truck debating whether I should trust my gut, or trust you."

"Trust me? About what?"

"I think you know something about that runaway girl. I can understand if you feel sorry for the kid, but she broke the law."

Mia tilted her head, her expression mocking him. "My, you're even tougher than I thought, Cade. So, the law's never wrong. Is that what you're saying?"

He cleared his throat. Her wide-eyed scrutiny made him feel like a teenaged boy wearing a fake mustache. "I'd like to take a look around inside the house, if you don't mind. The coffee shop, too."

"*Search* them, you mean?" She sounded baffled. "On what grounds?"

"Reasonable suspicion."

"Reasonable—?" Mia uttered a short sound of disbelief, then grinned. "Quit teasing me, Cade."

"Sorry, but I'm not teasing." Cade shifted, straightened. "You and Leanne were dancing around each other earlier like a couple of boxers. Aggie was nervous as a wet hen." He chuckled. "And all that nonsense about a packrat . . ."

He peered over her shoulder into the house.

Mia stepped onto the porch and pulled the door shut behind her. "That's silly," she said, her tone lighthearted. "What reason would any of us have to hide some runaway kid from you?"

He steadied his gaze on hers. "I don't know, Mia. Why *would* you do that?" Her amused look faltered.

Only for a second, but he caught it, that flicker of uncertainty, of apprehension in her eyes.

"You may have suspicions but they aren't the least bit reasonable." Shivering, Mia rubbed her palms up and down her arms. She wore a long-sleeved sweater under her baggy overalls, but no coat. "I'll be happy to let you search my place."

Cade couldn't hide his surprise. "You will?"

She nodded and smiled sweetly. "Of course. Right after you show me a warrant, Sheriff."

Sheriff. So they were back to that. Cade blew out a noisy breath. He'd hoped not to have to go to those lengths to gain her cooperation. How was a man supposed to convince a woman to see him socially when he was serving her with legal papers? He wished he could just forget Rachel Nye, follow Mia inside out of the cold, sit and talk to her about anything else but this. He wished he could do other things, too. Take her hair out of that braid, tangle his fingers in it, kiss her.

At least two months had passed since he last kissed a woman. Mary Lambert. A recently divorced court reporter in Amarillo. It had been nice, but Cade had a feeling kissing Mia would be *more* than nice. Much more. "If you've got nothing to hide," he said calmly, "then why are you making this so difficult? I'm a reasonable man."

"You're implying I lied to you." She shrugged. "Frankly, I'm a little insulted."

"Insulted or nervous?" Instantly regretting the quick comeback, he ran a hand across the top of his head and said, "Come on, Mia. I hate acting like a bully. Let's just get this over with."

Mia blinked once. Twice. She shook her head. "It's a matter of principle."

"You don't leave me any choice, then." Tugging his hat on, more frustrated than he'd been in a long time, Cade turned, stepped off the porch, then glanced back at her, hoping she'd change her mind and just come clean.

Mia stood with her arms crossed, a firm but polite expression on her face. She might look small and soft and fragile as a flower, but Mia MacAfee was one headstrong woman. Right now, with her green eyes staring into his and her mouth set in a stubborn line, he didn't know whether to grab her and satisfy his curiosity about that kiss, or shake some sense into her. "I'll be back soon." He swiveled around and started down the walkway.

"Cade," Mia called when he rounded his truck at the curb.

He opened the door and looked across at her.

"If you thought I was lying to you, why didn't you ask to search the coffee shop when you were there?"

"I wanted to believe you."

"But you don't."

He studied her. Mia had more strength of character, more heart, than anyone he'd ever met. But she was also vulnerable and soft-hearted. She was the type of woman who stood up for what she believed to be fair and right in the long run, popular or not. Once, years back, she'd stood alone against the entire school board, even her husband, insisting the star quarterback shouldn't play the biggest game of the year since he skipped class after a supposed final warning. The month before, the school suspended a girl for the same offense. In a community like Muddy Creek, where high school sports were the town's heartbeat—football especially—her actions took nerve. Still, Mia held her ground. And got her way.

But, would she break a *law* if she thought it was for a good reason? The right reason?

"I'm not sure what I believe, Mia. But it's my job to enforce the law. When my gut tells me something, I tend to listen. It's served me well in the past." He climbed into his truck and drove off.

At the end of the block, he stopped at the sign and glanced into his rearview mirror at her house.

Mia was gone.

At ten, Mia peeked in on Rachel and found her sound asleep, so she drove back to the Brewed Awakening to pick up Aggie.

Now, Aggie sat on a bar stool at Mia's kitchen counter with her sock-covered feet propped up on a matching stool. She wiggled her toes. "Lord, it feels good to be off my feet." Aggie gave a blissful sigh. "You don't really think Judge Brennan will give Cade a search warrant, do you? Won't he want some kind of evidence?"

"I don't know." Mia looked inside the refrigerator for something to fix Rachel for lunch. It was only ten-thirty and the girl was still asleep, but Mia wanted to have a good meal waiting when Rachel woke up. And she wanted to be the one to fix it. After all that had gone on today, Aggie needed some rest. "Maybe reasonable suspicion is all that's necessary."

"I'm not going to worry over it," Aggie said. "For heaven's sake, what could he tell the judge that would sound reasonable? He didn't see or hear anything. He's grasping at straws."

"Well he's right, you know. We *are* hiding the girl. That's against the law." Mia looked around the refrigerator door at her friend. "Are you okay with that?"

"Sugar, some laws are made to be broken. Besides, if they throw an old lady like me in the slammer for having a little compassion, then shame on them. And if they did, I'd feel sorry for the poor sucker who had to deal with Roy Cobb's wrath."

Smiling, Mia took out a pound of hamburger meat, thinking she'd make chili. "You're not an old lady."

"I feel like one lately."

"Leanne and I have both noticed you seem to be in a funk." Setting the meat on the stovetop, Mia went to the pantry where she gathered spices and canned stewed tomatoes. "We're worried about you."

Aggie stayed silent for a few seconds before saying, "The twins graduate from high school this May." Her voice wavered.

"You're kidding! Nicky and Natalie are seniors?" Mia referred to Aggie's granddaughters, her only grandchildren. The girls lived in Boston with Aggie's son Jimmy and their mother Sheila.

"The time's passed by in a blink, hasn't it?" Aggie

turned and stared out the breakfast nook window into the snowy front yard. "I always thought there'd be plenty of time to get closer to them." She met Mia's gaze. "We talked on the phone Christmas day, and we hardly had a thing to say to one another. They were polite, Mia. Like strangers."

Mia turned off the burner beneath the ground beef and went to sit beside Aggie.

"That's what they are. Strangers to Roy and me, and us to them. People don't grow to love one another through cards, e-mails and phone calls alone." Aggie blinked teary eyes. "My granddaughters don't know me. They don't love me, and they certainly don't need me."

"Oh, honey." Mia hugged her.

When they parted, Aggie pulled a tissue from the box on the counter, took off her glasses and wiped her eyes. "I'm so mad at Roy I could spit. And I'm mad at myself for letting him dictate every move I make. After that first trip to Boston when the girls were born, he refused to go again. '*It's too long a drive. Too many tourists in the summer, too cold in the winter, too much time away from the farm,*'" Aggie mocked her husband's gruff voice. "'*Let them come here.*'" She blew her nose.

"They *did* visit." Mia squeezed her friend's hand. "Remember that time we all went caroling on Christmas Eve?"

"Oh, sure. They spent the holidays with us some when the girls were little. A week in the summer from time to time, too. But when Natalie and Nicky started school, they just got so busy." Aggie teared up again. "They invited us to come up. I should've bought myself a plane ticket and gone without Roy." She laughed through her tears. "He would've had a fit."

Mia gave her a moment to cry.

Sniffing, Aggie waved her away. "Go on. Fix your chili. I'm just being silly and sentimental. Finish up and go help Leanne."

"I'll let her take care of things by herself today. I don't want Cade showing up with his warrant and you being here alone with Rachel."

"Sugar, I've got eighteen years on that man. I can handle Cade Sloan, don't you worry about it. Besides, he'll be a while. I saw his truck at the convenience store when we were heading over here, so he probably hasn't even left town yet."

"You did? I must have missed it."

Aggie nodded. "It's an hour's drive to Brody to the county courthouse. Who knows how long it'll take for him to convince Judge Brennan he's justified in his so-called suspicions? And I bet he'll want to grab some lunch before the hour's drive back."

"You think so?"

"More than likely, you'll be finished at the shop and home again by the time he shows up. *If* he shows up."

"He'll show up, warrant or no warrant." Mia returned to the stove and turned the burner on again beneath the skillet. "Cade follows through on his hunches." When the meat sizzled, she stirred it with a wooden spoon. "If he comes by here early, he'll wonder why you're at the house without me."

"He won't know. The Blazer's in the garage and I won't answer the door. He'll assume nobody's home."

"But would a warrant allow him to come in anyway?"

Aggie put on her glasses and frowned. "You mean *break* in? Cade wouldn't go that far, would he?"

"Who knows?" She shrugged. "Maybe. It wouldn't surprise me."

Nothing would now, Mia realized. Yesterday, if someone had told her she'd be harboring a fugitive today, she would have declared them crazy.

"Leanne suggested we get together over here before dinner under the guise of a Red Hat meeting," she said. "You think you can persuade Roy to let you come? The three of us haven't really had a chance to be alone and talk about all this."

Aggie nodded. "Don't worry about Roy. I'll be here, one way or another."

Around two o'clock, high school seniors with short schedules began trickling into the Brewed Awakening, backpacks slung over their shoulders and a day's worth of gossip ready to discuss. A couple of months after Mia and Leanne opened the coffee shop, they added trendy drinks to their menu to entice the kids. Chai teas, Italian sodas, fancy mochas with whipped cream toppings.

Behind the counter, Leanne took orders and Mia filled them. Soon, young people crowded the tables, their heads together over open books they'd already deserted in lieu of conversation.

Mia began wiping down the work area.

"Cade's back." Leanne nudged her with an elbow

and nodded at the big glass window overlooking Main Street.

Mia watched Cade's black Dodge truck ease slowly by on the road.

"You think he's been to your house yet?"

"Aggie would've called by now if he had."

"Maybe she can't." Leanne slid Mia a wry look. "Maybe he has her in custody."

"Call and let her know he's back. She can get Rachel out of there."

"Don't you think it's time we ended this? What good's it going to do?" Leanne tapped her boot against the floor. "We can't keep her hidden forever."

"Shhh." Mia eyed the kids at the nearest table. They seemed too caught up in their own drama to pay her and Leanne any mind. "I'd decided to tell him, but when he came by . . ." She shook her head. "I just couldn't do it. What if they put that girl away, Leanne? I couldn't stand it. We have to figure out a way to help her."

Mia waited for Leanne to break a dollar for a customer. When the boy was out of earshot, she said, "I still want to talk to Mack and Jesse. Maybe they'd be open-minded about not pressing charges if Rachel gives back their merchandise."

"Mack's gonna have a hard time selling half-eaten boxes of Pop Tarts and crushed up cookies."

"Okay, if she pays for the stuff, then."

"How do you plan to discuss any of that without raising suspicion?"

"I can be subtle." Mia shrugged. "Anyway, I want

more time to quiz Rachel. To hear what else *she* has to say."

"She'll say whatever it takes to win you over."

"You make her sound like some kind of con artist instead of a teenage girl."

"Girls like her *are* con artists, Mia. I should know. I *was* one."

"You weren't a runaway."

"No, but I bucked authority like she does. And I was a wildcat like her, too. You know that." Leanne averted her gaze.

Mia did know it. Though they were the same age and went through school together, she hadn't become close to Leanne until senior year. Prior to that, Leanne had run with a different crowd. Mia remembered sitting behind her in study hall one semester of ninth grade. Each day, Leanne spent the period whispering stories about her weekend antics: the smoking and drinking, the guys, the parties at Cooper Lake.

"But you had family," Mia said softly.

"That's the only reason I haven't blown her cover. *Yet.*" Leanne sighed. "I keep reminding myself that I had Aggie and Eddie when I hit rock bottom. Even my dad. He didn't have much left to give by then, but he was better than nothing. And that's what Rachel has. Nothing and nobody. That's why I'm willing to keep this from Eddie until we come up with a solid way to help her. Besides, you're right about him being a newspaper man. I don't want to place Eddie in an awkward position."

Mia wasn't surprised that, in addition to concern

for Rachel, Eddie's reputation played into Leanne's decision. She also was not surprised that Rachel had managed to uproot the sad memories that Leanne kept buried deep inside of herself.

A haunted look darkened Leanne's eyes. "If I could somehow help that kid get her life on track and avoid a tragedy like—"

"Call Aggie." Mia placed a hand on Leanne's arm and held her gaze. "We'll buy some time. Then we'll decide later how to straighten this all out."

Only seconds after Leanne disappeared into the kitchen to use the more private phone line, the bell over the shop door tinkled and Cade walked in.

He met Mia's gaze, then scanned the kids at the tables, speaking to this one and that one as he made his way to the counter. "Afternoon, Mia."

She straightened her apron. "Sheriff."

He pulled an envelope from his coat pocket, handed it to her. "I got what you asked for."

After opening the envelope, Mia skimmed the warrant, her pulse thumping. "So where would you like to start?" She swept an arm in the direction of the entryway leading behind the counter. "Help yourself."

He came around and headed for the swinging doors to the kitchen.

"Don't forget these cabinets under the work station," she said with a hint of teasing sarcasm, tapping her knuckles against the stainless steel. "How old did you say the girl is? Thirteen? Fourteen? A child that age could probably squeeze under here."

His stare made Mia ask herself why she was being

so hard on him. Why did it irritate her that Cade didn't trust her? He *was* only doing his job. And, in truth, she was guilty of what he suspected. Besides, she didn't trust him, either, did she? If she did, she would simply turn Rachel over and let him handle the matter.

Still, she hoped that Leanne ended her conversation with Aggie before Cade got back there. Or at least talked softly so he wouldn't hear. Mia understood why she and her friends would risk themselves to save a girl they'd never laid eyes on before. The reasons were all tangled up in their pasts, in mistakes they'd made. Maybe, for all of them, Rachel represented a second chance to do things right.

Ten minutes later, after looking in every closet, the storage room, a couple of kid-sized boxes and out in the Dumpsters lining the back alley, Cade gave Mia a curious glance. Then he went out front and checked under the work area cabinet like she'd teasingly suggested. Mia supposed the thought crossed his mind that she might've been trying to throw him off guard by stating the truth.

"You satisfied?" Leanne asked when he came back into the kitchen. She pursed her lips, one fist perched on an out-thrust hip.

"I'll grab my purse and follow you to the house so you can look there, too," Mia said, starting for the back door.

"I've already searched it." He sounded disgruntled, impatient, ready to strangle somebody.

Pausing with her hand on the coat rack, she looked back at him. "You broke into my house?"

Behind Cade, Leanne winked and cocked her head toward the phone.

"Aggie let me in."

"She did?"

"You sound surprised." He crossed his arms, scowled. "What was Aggie doing at your place by herself, anyway?"

Mia's stomach slid slowly down to her toes. "Didn't she tell you?"

"Yes, she did. What's *your* version of the story?"

"She felt a migraine coming on," Leanne said calmly.

Cade glanced back at her. "I was asking Mia."

When he turned around again, Mia said, "She had a migraine."

Leanne stepped forward. "Aggie didn't want to start the drive to the farm and have a headache hit her like a freight train halfway there."

"And so she went to my place to lie down until it passed," Mia finished, picking up on the lie Aggie had obviously relayed to Leanne over the phone.

"That's what Aggie said." Cade didn't appear convinced. "Apparently potato chips and rock videos are good therapy for her headaches. Oh, and pizza. A small sausage, pepperoni and mushroom arrived right after I did."

Behind Cade, Leanne grinned and turned away. "Well," Mia said, "Aggie can't let her blood sugar get low."

"Or her cholesterol, apparently," Cade added.

She cleared her throat. "So I take it you didn't find anything?"

"Does that surprise you, too?"

"Of course not. Just stating the obvious."

Cade started for the swinging doors. "I'll be watching you, Mia."

"You'll be wasting your time."

"You, too," he said to Leanne when he passed her.

Leanne winked and smiled at him. "I'm flattered, Cade, but I'm a happily married woman. You know that."

Without smiling back, he pushed through the swinging doors and disappeared.

Air rushed from Mia's lungs and she staggered back against the refrigerator, one hand pressed to her pounding chest.

Leanne laughed quietly. "Aggie thought he was the delivery guy from Papa Roni's Pizza," she whispered. "That's why she opened the door."

"How on earth did she hide Rachel from him?"

"She didn't. Aggie said she was sure we were caught. But the only signs of Rachel in the house were an empty potato chip bag and MTV on the television. She even took her backpack with her. Luckily, Aggie had made her bed earlier." Leanne chuckled. "Aggie didn't call us right away because she went looking for Rachel. She didn't have any luck, but when she returned to the house, she found her in front of the television chowing down on pizza."

"Where had she been?"

"In somebody's storm cellar a few streets over from you."

"The Nelsons'." Mia sighed. "Sneaky girl."

"Lots of experience at it, I'm sure."

"So they're both at the house now?"

Leanne nodded. "Aggie says she'd better get home soon, though. She told Roy she was working late then running some errands, but that was hours ago. How many errands can you do in Muddy Creek?"

The phone interrupted their conversation. Leanne reached for it. "Brewed Awakening." She winked at Mia and pointed to the receiver. "No, Roy, she left a while ago to run some errands."

Mia giggled.

"I'm sure she's fine." Leanne paused, then said, "No, she didn't say what she had in mind for your dinner. It's not even three o'clock yet." Shaking her head, she crossed her eyes at Mia. "What are you doing home so early, Roy? Shouldn't you be farming?" Leanne winced. "Oh, no . . . are you okay?"

Concerned that Aggie's husband might be hurt, Mia sobered and stepped closer to the phone.

"Your finger? Well, maybe she's out buying Band Aids right now," Leanne said into the phone, stifling a laugh.

Relieved, Mia snickered.

"Did Aggie tell you we're having a short Red Hat meeting later this afternoon?" Holding the receiver away from her ear, Leanne winced again. Mia heard Roy's booming voice; he sounded irritated. "Well, it was planned on the spur of the moment," Leanne told him. "That's probably why she forgot to mention it. We'll be finished before dinnertime; we're just having refreshments." She said goodbye and hung up the phone. "Speak of the devil."

"You'd think the woman was ten years old, the way Roy keeps tabs on her," Mia said with a laugh.

"He calls out the cavalry if she's gone more than an hour and he doesn't know where she is."

"Let's put the sign on the door and go ahead and close up. It's been a long day and we have things to do."

"Good idea. I'll shoo those kids out."

Chapter 5

"Would you like more lemonade, Rachel?" Mia asked.

"No, thanks." Rachel pushed away from Mia's dining room table. She crossed the room, took Aggie's wide-brimmed red hat off the buffet, put it on, then traded it for Leanne's. "Why did y'all bring these?"

"We ran home to get them and change clothes so our husbands would think our chapter's having an afternoon tea." Aggie lifted her cup. "Which is true enough. Just not the *entire* chapter."

Studying her reflection in the mirror over the buffet, Rachel asked, "What's a chapter?"

"A lady's organization," Mia explained.

"A dress-up club?"

Mia nodded. "You could say that."

Rachel glanced at all of them and asked, "Is that why you're wearing purple?"

"That's right, sugar."

"I didn't know grown women played dress-up. I'd feel stupid. I mean, even *I'm* too old for that."

Aggie *tsk*ed. "You're never too old for a little good, silly fun."

Squinting, Rachel assessed each of them then returned her gaze to the mirror. She tilted the hat to one side to cover her right eye then struck a pose, her hand on one hip. The lashes on her exposed eye fluttered dramatically. She giggled. "Must be a weird club. Can I join?"

Stretching both arms overhead, Leanne yawned and said, "Get back to us in thirty-six years."

"I didn't *really* want to join the stupid club." Rachel stomped to the table, jerked off the hat and threw it down.

"Oh, sugar . . . don't be hurt. Come back and sit with us." Aggie motioned to the chair beside her. "We'd let you join if we could. You're just not old enough yet." She smiled at Rachel. "When you are, I bet you'll fit right in, though. You looked sassy as can be in that hat. Didn't you think so, Mia?"

Too *sassy*, Mia thought. *Too cute. Too sweet.* Which made it all the harder to think about turning her in. Rachel had just given them a glimpse of the soft, vulnerable little girl beneath the scrappy, streetwise teenager. Mia knew she and Aggie weren't the only ones who'd been charmed by Rachel over the last hour; Leanne had a smitten look in her eyes, too.

Leanne sipped her tea and muttered, "She looked flirty, if you ask me."

"If that's not the pot calling the kettle black, I don't

know what is," Aggie said, exchanging a look with Mia and laughing.

It was already five-thirty and they had made no progress in deciding how to handle Rachel's situation. In fact, they hadn't even discussed it. Rachel had more important topics to talk about. Not that she'd been eager to talk initially. At first, she'd been as closemouthed and edgy as when they first found her, but as she became more comfortable around them, she'd loosened up. They had learned her favorite movie was *Lord Of The Rings*, that she "like *really, really*" wanted to pierce her belly button, that "older guys" who were sixteen and seventeen were so much hotter than guys her own age.

Rachel wandered over to an empty chair where Leanne and Aggie had laid their coats. She touched the fur trim on Leanne's. "Is this from a real leopard?"

Leanne shook her head. "No, it's fake."

"Good. I don't like animals getting killed." Rachel nibbled her lip and gave Leanne a tentative look. "Can I try it on?"

"Sure. Go ahead."

The coat was too big, but Rachel's eyes lit up when she pulled it around her. "It *feels* real." She glanced at her feet. "You know what would look totally cool with this?"

Leanne lifted a brow and smiled. "Those boots from Jesse's?"

Rachel nodded. "Only in brown suede instead of pink."

"That's just what I was thinking." Leanne smiled. "I'm just wild about those boots."

"I bet this coat's expensive," Rachel said, sounding dejected. "All the clothes I like cost too much."

"There are ways around that." Leanne left the table and walked over to her. "When I was your age, I made most of my outfits. Sometimes I even took hand-me-downs and reworked them." Facing Rachel, she zipped up the coat, reached around her and pulled the extra fabric together in back so that it fit her body more snugly. "A little nip here, a tuck there . . . I could make it my own design."

Rachel gazed up at her. "Did your mother teach you?"

Still holding the coat in place at Rachel's back, Leanne leaned away to take a look at her handiwork. "No, my mother died when I was eight."

Warmth spread through Mia as she watched them together. She saw their gazes meet briefly before Leanne averted her eyes.

"I learned to sew in a homemaking class I took in junior high," Leanne said. She turned Rachel around, moved her slightly so that she could see herself again in the mirror over the buffet across the room.

Though the shoulders were still too wide, the sleeves and hem too long, Rachel smiled at her image. "I don't have a sewing machine," she said, running her hand across the fur lapel.

Aggie sat forward. "I have an old one I never use. You'd be welcome to it."

"Who'd teach me to sew?"

"Leanne could teach you."

Leanne let go of the coat and scowled at Aggie.

Aggie seemed not to notice. "The machine's portable. I could bring it over here tomorrow and you could give her a quick lesson, just to get her started."

"Would you?" Rachel blinked wide eyes at Leanne. "I want to make some halter tops for this summer. The older girls at my school? They wear them all the time when it's hot. Not to school, though. They're not allowed. But to movies and stuff. They look like they'd be really easy to make."

"I don't know, Rachel." Leanne returned to the table, her back to the girl. "It'll depend on what happens tomorrow."

The excitement in Rachel's face disappeared. She slipped the coat off and carried it back to the chair. "You mean, it'll depend if you tell the sheriff about me or not." She turned and ran from the room.

"Rachel—" Mia pushed back her chair and stood.

Aggie touched her arm. "Let her go. That was my fault."

Leaning against the table, Leanne sighed. "What were you thinking, Ag?"

"I wasn't. It's just so much fun having a young girl around. I suppose I was wishing she *could* stay. She makes me think of my granddaughters."

A sense of helplessness swept through Mia. "So what are we going to do?"

"Don't look at me," Leanne said. "I'm more confused than ever."

"Maybe we should just sleep on it tonight." Aggie began gathering the teacups. "Surely the answers will be clear to us in the morning."

• • •

Two hours later, Aggie carried a couple of bowls of chili to the kitchen table where Roy sat reading the newspaper. Mia had the right idea at lunch, Aggie thought. It was chili weather. Cold, snowy and gray. Aggie had passed up the chili Mia made for Rachel's lunch, since she had consumed two sweet rolls, a carton of yogurt, and an apple that morning. But now, after the close call with Cade followed by Rachel's emotional scene, she was in dire need of some stress relief. Nothing worked better for that than a big ol' pot of Texas comfort food.

Besides that, chili was Roy's favorite, and she wanted him in a good mood when she told him the idea she'd come up with on the way home from Mia's house. When it came to convincing Roy of anything, she knew to lay her groundwork first then ease into it.

She set Roy's bowl in front of him, put hers at the place beside him then went to take a pan of cornbread from the oven.

Roy folded the section of paper containing the evening television programming and tossed it aside. "We might as well just throw the set out the window," he rumbled. "Not a damn thing worth watching these days. Nothing on but that reality crap. If eatin' worms and runnin' races half nekkid on some beach with a bunch of strangers is the world's new reality, we're moving to the Twilight Zone."

"Ha!" Aggie pulled out her chair and sat. "The U.S. Army couldn't drag you off this farm." She sliced the cornbread and served him a piece. "How'd the fence building go today, anyway?"

"Same as yesterday." Roy tasted the chili, licked his lips, frowned. "You go a little crazy with the cayenne pepper, Aggie girl?"

"I made it same as always."

In answer, Roy grunted and took another bite. "You know I don't like eatin' this late. It gives me indigestion."

Aggie lifted her spoon. "Sorry. The girls and I got to talking and the time slipped away from us."

He eyed her purple blouse. "You wear that to the shop this morning?"

"No, I came home to change for the meeting after I ran my errands."

"Must've just missed you." He lifted his left hand and showed her his bandaged index finger. "Cut it on some barbed wire and ran home to fix it up; you weren't here then."

She looked at him sympathetically.

Swallowing, he rolled his shoulders then tilted his head side-to-side. "Dad-gum crick," he muttered.

"I'll give you a back rub later." Aggie smiled at him.

Roy looked up briefly from his bowl and smiled back.

"It's nice havin' you home earlier these days," she said.

"Nothing too pressing in the winter. You know that."

"Seems to me, hiring J.P. took some of the load off, too." Their nephew had moved back to Muddy Creek a year ago, and Roy had hired the young man to help out with the last harvest. Afterward, he kept J.P. on. "I guess he's working out?"

"You kidding? J.P. could run the place single-handed."

"Good. You don't need to be putting in the long hours you used to, winter or not." Aggie knew better than to remind him that the doctor had ordered as much. Last year's "little flare-up," as Roy called it, was a touchy subject for him. He liked to pretend the chest pains he'd had, not to mention the test results showing off-the-charts cholesterol, didn't mean anything. She also never mentioned that they now ate ground turkey instead of ground beef, that the milk he drank these days was skim rather than whole, and a hundred other little healthy adjustments she'd made to her cooking.

"I heard you had to swing by Mia's today and lay down."

Aggie lowered her spoon. "I swear, a person can't burp in this town without everyone knowing ten minutes later what it smelled like. Who told you that?"

"Buck Miller. He called while you were at your meeting to see how you were feelin'."

"Well, that makes sense." Mia's widowed seventy-something next-door neighbor had been shoveling snow off his front walk when the Sheriff showed up unannounced. The man might be half-blind, but his hearing obviously wasn't suffering. "Poor old man needs something to occupy his time now that Martha's gone. To keep him from eavesdropping."

Roy huffed. "Snoopy s.o.b. couldn't mind his own

business when the wife was alive, either. He said Cade Sloan stopped by Mia's twice today. What's up with that?"

Aggie buttered her cornbread. "I didn't ask. It's none of my business."

"That's never stopped you before." Roy crumbled cornbread into the big glass of milk Aggie had poured for him. "Since when do you get migraines?"

"Since about eleven-thirty this morning. You mean Buck didn't tell you the time?"

With half the cornbread broken up, Roy used his spoon to dunk the crumbs into the milk. He nodded at his glass. "You were a little stingy with the milk, hon. How 'bout a top off?"

Aggie pushed away from the table and headed for the refrigerator, wondering if the time was right to tell Roy her idea. He didn't know it, but she'd recently opened her own savings account at the bank and, for the past month and a half, she'd been depositing her coffee shop earnings. She had planned to use the money to buy two tickets to Boston for their granddaughters' graduation in May. But now, after spending time with Rachel this afternoon and realizing all she'd missed out on with the girls living so far away, she didn't want to wait another four months to see them. She might not have enough money yet, but they could use what she had to pay for some of the trip, and Roy could spring for the rest.

And after they went and Roy realized how much he, too, had missed seeing Jimmy and the girls all these years, she'd insist they go back in May.

Aggie returned to the table with the milk carton, considering how to broach the subject. "What do you want to do tonight?" she asked while pouring a stream of white over the cornbread in Roy's glass.

"I don't know." He shrugged. "Watch TV, I guess."

She emptied the carton and sat. "You said nothing was on."

Roy spooned a bite of soggy cornbread into his mouth. "We still got time to go into town and rent a movie."

"You'll only fall asleep watching it."

Leaning back in his chair, Roy settled his hands atop his round belly, right above his belt buckle. "Why don't you just tell me what you've got planned for me, Aggie girl?" His dark eyes held a twinge of amusement, and a whole lot of wariness.

"Well . . ." Aggie leaned over and pinched a crumb from the corner of her husband's mouth. "Since winter's slow for you around the farm, and you said J.P. can run the place single-handed anyway, I was thinking we might get on the Internet and check out flights to Boston."

Beneath the sparse strands of hair atop Roy's head, his scalp turned fire-engine red. "Are you crazy, woman? Do you know what they're charging for plane tickets these days?"

"Not all that much." Unsurprised and undeterred by his outburst, Aggie scowled at him. "To hear you talk, you'd think we're on our last dime. We've got plenty of money in the bank, Roy."

"I don't care how much money we've got, I'm not

paying some airline hundreds of dollars for a five-hour ride and a package of stale peanuts."

"What if the tickets don't cost you anything?"

He gave her a look of disbelief. "Where do you think you're gonna get free tickets to Massachusetts?"

"Just *what if?*"

"That's the dangedest thing I ever heard, Aggie. Why would anyone want to go to the Northeast in January?" He crushed his paper napkin and tossed it into his bowl. "It's colder than a witch's tit up there this time of year."

Aggie shoved her chili to the center of the table and crossed her arms. "It's cold here, too, if you haven't noticed."

"There's a difference between Yankee cold and Texas cold."

She'd promised herself she wouldn't let his stubbornness reduce her to tears. But, like always, when Aggie's frustration with her husband reached its limit the waterworks started. "Why would anyone want to go up there?" Pushing her chair back, she stood and glared down at him. "To see granddaughters, that's why. To see a son and daughter-in-law. What's wrong with you, Roy Cobb? Don't you have a heart? Have you forgotten the meaning of family?" She stormed from the kitchen.

Behind her, chair legs scraped the linoleum, and she heard the thump of boots against the floor. "Aggie, come back here. What's got into you?"

As she entered their bedroom, Aggie turned and slammed the door in Roy's startled, red-splotched face. Then she locked it.

He rattled the knob. Pounded on the door. Waited several seconds. Knocked more softly. "Aggie, honey," he said with what she knew was forced calm. "Open up."

"Don't you 'Aggie, honey' me." She threw a pillow at the door. "Is this how it's going to be, Roy?"

"How what's gonna be?" His voice became louder and more exasperated with each word.

How could the man have lived with her forty-seven years and be so out of touch with her heart? "The rest of our lives. The two of us alone in this house, me waiting on you hand and foot while you gripe about everything from what's on TV to the way I cook."

"I love your cooking, hon. You know that."

"This isn't about my cooking," Aggie said between gritted teeth, trying not to scream.

"Damn it, woman." Roy sounded baffled. "What's it about then?"

"I want more, Roy."

"More what?"

"More in our old age than staring at each other from a set of matching recliners every night."

A long silence, then, "Like what?"

Aggie closed her eyes, puffed out her cheeks, let the air seep slowly from between her lips. "Like a simple night out every now and then. Like an occasional trip. Maybe even across the blessed state line. Like visits with our family. I want—"

"What you're really saying is you want more than

me," Roy exploded. "That you're not happy with *me* anymore."

"I didn't say I wanted to go alone." When she heard him stomp off, Aggie unlocked and opened the bedroom door. He stood across the den in the front entry hall, snatching his coat and hat from the rack. "Where are you going?"

"To Joe Pat's," Roy answered, his back to her.

Aggie's irritation shifted, making space for a slice of concern. Roy hadn't played pool in years. And he didn't drink. "You never go to Joe Pat's."

He opened the front door, glanced over his shoulder at her. "Maybe it's time I started."

Chapter 6

Cade stood on Mia's dark front porch, holding a small gift bag. He still believed she knew something about Rachel Nye's whereabouts. Was certain of it. But after coming up empty-handed this afternoon, he'd called Judge Brennan. The old man was bullheaded. He refused to grant any more search warrants unless Cade presented hard evidence instead of mere suspicion.

So Cade decided he'd be smart to do a little damage control. He had two reasons for wanting to soften Mia up; one personal, the other professional. Both involving trust.

He had set out to buy flowers, then came up with a better idea. At least he hoped this gift was better than a bouquet of tulips. Cade rang the doorbell and stared down at the small, glossy red bag he held, left over from the store's Christmas stock, most likely. He'd find out soon enough if he'd chosen well, he thought, when the porch light came on.

The door opened and Mia peeked out. Her brown hair was loose; it brushed the tops of her shoulders. "Cade." She shook her head at him. "You never give up, do you?" When the door opened wider, he saw that she held a staple gun.

"Don't shoot." He lifted the sack with one hand while removing his hat with the other. "I brought a peace offering."

She looked from him to the gift and back. "You didn't have to do that."

"Oh, yes I did. Open it. You'll see."

They traded items; he took the staple gun, she took the sack. Mia reached inside and pulled out the CD. "Oh my gosh!" A laugh bubbled out of her. "Carole King's *Tapestry*."

"It may take three decades or more, but I always return what I borrow."

"Where'd you get this?"

"After I left the coffee shop this afternoon, I had to run into Amarillo to tend to some business. I stopped by a music store before I came back. I must've tossed out your old eight-track tape some time or another and they don't carry them anymore. Sorry. Hope the CD will do as a replacement."

"Of course it will. I don't even have an eight-track player now. Does anyone?" Clutching the CD to her chest, Mia laughed. "You can't fool me, though. You didn't toss the tape, you wore it out on all your parking excursions. I remember your smooth high school reputation with the girls."

"Yeah, well . . . I always thought I retained a little

of that old magic, but you're starting to make me wonder."

Her laughter drifted away on the chilled night air. The only warmth he felt came from the light in her eyes as she leaned against the doorframe and watched him.

A radio or stereo played inside. The music thumped with bass. "Can I come in, Mia?"

"It's late." Tensing, she took the staple gun from him. "I'm in the middle of a project. Reupholstering an old dining room chair."

"I've reupholstered a chair or two in my day. I could help."

"Thanks, but I don't need any more—" She cut the sentence short. "I don't need any help, Cade. I'm about to call it a night."

Any *more help*. That's what she'd started to say. Meaning someone was already in there helping her. He *knew* it. "I realize you've turned me down the last couple of times I've asked. I should take the hint, but I guess I'm either determined or a sucker for punishment." He cleared his throat. "Why don't we go out for some supper tomorrow night?"

"Cade . . ." She averted her gaze. "I'm sorry. I'd better not."

"So much for my smooth reputation with the ladies." He smiled and rubbed his chin between his fingers. "Guess I can't complain. It served me well until I got out of college and married Jill. Then, *poof*, it disappeared. Just like that."

"It's not you. I'm just not ready to date. Not anybody. I've told you that."

He narrowed his eyes. "You mean to say if Brad Pitt or that Clooney character asked, you wouldn't jump at the chance?"

"*Well . . .*" She pursed her lips, as if pondering the question. "That would be a tempting offer, but I'm sure those two wouldn't give me a second look."

"Then they'd be fools."

She watched him a minute then said, "You know what I think?"

"I wish I did."

"I think this sudden impulse of yours to date me might have something to do with the fact that I'm the only unattached woman in town over the age of nineteen and under seventy."

"That's not true. What about Janice Dubinsky?" he asked, referring to the middle school girls' P.E. teacher.

Mia smirked. "Janice isn't interested in men."

Cade feigned surprise. "Nobody ever told me that."

"They won't, either. But everyone knows it's true. Even you."

When a crash sounded somewhere in the house, he peeked around her shoulder, trying to see in. "You got a packrat here, too?"

She jerked, leaning to block his view. "My cat. She's always jumping up on the furniture and knocking stuff off. Picture frames, vases, you name it."

"I didn't know you had a cat."

Mia looked flustered. "Got it for Christmas. It's a kitten, really. From Aggie. Her cat had a litter." She blurted a short laugh. "Not something I'd planned on, but what could I say? Aggie's always afraid I get lonely."

"Do you?" When her eyes flicked away from his, he wished he hadn't asked such a personal question.

"Sometimes." She shivered. "I'm still not used to living alone."

"It gets easier with time. Did for me, anyway." When another rattle sounded behind her, he said, "You sure I can't come in? Maybe put that CD on and see if it has the same effect on women it had on sixteen-year-old girls back in the day?"

"Nice try, Cade." She smiled. "Maybe another time."

"Now we're getting somewhere." He put on his hat, shrugged. "Another time is better than never." Turning, he started down the walkway. "Goodnight, Mia."

"Cade?"

Pausing, he looked back at her.

She held up the CD. "Thanks."

Cade grinned. "I should be the one thanking you."

"Oh, *really*." She propped a fist on one hip. "I suppose a lot of women from Muddy Creek High's class of '72 would be thanking me, too, if they knew I was the one who loaned it to you."

"Not so many." His gaze lingered on her silhouette in the doorway and, for the first time in a long while, Cade felt lonely, too. And more determined than ever. "Besides, I want to listen to the music with *you* now, not them."

Mia's hand slowly lowered from her hip.

"And Mia?"

"Yes?" Her voice was quiet.

"Back in school? Your hair always smelled like strawberries. I never forgot that."

Leanne removed her eye makeup then washed her face and applied moisturizer. She was slipping into her nightgown when the bathroom door opened and Eddie walked in, carrying his shoes.

"Hey." He glanced at her as he walked past, headed to the closet, pulling his shirttail from the waistband of his pants.

"Hi. Where've you been?"

He opened the closet door, put his shoes inside, then began unbuttoning his shirt. "Shooting pool at Joe Pat's."

"All night?" Leanne crossed her arms.

Eddie shrugged. "You were at your meeting." He took off his shirt, tossed it toward the dirty clothes basket then unbuckled his belt, avoiding her eyes.

His dismissive attitude stung. "I cooked."

"I wasn't sure you'd be here for dinner."

"I told you I would." When he didn't respond, she said, "I was here."

"Were you?" He looked up at her as he bent to step out of his pants. "Physically, maybe. I doubt if you would've noticed me sitting across the table."

"What's that supposed to mean?"

Without answering, Eddie walked past her wearing only his boxers.

She followed him into the bedroom, watched him pull back the comforter on the bed then climb beneath the covers. He plumped the pillows, leaned back against them and reached to the nightstand for the novel he'd been reading the past few nights.

For a moment, Leanne just stared at him. Time had been easy on her husband. The silver threaded through his dark, wavy hair and the faint lines fanning the bronzed skin at the sides of his eyes only made him more handsome. Eddie wasn't tall—only five-ten—but he was broad shouldered and as fit as he'd ever been, thanks to all the sports he continued to play, week in, week out, all through the year. An adult basketball league in the winter. Baseball in the summer. And in the spring he volunteered as coach for an elementary school boy's soccer team, where he ran up and down the sidelines, cheering the little guys on.

Leanne climbed into bed beside him. Eddie was right; she hadn't been here in a long time, not really. Not since Christmas. Along with the shopping and carols and twinkling lights, the holidays had brought the reality of her future into focus. She and Eddie were both only children. Her parents were gone, and so were his; his father had died over the summer. They had no other family left besides Aggie, and Aggie was fast approaching seventy. Someday soon, their lives would truly be empty.

Leaning back against the pillows, Leanne closed her eyes, and there it was . . . the memory that had kept her awake for more nights than she could count. Thirty-four years ago . . . driving home with Eddie from a party at Cooper Lake on a Saturday night, both of them blind drunk. God, they were so young; she was sixteen, Eddie was seventeen. Leanne was behind the wheel; she'd charmed him into letting her drive his new car. Even now she could hear their carefree laughter, feel Eddie's hand on her thigh. She could see his hazy dark eyes, then the startling flash of an animal in the headlights when she looked back at the road.

Leanne's heartbeat kicked up as she remembered Eddie's yell, her scream, her hand jerking the steering wheel. The looming tree, the impact. Eddie pulled her from the wreckage before anyone arrived, then took the blame.

Leanne opened her eyes and glanced over at Eddie, aching for him to hold her. They had lost a baby that night, a child she hadn't known about until she miscarried. A child no one except Eddie, Aggie, and Mia knew about even today. She had also lost the ability to bear more children.

There'd been a time when she and Eddie had discussed adoption. Twenty years ago, they had even applied to be foster parents, but never went through with it. Leanne started therapy instead. She faced up to what she'd done, accepted her fate and moved on.

Or so she'd thought.

She knew she should share her concerns with Eddie, let him help her figure out how to fill the gaping hole that had reappeared in their lives. But she didn't know how to explain the emptiness in her heart without hurting him like she had in the past. So she stayed quiet. And as her unhappiness grew, so did the tension between them.

Leanne took a book from her nightstand drawer.

Sometimes she caught him studying her instead of the pages when they read at night. Same thing when they watched TV. As if he was searching for a sign in her face that her prior instability had returned. What did he expect to see? A tic? An outbreak of hives or tears? Was he afraid she'd have a sudden deranged fit, tear off all her clothes, run naked into the street? How could she convince him she wasn't headed for another breakdown? That she'd never again disappear on him like she had all those years ago? She felt bad about worrying Eddie, but his constant scrutiny was wearing her nerves thin. If he didn't stop soon, she'd snap, all right.

After several minutes of silence, Eddie reached over, nudged beneath her chin with the pad of his thumb until she looked at him. "I'm sorry, baby."

"Me, too." She managed a slight smile. "Let's start over, okay?"

He nodded, his mouth curving up at one corner. "You first."

She closed her book. "What went on at the paper today?"

"Not much." He bent his neck from side to side, as if working out the kinks from long hours spent at his desk. "A runaway kid shoplifted from a couple of the stores in town yesterday."

Leanne's heart skipped. "I heard about that. Cade Sloan stopped by the shop this morning to ask us to keep an eye out for her."

"Shoot. She's long gone by now. I bet she caught a ride with some trucker and is halfway to California."

"What's a kid like that looking for, I wonder?" She

thought of Mia's daughter, Christy. A moody, creative loner; a puzzle piece that never quite fit into Muddy Creek's picture. Then she thought of tiny, hollow-eyed Rachel. The girl was too thin, too bleached and made-up, too smart-mouthed and needy. Too everything.

Just like Leanne at fourteen.

Leanne shook her head. "It's not easy being a kid . . . growing up."

He pushed a strand of hair behind her ear.

"What about you? How was your meeting this afternoon?"

"Good." She laughed. "I'm still a little blown away that I'm old enough to be a full-fledged Red Hat member. I'm *fifty*, Eddie. How's that possible?"

He winked. "Happens to the best of us."

"Did you think our lives would be different than this by the time we reached half a century?"

"I'm not sure I ever thought about it." The space between his brows puckered. "Did you?"

Shrugging, Leanne said, "I don't know. It's just . . . nothing much has changed when you think about it. We live in the same old town where we were both born, in the same old house I grew up in." Which had belonged to her ever since her daddy died just after her eighteenth birthday.

Eddie's body tensed. "And you're married to the same old guy you used to date in high school."

Leanne tilted her head to one side. He was too sensitive. Any time she even hinted at something amiss, he assumed he was the cause. "I wasn't gonna say that, Eddie."

"But is it what you're thinking?"

She shook her head. "No . . ."

"Then what?" Eddie touched her cheek.

"I guess I always thought—" She brushed a finger across his chest. *That there'd be more time. That somehow or another, we'd have a family. That this house wouldn't be so quiet . . . so empty.* "Nothing," she said, and opened her book again. She felt Eddie's stare.

"My football reunion's in a few weeks," he said. "I was thinking . . . instead of driving home afterward, why don't we stay over in Amarillo for the weekend? Someplace nice. We could have ourselves a little mini-vacation. It'll be good for us."

Leanne nibbled her lower lip. She'd forgotten about Eddie's reunion. Back in the seventies, he'd played for West Texas A&M, a school located two hours away in Canyon. A group of the guys and their wives got together every five years in Amarillo for dinner, drinks, and reminiscing.

"You up for it?" Eddie asked.

Leanne looked at him, hesitated then answered, "Not really. I mean, staying over would be nice, but I'm not looking forward to the reunion." She winced. "Would you mind if I skipped it this year?"

His eyes dulled and the muscle along his jaw line jumped. "Do whatever you want to do, Lea. I don't care."

She sighed. "I'm sorry, Eddie, but it's the same thing every time we get together with the old crowd. I get to hear about their kids and they look at me with questions in their eyes."

"That stopped a long time ago, Lea. They know by now we're not having kids."

"They may have stopped asking, but they still wonder why we didn't." His irritated look told her she was being paranoid. "I'm not imagining it, Eddie. I was forty-five last time we met and Scott Whitlow's wife still asked me why we didn't ever go through with our plans to be foster parents."

"So what? You don't have to explain anything to anybody. Besides, things will be different this time. Most of their kids are grown. Hell, Marcus and Bobby are granddaddies now."

Leanne grimaced. "Oh, boy. You know what that means: baby pictures."

"Well, I'd rather go without you if you're going to be all moody and ruin everyone's good time."

Eddie tossed his book onto his nightstand and switched off his lamp. Turning away from Leanne, he tugged the blanket over his shoulder.

"Good night," Leanne murmured to the back of his head. When he didn't respond, she started to add, *I love you,* but instead she blinked back tears and switched off her lamp, too.

Chapter 7

On Saturday morning, Mia didn't want to leave Rachel alone at the house when she left for work, so the two of them devised a plan. Or rather, Rachel did. The girl had a shifty mind, which made Mia nervous, but in this case, thankful, too. Rachel had spotted several empty boxes in the garage. They'd once been packed with coffee shop supplies. But at five-thirty A.M. on January 8th, the largest of the collection sat in the back of Mia's Tahoe, packed with eighty or so pounds of Rachel Nye.

"You okay back there?" Mia called over her shoulder, as she cruised down her dark, quiet neighborhood street.

"Yeah," came a muffled reply, followed by a giggle.

Rachel considered the method of transfer from the house to the coffee shop a wild adventure. She was having the time of her life.

But the escapade brought reality crashing down on Mia. Not only did she feel like a criminal, she *was* one.

Questions she'd previously ignored raced through her mind. Would a person only be fined if convicted of harboring a fugitive? Or would jail time be the punishment?

She stared ahead at the snowy road, shivered, adjusted the heater vent so that warm air blew directly on her. How many blankets did they give you in jail? Would they allow you to bring your own pillow? She couldn't sleep without her Beautyrest goose down.

"Why do y'all have to go to work so *early*?" A noisy yawn then a groan emerged from the box. "Who drinks coffee at five-thirty in the morning?"

"I do." Were prisoners served coffee, Mia wondered? If so, probably only one cup. And instant. She shuddered, then echoed Rachel's yawn. How would she survive a day on one cup of instant coffee? Mia turned onto Main. "You're only staying at the shop until Aggie's ready to leave. I'm afraid you'd get bored stuck in the kitchen all day. Or someone might catch a glimpse of you. Aggie will take you to the house and stay with you there."

Which undoubtedly meant more speculation for the gossipmongers, courtesy of her neighbor. A tense-sounding Aggie had called last night and relayed Buck Miller's conversation with Roy. Aggie spending time at the house two days in a row while Mia was at the shop would start Buck's tongue wagging again, no doubt about it.

"What about Leanne?" Rachel asked.

"We take turns working Saturdays. This is her day

off. She has errands to run and a manicure appointment."

Since it was Saturday, Aggie would only be able to stay at the house a short while. Roy would be home earlier, expecting her to dote on him. Mia made a mental note to call Leanne to see if she could take over when Aggie left. If Leanne couldn't make it, Mia wasn't sure what she'd do. In addition to her apprehension about Rachel running off, she had her property to consider. Mia chewed her lower lip. She hadn't thought to hide her jewelry. Or anything else.

"If it turns out you have to spend some time alone at the house, I don't have any reason to worry about that, do I, Rachel?" She glanced into the mirror. The box shifted and she heard a knocking noise, as if the girl's elbow or knee hit against the side.

"*Duh-uh*. I'm only gonna steal all your old-timey records and sell 'em on Ebay."

Sarcastic little snot. Mia bit back a laugh. For some odd reason, she trusted the girl. That would earn her a "crazy" label from Leanne, but what else could she do? "Get me a good price, okay? They're antiques," Mia teased. When she didn't get a response, she added, "I hope you know I'm kidding. You wouldn't really sell my stuff, would you?"

"I'm *not* retarded." Rachel didn't laugh. "I'm *getting* a *cramp*." The whine in her voice indicated that her excitement over this little adventure was waning fast.

Mia halted at the intersection stop sign at the same

time Aubrey Rickett's rattletrap truck pulled to the facing sign.

He waved and squinted.

She waved back and, without moving her lips, said, "We're almost there." She eased across the intersection. Glancing in the rearview mirror, Mia saw the box tip to one side as Aubrey crept past, eyeing her back window. "Be still," Mia hissed.

"*Man.* If I have to stay alone at the house, what am I supposed to do? Besides not steal, I mean."

Okay, she deserved that. She'd thought it, after all. "Read those magazines I saw in your backpack."

"I've already read them a million and one times."

Mia pulled into the parking lot beside the Brewed Awakening and eased toward the alley. "After the morning rush, before Aggie leaves, I'll make a quick trip to the grocery and buy you some more. I need to pick up something for supper, anyway." And it would give her a chance to talk to Mack about whether or not he was seriously considering pressing charges against Rachel. "Leanne and Aggie are coming over again." She hoped they'd have better luck devising a plan than they had yesterday. "How about tacos? I make great guacamole."

"Tacos are good. But not guacamole. I don't eat anything green. Or anything with 'loaf' in the name."

"Like meatloaf?"

Rachel made a gagging sound then said, "Can we have a slumber party?"

Mia chuckled. "With Aggie and Leanne?"

"Yeah. I used to have slumber parties all the time.

My mom would make us popcorn and brownies." She paused for a few moments then added, "And hot chocolate." Another pause. "Me and my friends? We'd dance and have pillow fights and do each others' makeup and stuff."

A slumber party. Mia moved slowly through the alley. She hadn't hosted one since Christy was in fifth or sixth grade. She hadn't been a *participant* since her own high school days. "That sounds like fun to me. We'll see what Aggie and Leanne think."

The box wobbled and produced a series of knocks and thumps.

Mia parked the Tahoe at the shop's back door. "We're here. Remember, you have to stay in the kitchen. And when we open for business, you'll have to be quiet."

Another few thumps against the cardboard, an "*ouch*," then, "Whatever."

Aggie was ready for them. The back door opened, spilling light into the alley. The older woman stuck out her silver-gray head as Mia climbed from the Tahoe. "Tell me you have a strong, healthy heart, Ag."

"Strong as an ox. Why?" Before Mia could answer, Aggie peeked into the windows of the vehicle and said, "Where's—?"

"You'll see." She opened the Tahoe's rear door. "Your back strong, too?"

Aggie looked at the box. Understanding dawned in her expression. She smiled. "Sugar, I'm a farm wife, remember?"

• • •

As promised, Mia visited Mack's Grocery later that morning. The small store buzzed with shoppers, and she recognized all the faces.

Missy Potter, the woman whose tree Aggie toppled day before yesterday, cornered Mia on the toilet paper aisle to ask about Aggie's mental stability. Apparently, old man Miller told the woman about Aggie bursting into tears at the coffee shop for no particular reason, and also that she'd had to rest at Mia's yesterday before driving back to the farm. Missy let it be known she thought Aggie's license should be taken away.

Then Aubrey Ricketts, who Mia was starting to wish had never retired from his thirty-year stint guarding the bank, headed her off just short of the periodicals to tell her about his gout. During the conversation, he asked about the box she'd been hauling in the backseat of her Tahoe on the way to work. He "coulda swore" he "saw the blasted thing move."

Mia made excuses then made her escape, telling herself she, Leanne, and Aggie must be insane to think they could keep Rachel's presence in Muddy Creek a secret for long.

Mia tossed a movie magazine into the cart then a *Seventeen* and one called *Fashion Trends*. All requested by Rachel. Then she started for the food aisles. She picked up taco makings, lemonade, popcorn, instant hot chocolate and brownie ingredients. Everything Rachel had mentioned her "mom" providing at previous sleepovers, plus more. If Mia were betting, she'd put money on the probability that Rachel had never in her life had girlfriends over for the night at any of her foster homes. That suspicion twisted her heart. She wanted to make tonight special. An event.

When Rachel invited Aggie to the slumber party earlier, Aggie had squealed like a teenybopper. So Mia had called Leanne and, after a fit of laughter, she agreed to join in. She also relieved Mia by saying she'd come over to sit with Rachel later this afternoon when Aggie left for the farm.

On the hygiene aisle, Mia scanned Mack's sparse selection of cosmetics and, on impulse, chose a bottle of pale purple nail polish for Rachel. Moving onto the lipstick, she considered fat tubes of fruit-flavored gloss. At Rachel's age, she had preferred candy apple. And she'd used strawberry-scented shampoo. Recalling Cade's comment about the scent of her hair back then, Mia smiled. That he'd remember such a thing both amused and flustered her. Of course, as a teenager she probably smelled like a walking fruit market, considering the fact she'd also used coconut hand lotion. No big surprise Cade hadn't forgotten.

She decided on bubblegum-flavored lip gloss for Rachel. Buying the cosmetics seemed silly, since the girl already had enough makeup stashed in her backpack to open a store of her own. What Rachel *really* needed was a change of clothes, socks and underwear, a coat that fit, another pair of shoes. But those items required that she be along for a fitting. Which meant they'd have to shop somewhere besides Muddy Creek so as not to be caught. Shopping in Amarillo, the closest city of any size, was a risk, too, since Rachel had lived there. Someone might recognize her.

A disturbing realization hit Mia. She had watched the Amarillo news last night and had read the city's paper. There'd been no mention of Rachel. Nothing. Eddie had written a short piece in *The Muddy Creek Chronicle*, but that was it. Didn't lost foster kids receive the same attention as those with families?

Mia reversed the cart as an idea crossed her mind. Maybe shopping in Amarillo wouldn't be that big of a risk, after all. And as for anyone recognizing Rachel . . . Pausing at a display of hair color she'd previously passed by, Mia chose three different shades. Getting rid of Rachel's distinctive white-blonde, black-rooted hair would drastically alter her appearance. But buying only one color would be a mistake. Rachel possessed definite opinions about everything.

It amazed Mia how quickly the girl had opened up to her, Leanne, and Aggie at their pretend Red Hat meeting. She supposed that Rachel's history of moving from family to family, and school to school, had made her an expert at adjusting to new people and new situations. Rachel didn't put on airs. In fact, the only things the least bit artificial about her were her hair color, makeup and her imaginary family background. Those disguises, though, failed to hide the vulnerability underneath, her desire to belong, to be important to someone, accepted. Her pretense of a prior stable home was understandable, but heartbreaking, too. Rachel needed a safe, familiar place where she could retreat, if only in her mind.

On the canned goods aisle, Mack unloaded a crate of green beans. Mia rolled her cart over. "Hi, Mack. I hear you had a little excitement around here the other day."

He turned away from the shelves and faced her, his bald head gleaming beneath the overhead lights. "You mean the shoplifter?"

Nodding, she said, "The sheriff told me you caught her."

"Red-handed." He chuckled. "She was about to slip a jar of peanut butter into her bag. Don't know where she planned to put it; the thing was already crammed full."

"Peanut butter, huh? That's not the sort of thing kids usually steal, is it? She must've been hungry."

"Candy's usually the item of choice for kids. I think she just hadn't made it to that aisle yet."

"So, what else did she take?"

"Pop-Tarts. Cookies. A couple of apples. A jar of grapefruit juice. Stuff like that."

"Sounds like a kid in trouble to me. Not just out to pull one over on somebody."

Mack set a can on the shelf behind him then scratched his chin. "Maybe. She was a skinny little thing. She looked scared and lost."

"When she's found, you planning to press charges?"

His cheek twitched. "Well, Mia, I hate it, but I feel like I have to. I can't be giving away merchandise and stay in business."

Mia smirked at him. "Now, Mack. How many times have you opened a bag of pet food to feed that stray dog that hangs out around here?"

He started to respond then looked beyond her. "Hey there, Sheriff."

Turning, Mia found Cade behind her, a soft drink in his hand.

"Mia. Mack." He popped the top and lifted the can. "Stopped by for a Coke."

She pursed her lips and stared at him. *And just happened to end up on the same aisle as me.* She knew for a fact the drink machines were out in front of the store. "Well, I'd better get back to work," she said.

Cade smiled. "I'll walk you out."

"Aren't you here to talk to Mack?"

"Just to tell him still no word on that girl."

"I figured as much," Mack said. "Now Mia's got me feeling all guilty about making the kid face the music."

"You do whatever you think's right, Mack." Avoiding Cade's stare, Mia nodded at the grocer and started to push her cart past him. "Nice talking to you."

Cade, too, said goodbye to the man then caught up to her. "You care to explain why you're so concerned over Mack pressing charges against Rachel Nye? Seeing as how you don't know a thing about her whereabouts, I mean."

Rachel wasn't the only sarcastic snot in town, Mia decided. "No, I don't care to explain." She maneuvered the cart around Aubrey Ricketts, who stood center aisle, staring at them. "Were you eavesdropping?" she asked Cade.

"I couldn't help but overhear. You two weren't whispering."

"I was only making conversation. How'd you know I was here, anyway?"

"What makes you think I knew? I was buying a Coke, like I said." He slid her a sideward glance. "I saw Missy Potter out front. She mentioned running into you."

"Isn't there something you should be doing?"

"I can't imagine what."

"Well I, for one, didn't elect you to office so you could spend your days stalking women and drinking Cokes."

He grinned. "So, you voted for me?"

Mia shook her head. "You're incorrigible, Cade."

"So I've been told." He took a drink, eyeing her basket. "That's some interesting stuff you've got there." He reached inside and pulled out the bottle of polish. "I never noticed you with painted fingernails before. And I sure didn't peg you as the purple type." Lifting the lip gloss, too, he muttered, "Bubblegum."

The smug certainty on his face didn't escape Mia. "You don't know everything there is to know about me, Cade."

"I've been trying to do something about that. You don't make it easy."

When they arrived at the checkout, everyone in the store, from the two checkout clerks, to the sackers, to the six or so other customers up front, watched her and Cade. Within half an hour, the entire town would think they'd gone grocery shopping together and have them shacking up.

Beside her, Cade said, "What? No food for that new kitten Aggie gave you?"

Mia's pulse skipped. "I bought plenty of cat food when I was in here last week."

The checker glanced up as she scanned a box of microwave popcorn. "I don't recall you buying cat food, Mia."

Ignoring the girl, Mia bit the inside of her cheek.

Cade coughed, looking more smug than ever. "Sure you won't change your mind about supper tonight?"

"I'm sure. I have plans."

"To paint your nails purple, eat tacos, and read movie magazines from the looks of it."

She stared straight ahead. "Exactly."

"And listen to Carole King, I hope."

In spite of everything, Mia felt on the verge of laughter. "Maybe."

"Have fun."

"I plan to."

Cade handed her the polish then the lip gloss. Their fingers brushed. Every nerve ending in Mia's body sprang to attention.

"Bet that bubblegum stuff tastes good," Cade said quietly. "Something like that on a girl would've driven me to distraction when I was . . . I don't know . . . fourteen? Fifteen years old?"

Refusing to look at him, she handed the magazines to the clerk.

"That along with your strawberry hair . . . I would've been a goner, for sure."

When the young checker giggled, Mia began plotting Cade's murder.

Chapter 8

*M*ia pulled a pan of brownies from the oven. The shades were drawn, the tacos eaten, the dishes put away. When the high-pitched hum of the hair dryer stopped, she glanced toward her kitchen table where Leanne, Aggie, and Rachel played beauty shop.

"Look at you, sugar!" As Leanne fluffed Rachel's hair, Aggie clapped her hands together.

Leanne had rinsed "toasted chestnut" coloring through Rachel's hair at the kitchen sink, then dried her wet head at the table. The warm tone softened the girl's face and brought out the flecks of gold in her huge brown eyes.

Setting the brownies on the counter to cool, Mia walked to the table and pushed a button on Christy's old makeup mirror. The tiny lights surrounding it flickered to life.

Rachel studied her reflection with uncertainty. "Oh . . . my *God*!"

Beaming, Aggie said, "She looks sweet, doesn't she, Leanne?"

"Sweet?" Rachel's face twisted in disgust.

"She means *sweeeet*, Packrat," Leanne quickly interjected, in a weak imitation of a surfer dude. "As in, *radical*."

Rachel's brows drew together, like they'd been pulled by a thread. She groaned and rolled her eyes.

"At least give me credit for trying," Leanne said dryly.

Aggie only looked baffled by the comment, since what she'd *meant* was sweet as in "nice and prim."

What Rachel looked, Mia thought, was fourteen and pretty, rather than fourteen trying to appear twenty-five.

Stepping back from Rachel's chair, Leanne said, "You fix it like you want it. I'm not good with styles."

Mia reached for the cordless phone when it rang then sat in the chair beside Aggie. She pushed the button.

"Hey, Mom." Her youngest son's deep voice vibrated at the other end of the line.

"Trey!"

Everyone at the table fell silent.

"Is something wrong?" Trey asked. "You sound funny."

Her heart thudding out of control, Mia watched Rachel grab a bottle of hair gel from the center of the table, one she'd pulled earlier from the virtual beauty salon she kept hidden away in the depths of her backpack. "Nothing's wrong. I'm just surprised to hear your voice."

"It hasn't been that long since we talked."

"That's why I'm surprised." Knowing she made no sense, Mia gave a jittery laugh.

"I was thinking," Trey said after a moment of silence. "Why don't you let me fly you to Dallas next Saturday? You can see my new place. Maybe help me with some of the decorating."

"Oh, honey, that sounds fun. Thanks for the offer, but I don't know if I can get away from the coffee shop." Normally she'd jump at the chance to spend time with her busy son.

"That's your Saturday off, isn't it?"

"Well yes, but . . . Let me call you midweek, okay? We'll see how I feel. I still haven't recovered from the holidays."

"We weren't that bad, were we?" His laugh sounded a tad wounded.

Mia cringed inside. Trey referred to himself, his brother, and Brent's family. She hated that she'd given him that impression. "Of course not. I loved having all of you. You know that. I just have a little cold."

After promising to call him on Wednesday, Mia hung up.

"Who was that?" Rachel asked, adding more glossy goo to her fingertips.

"My youngest son."

Leanne unplugged the hair dryer. "Everything okay?"

"Trey wants me to fly there next Saturday to help decorate his new condo."

"Go," Aggie said. "We'll be fine." She slid a glance toward Rachel.

"We'll see," Mia told them.

Leanne changed the subject as she wound the cord around the hairdryer. "Was Roy okay about you spending the night, Ag?"

Aggie's chin lifted a fraction. "No, but he can just go drown himself in root beer floats at Joe Pat's again like he did last night. He drank so much of the stuff, he was up and down going to the bathroom 'til the wee hours."

Rachel giggled. "He was weeing until the wee hours, you mean."

Laughing along with the others, Mia asked, "What was Roy doing at the pool hall? You two have a spat?"

"He was being mule-headed, as usual. It's not worth talking about." Aggie pursed her lips.

"Maybe you'll get roses." Rachel picked and pulled at tiny strands of her hair, spiking it out in every direction. "When my dad was mule-headed he always bought my mom flowers."

"Your foster dad?" Leanne placed the dryer on the table.

Rachel barked a short, sharp laugh. "Ricky? No way. He wouldn't buy Pam flowers in a million years. I'm talking about my *real* dad."

When Leanne and Aggie both frowned at Mia, she sent them a quick wink, hoping they'd let it go. For now, at least.

"There," Rachel said. After a final inspection in the mirror, she sat back and looked at the three women.

The wild style didn't seem as startling with Rachel's new, more natural hair color. Mia liked it. The spikes fit the girl's personality. "Dahling, you look mahvelous," she told her.

Rachel reached for her cosmetic bag.

While she went to work on her face, Aggie rose to cut the brownies. Meanwhile, Leanne and Mia flipped through the new magazines from the grocery store, as well as the ones Rachel had acquired using a five-finger discount.

Leanne turned a page in *Seventeen*. "I notice these models are going subtle on the eye makeup. Light brown liner instead of black. Easy on the shadow." She thumbed another page without looking up. "I know that's not your style, though, Rachel."

"Let me see." Rachel lowered her black eyeliner pencil and took the magazine from Leanne. She flipped through the pages. "Less *is* better with this new hair color. I knew that."

Leanne tilted her head and studied her. "Whatever you think." She shrugged. "I guess you could give it a try."

Handing the magazine back to Leanne, Rachel dug around in her cosmetic bag for a brown pencil. Minutes later, her eyes finished, she brought out a lipstick so dark it appeared almost black.

"Wait a minute," Mia said. "I bought you a little something today." She left the table and went to the utility room where she had left the grocery sack. From inside it, she pulled the lip-gloss tube and the bottle of purple nail polish. She carried them to Rachel.

"What's this?" Rachel took the bottle, a pleased look on her face that she quickly covered.

"The purple made me think of you. You may not like the lip gloss, though. It's just a touch of color, and I know you like the darker stuff."

"Give it a try. Tonight's for experimenting, sugar," Aggie encouraged.

"It tastes good." Rachel smacked her lips after applying a thin layer. Then she looked into the mirror again, her eyes widening when she saw herself.

Leanne whistled.

"Watch out, boys," Mia said with a laugh.

"Yeah, right." Rachel blushed. "Guys my age? They don't know you exist unless you have boobs. Trust me."

"That'll come soon enough, Packrat." Leanne tossed back her hair. "And *you* trust *me*. Sometimes, they're more trouble than they're worth. Besides, you're a head turner without 'em."

Rachel didn't appear convinced. "Some clothes just look better with boobs."

"Well, now that you mention it, a girl *should* keep a few tricks up her sleeve for special occasions. For instance, if you have to wear a strapless gown to prom or something like that." Reaching into the pocket of her jeans, Leanne pulled out a tissue. "These aren't necessarily just for blowing your nose, kiddo."

Rachel turned beet red and everyone laughed. She

blew out a noisy breath as she turned off the mirror and faced Aggie. "Your turn."

"Me?" Aggie frowned.

Grabbing a magazine from the table, Rachel flipped to an ad featuring a casual, but sharply-dressed woman about Aggie's age. "See her? I think you should copy her."

"Copy her?" Aggie's face paled. She blinked at the page.

"Yeah." Rachel slid the magazine over for Leanne to see. "Don't you think those kind of jeans would look good on her?"

Leanne agreed. "Aggie, you're built just like this model."

"She sort of *looks* like her, too." Rachel glanced over at Aggie, tilted her head, squinted. "Or you *would* if you'd change a few things. I mean, no offense, but you could *totally* use a makeover." She pointed to one of the hair color boxes Mia had bought. "You should use that one. It's like the picture."

Mia picked up the box and read, "Autumn Kiss."

"Oh, good Lord." Aggie bit her lip. "I've been gray for years. What would Roy think?"

"Lady, you go home looking like that," Leanne nodded at the picture in the magazine, "Roy'll think he died and went to heaven. Even those funky little glasses she's wearing would look good on you."

Aggie let loose a nervous laugh. "You think so? They're *reading* glasses. If I started using those, I'd have to wear my contacts."

"You should." Rachel popped her knuckles and shifted to look at Mia first, then Leanne. "Okay, we better start so I'll have time to help you two."

Amused with Rachel's sudden take-charge attitude, Mia asked, "We need makeovers, too?"

"*Duh-uh.* Especially you, Mia. I mean, Leanne already has cool clothes. And her hair and makeup look sort of decent for someone old."

"Wow." Leanne arched a brow. "Decent. For someone old. Thanks."

Rachel took the towel Leanne had used to dry her hair and wrapped it around Aggie's shoulders before guiding her to the kitchen sink. "You should play that CD your boyfriend bought you, Mia."

"Boyfriend?" Leanne and Aggie both blurted at once, turning to her.

"It wasn't a boyfriend, it was Cade." Mia scowled at Rachel, who grinned. "He stopped by to snoop last night."

"And to give her that CD," Rachel added, turning on the faucet and testing the water.

Aggie slipped off her glasses, her eyes widening. "We told you that man has a soft spot for you. Didn't we, Leanne?"

Mia felt a hot flash coming on. "He was returning something he borrowed a long time ago, that's all."

"It was brand new," Rachel announced. "Still in the wrapper."

"A brand new CD?" Aggie frowned. "That's an odd thing to borrow."

"It's a long story. He borrowed it way back in high

school." Mia flipped through the magazine, not seeing the pages.

"Hmmm." Leanne tapped a finger on the table and smirked. "You and I both know CDs didn't exist when we were in high school."

Making a face, Rachel positioned Aggie's head beneath the faucet. "How long ago *was* that?"

Leanne raised her brows and said sarcastically, "So long only a few people had even *heard* of music, wise guy."

Closing the magazine, Mia tossed it aside. "Would y'all just drop it? Cade used the CD as an excuse to snoop, but he didn't get past the front door."

An hour later, Aggie had Autumn Kiss Auburn hair and firm instructions from Rachel to (1) start wearing her contact lenses every day instead of just on special occasions, (2) buy some funky little reading glasses like the ones in the magazine to replace the "old lady" ones, and (3) ditch the polyester pants.

Then it was Mia's turn. Rachel conferred with Leanne and they agreed that Mia should stop wearing baggy overalls so much. With their heads together over the fashion magazines, the two pointed out slim, flared slacks and fitted jackets in feminine colors that would show off Mia's figure and brighten her complexion.

Rachel decided Mia should wear her hair down when not at work. She should also wear a darker shade of lipstick rather than her usual clear gloss since, "you could, like, *totally* use some color to make you not look so tired." According to Rachel, Mia's nails needed attention, too. She wore them clipped short and never bothered with polish. So, in the spirit of experimentation, Mia let Rachel paint them purple. She could hardly wait to flash her fingers at Cade.

As it turned out, Leanne's big hair was *her* only beauty flaw of any consequence since, "That went out, like, with the dinosaurs. Even in Texas."

Close to midnight, wearing pajamas and stuffed with brownies, popcorn, and hot chocolate, Mia sprawled at one end of the couch while Leanne sprawled at the other. They cheered Aggie on as Rachel taught the older woman hip-hop dance steps to the rap music blaring from the living room stereo.

Mia listened to Rachel's laughter, noted the sparkle in her eyes. Eyes that, only yesterday, had looked dull and lifeless and lost.

"What are you thinking?" Leanne asked, scooting closer to Mia's end of the couch.

"I'm thinking Aggie better stick to square dancing."

Aggie jerked and gyrated in her fuzzy pink house shoes, singing, "*Whoop, whoop . . . Whoop, whoop . . .*"

Leanne stifled a laugh. "That's not what I'm talking about."

"I know it isn't." Mia faced her. "I've decided to tell Cade the truth tomorrow. I'm afraid to, but I'm at a loss. We'll just have to trust him to do what's in Rachel's best interest. He's a good man. He must know something about kids. He raised two boys who seem to respect him and enjoy his company."

Mia had seen Cade shopping with his sons in town

over the holidays, laughing and joking with one another. Watching them, her heart had ached over the fact that her own sons no longer had their father's companionship, and that her relationship with her daughter wasn't a close one.

"I talked to Mack today," she said, her gaze on Rachel. "I think he's wavering about pressing charges. And Jesse's a soft heart. I bet if Rachel returned those boots, she'd change her mind, too."

"You're making the right decision, Mia. What's the alternative? Raise her on the sly until she's of age?"

Mia sighed. "I'm just sorry I got you and Aggie into this. Hiding Rachel was a knee-jerk reaction on my part. She brings back all the stuff from when Christy ran off, you know?"

"I understand. I went along with it because she brought back my past, too. You want me to go with you tomorrow when you tell Cade about her?"

The song on the stereo ended just as Leanne asked the question, and Rachel jerked her head in their direction, having heard Leanne's words. "You're going to tell him?" She blinked back tears. "I *knew* I shouldn't have believed you." She looked from Mia to Leanne, then at Aggie beside her. "I'm *so* retarded."

As Rachel darted toward the door, Aggie ran after her. "Rachel . . ." Aggie caught the girl in a hug.

Rachel's arms remained pressed to her sides. "I'll go to jail," she choked out.

Over Rachel's shoulder, Aggie blinked teary, confused eyes. "Nobody's taking you to any jail. I won't let them."

"The sheriff told us stealing those things in town made for your third strike," Mia said. "A judge could put you in a juvenile placement facility if the merchants press charges, but those aren't anything like the jails you're picturing."

"How do you know?" Rachel stepped from Aggie's embrace. "That's not what Pam and Ricky said. I knew someone who went to juvy and it wasn't like Pam described. But when I told her that, she said there's different kinds, depending on what you did wrong. She said sometimes all the girls have to shower together, just like prisons in the movies. And they lock you into a cell at night."

"I used to be a teacher." Disgust for Pam Underhill tinged Leanne's voice. "I've toured the Amarillo facility and Pam's wrong. It's no hotel, mind you. You don't want to spend time there if you can avoid it."

"Since you're so afraid of it, honey," Mia asked, "why do you keep breaking the law? Stealing things and drinking and running away?"

"I don't drink. I was only *trying* a beer at a party. So what? I wanted to make friends, but then the cops came and busted everybody." Rachel sank to the floor, crossed her legs, and buried her face in her hands. "I don't know why I steal things. I took the food because I was hungry. But the boots . . . I just liked them. And I told you why I ran. They locked me out. Pam hit me. It wasn't the first time, either. She hit me any time I made her mad, which was a lot. Pam went to work at the furniture store and Ricky would go to his job, and I was stuck at home taking care of the house and everything else they told me to do, *or else*. Just like stupid Cinderella." The words tumbled out of her like rocks in a landslide.

Aggie sat on the floor beside Rachel. Mia scooted to the edge of the couch. Leanne stood and started to pace.

"Why didn't you tell us before that she hit you more than that one slap?" Mia asked. Not that a slap wasn't bad enough.

"I don't know." Rachel looked up at them, mascara streaking her cheeks. "You want me to prove it?" Standing, she lifted the hem of the gown Mia had loaned her. She pulled up the elastic around one panty leg. Bruises covered her bottom.

Tears burned Mia's eyes. Anger ignited in her chest.

Aggie's intake of breath was sharp and loud. "Oh, you poor girl." She pressed a palm against her chest.

"Why didn't you call your caseworker, Rachel?" Mia asked.

"They'd just put me with some other stupid family. I'd have to get used to things all over again. It never works. Even when they're nice to me. Something always happens and I get dumped." She lowered the gown and turned away. "I'd rather be on my own."

Trembling inside, Mia looked from Aggie to Leanne. In their faces she saw the same certainty she felt in her heart. Rachel spoke the truth.

They couldn't confide in Cade. Not now. Not yet. No matter how compassionate toward the girl he might feel, he was an officer of the law, sworn to follow the rules. He would have to turn Rachel over to the proper authorities and ask questions later. No time would be taken first to gather evidence that proved Rachel had been forced into a situation where running away and stealing had seemed her only options for survival.

Quiet tension radiated from Leanne. "Does anyone else know what Pam did to you, Rachel?"

"Only one girl. This skank from my school named Lacy Oberman."

Aggie flinched. "*Rachel*."

"Well, she *is* a skank. She acts like I eat toe jam for breakfast or something."

"How does she know Pam hit you?" Leanne prodded.

"Our teacher put us together to work on a project. Otherwise, Lacy would've never spoken to me. She thinks she's all hooty hooty and I'm nothing." Rachel wiped her eyes on her hand, smearing the mascara more. "When she came to my house to do homework? She saw Pam hit me. So did her mom. Pam didn't know they were there until she'd already slapped me."

Leanne kept pacing. "Do you know Lacy's mother's name?"

"No." Rachel shook her head. "But the next day at school? Lacy pretended to be really nice to me. She asked if Pam had hit me before and I showed her some bruises. Pam only left marks in places she thought nobody would see." Rachel's face hardened. "After I showed Lacy? She, like, told the whole stupid school."

Mia cleared her throat, hating the humiliation Rachel had suffered. Hating the shame she'd been made to feel for something that wasn't her fault. Hating Pam Underhill most of all. "You said Pam works at a furniture store?"

Sniffing, Rachel said, "Yeah."

"Does she work Sundays?"

"Most of the time."

Mia turned the situation over in her mind. "Okay, we'll wait a while before talking to Cade." She stood and crossed to Rachel, put an arm around her shoulder. "Why don't you go wash your face? Then we'll watch that movie Leanne brought, okay?"

"Okay." Her tiny body trembled beneath Mia's embrace.

When Rachel left the room, Mia faced the other women.

"I need a smoke," Leanne said, but made no move to go into the kitchen where she'd left her purse.

"I'm driving to Amarillo tomorrow to pay Rachel's foster mother a visit at that furniture store." The coffee shop was always closed on Sundays. Mia could think of more enjoyable ways to spend her day off but, right now, nothing seemed more urgent than meeting Pam Underhill face-to-face.

"I'll go with you." Aggie's voice shook with rage.

"What are you two planning?" Leanne finally sat down. "A lynching?"

"That's a good idea," Aggie said. "Roy has a rope in the barn that'd be perfect for the job. And I know just the rafter to use, too."

"We can't say anything to tip the woman off about

Rachel," Mia said to Aggie. "No accusations, no hints, nothing like that."

Leanne crossed her arms. "Then what's the point?"

"You said yourself that kids like Rachel say whatever it takes to win a person over, Leanne."

"That's true. But this time, I believe her."

"Surely you do, too, Mia." Aggie shuddered. "You saw the bruises."

"I do believe her," Mia said. "But hiding an underage fugitive is no small thing. If we don't play this right, we could be the ones who go to jail."

"You have a point," Leanne conceded after a moment. "Guess it won't hurt to make sure her story still rings true after meeting the foster mother."

"My thoughts exactly," Mia said.

Leanne sighed. "Okay, I'll go along, too. It's going to take some doing. Eddie already thinks something's going on with me. When I told him I was spending the night over here, he didn't give me a chance to explain before he got all bent out of shape."

Mia frowned. "You sure you want to add fuel to that fire? It's okay if you don't go."

Leanne shook her head. "He probably won't be at home much tomorrow, anyway. While y'all are at the furniture store, I'll stay at the mall with Rachel and help her pick out some of the things she needs." She blinked at Aggie and added, "And bring that sewing machine over when you get the chance. If she's going to be around for a while, I might as well start teaching her to sew. It will give her something to do."

Mia smiled at Leanne. "Good idea."

"I'm also going to call a lawyer friend of mine in Amarillo and make an appointment to see him next week," Leanne continued. "Jay will answer my questions about Rachel's situation without asking too many of his own, if you know what I mean. I trust him."

Cold all of a sudden, though the house was warm enough, Mia said, "Eventually, we'll still have to trust Cade with this, too, though."

"Not until we do whatever's necessary to make sure Rachel's case is taken seriously." Aggie lifted her "old lady" glasses and wiped her eyes. "I'm not gonna let that girl slip through the cracks. If some judge locks her away, they're gonna have to take me with her."

Mia looked from one friend's determined face to the other. "I think that makes three of us, Ag."

Chapter 9

$\mathcal{M}$ia hated malls almost as much as she hated mornings. But her shopping companions felt altogether differently.

By two o'clock on Sunday afternoon, Aggie was the happy new owner of two pairs of curve-hugging stretch jeans—one denim, the other khaki—and a pair of tiny, red-framed reading glasses to wear with her contact lenses. Following Rachel's advice, she'd worn them today.

Leanne had purchased two pairs of shoes, made a haircut appointment for later in the day at Reynaldo's Salon and had scored and turned down two coffee invitations from men she met while window shopping at Victoria's Secret.

Mia, however, had only acquired a tension headache from looking over her shoulder every five minutes. In spite of the drastic change in Rachel's appearance and the fact that so far, no one had given them so much as a curious glance, she worried someone might recognize the girl.

"Now that you've shopped them into shape," Mia told Rachel, "Leanne can help *you* pick out a few things." So many people crowded the food court she almost had to shout to be heard over the laughter, chattering, and crying of babies. The place smelled of spilled sticky-sweet drinks and stale corn dogs.

Rachel popped a French fry into her mouth. "What about you?"

"Hey, my nails are purple." Mia wiggled her fingers in the air. "That's a start. You'll have to ease me into this makeover thing. I don't do change easy."

"Mia and I are going to run an errand while you and Leanne shop," Aggie told the girl, sounding upbeat. "We won't be long."

Rachel stopped chewing and frowned, shifting her attention between each of the three women. "You aren't going to see my caseworker, are you?"

Smiling, Mia shook her head. "I told you we wouldn't." Last night's incident had shaken the girl's trust in them. It wasn't the first time today Rachel had expressed fear about the caseworker. And, twice, she had required assurance that they wouldn't confide in Cade.

"We just have a couple of things to take care of here before we head back to Muddy Creek," Aggie explained, reaching into her purse when her cell phone rang. She pulled the phone out and answered it. "No, Roy," she said. "We're still in Amarillo. You'll have to fix your own lunch. I'll be home around six."

Mia and Leanne exchanged smiles before Mia checked her watch. "Aggie and I will meet you two at Reynaldo's in an hour." She narrowed her eyes at Leanne. "Don't go *too* crazy, okay?"

Leanne feigned offense. "Hey, don't worry about it. We're splitting this bill. Besides, I can bargain shop if I have to."

"Right." Mia nodded at the boxes on the floor beside Leanne's chair. "I saw what you spent on those shoes."

Aggie turned away from the table, the phone still pressed to her ear. "No, Roy," she said with quiet exasperation. "We can't come home earlier. We still have shopping to do . . . no, I'm not spending all your money. Go tinker around in the barn or something. I'll be home before you know it." Ending the call, she faced them again and returned the phone to her purse. "I swear . . ." She shook her head. "That man is something else."

During the short drive to the furniture store, Mia and Aggie rehashed last night's conversation. Before starting the movie, they had managed to coax more information from Rachel about her foster mother. She'd told them the name of the furniture store where Pam worked. That the woman was tall and thin, with short, dark, curly hair and glasses. That she liked to talk and tell "her whole, stupid, boring life story" to anyone willing to listen.

After finding a parking spot, they entered the store and wove a pathway through bedroom suites and dining room tables.

Aggie nudged Mia with an elbow and whispered, "I bet that's her. See? Over by the couches?"

A woman fitting the description Rachel had provided paced in front of a leather love seat, hands clasped behind her back.

"Remember our plan," Mia said to Aggie as they started toward the woman. "Let me do most of the talking."

The sales clerk smiled as they approached. "Afternoon, ladies. Are you looking for something in particular today?"

Mia's heartbeat kicked up as she read Pam Underhill's nametag. "I'm helping my mom shop for a living room couch."

She studied Rachel's foster mother. Late thirties, piercing blue eyes behind a pair of oval glasses, a scatter of freckles across her nose. Her voice sounded like a scratchy record album, but friendly enough. She looked benign, like anyone's middle class next door neighbor. Hard to imagine that someone like her would hit a child hard enough to leave bruises. But Mia wasn't naïve. Human monsters didn't have horns and a tail. As often as not, they looked like teachers and preachers . . . or sales clerks in furniture stores.

Pam turned to Aggie. "I'm sure I can help you find something. Tell me about your living room. Is it formal? Informal?"

"Informal," Aggie blurted at the same time Mia said, "Formal."

Pam eyed them curiously.

"Mother, it's—"

"You really think it's formal, sugar?" Aggie's eyes fluttered as she shifted from Mia to Pam. "Maybe it is. I do like fancy things."

Pam's gaze flicked over Aggie, from her polyester pants, to the sweatshirt the twins gave her, years back, with "Grandma" embroidered across the chest. "I'm a little surprised. You look so down to earth."

"Do I?" Aggie chirped, dipping her head, shooting a sharp look at Pam over the top of her new reading glasses. "Well, people aren't always what they seem, now are they?"

Pam flinched. "I meant that as a compliment, ma'am. I like down-to-earth people. I consider myself one."

A spark of fury flashed in Aggie's eyes. Mia doubted Pam noticed it, but *she* did. She was almost relieved when Aggie's cell phone rang. Maybe a call would give her time to calm down.

Aggie looked at the caller I.D. then answered the phone. "What now, Roy?"

The sharpness in her voice startled Mia. She had never heard Aggie use that tone with her husband.

"I can't talk now. The scissors are in the kitchen junk drawer." She sighed. "Well, keep looking." Aggie punched the phone's off button.

"Everything okay?" Mia linked arms with her friend.

Aggie's smile appeared forced. "Just fine. Now where were we?"

Returning her attention to Pam, Mia said, "Mother

just had the room redone. It's all very Mediterranean. Dark reds and greens and golds. The couch should be classy."

"But comfortable," Aggie added.

Mia chuckled. "Like Mother."

"I have just the thing." Pam started across the aisle. "Follow me."

Snagging Aggie's attention, Mia frowned, jerked her head toward Pam and mouthed, *be nice*. Their goal was to make the woman comfortable with them so she would open up, not to make her wary by spouting innuendoes. While they walked, Mia pointed out couches that Aggie rejected. They bantered back and forth like a mother and daughter. "Excuse us," Mia said to Pam. "We're both out of sorts today." When Pam glanced back at her, Mia shrugged and said, "My teenaged daughter is driving us crazy."

Pam's fake smile turned into a sympathetic one. "I hear *that*."

"We've been staying with Mom since my divorce but, thanks to my daughter, I think we've about worn out our welcome."

"She's a handful, that's for sure," Aggie agreed, arching a brow. "The girl didn't come in until two o'clock this morning." She turned to Mia and said, "You're too easy on her. If she were *my* child, I'd—"

"What, Mom? Spank her like a three-year-old? She'd only laugh at me. Ground her? I've tried that. She sneaks out the window."

Playing the part of the opinionated grandmother,

Aggie lifted her chin. "I was about to say I'd take away her car privileges."

"I've tried that, too. She has plenty of friends who drive." Mia sighed. "I don't know what I'm going to do with her. I'm about ready to lock her out of the house and throw away the key." She held her breath, waiting for Pam's reaction to that idea.

Pam slowed her step until Mia and Aggie caught up to her. She laughed. "Maybe you should."

"Lock her out?" Mia laughed, too, though it wasn't easy. She found nothing remotely funny about what Rachel had endured. It took every ounce of composure she could summon to be cordial to Pam Underhill. "You have kids?" she asked.

"I had a foster daughter. Fourteen. Talk about a pain." Pam stopped in front of a couch covered in muted stripes of cranberry and gold. She looked at Aggie. "Here we go. What do you think of this? The colors are right and you won't find one of better quality."

"*Ohhh.*" Aggie tilted her head and winced. "All those stripes . . . it looks a bit like a circus tent awning to me." She sent Pam an apologetic smile. "No offense, dear. You know what they say . . . one woman's treasure is another's trash. Or something to that effect."

Pam's face turned the same shade of cranberry as the dominant stripe in the fabric.

"*Mother.*" Biting back a smile, Mia nudged Aggie with an elbow. "It's a lovely couch. Maybe you should be more specific about what you want. The woman can't read your mind."

Aggie cut her eyes at Pam then turned away. "We *were* specific," she said, barely lowering her voice. "You said classy, and I said comfortable."

Pam flinched again. "I have some others to show you."

Mia moved closer to Pam as she led them further into the store. "I'm sorry," she said quietly, glancing back at Aggie. "Mother isn't herself today." *That* was a gross understatement. Mia had never seen Aggie on such a roll, never known her to try so hard to get under another person's skin . . . like a rash.

Adjusting her glasses, Pam cleared her throat. "I understand." She blinked and offered a taut smile. "I know how trying kids can be. Sometimes they bring out the worst in a person."

"So the foster parent thing was a bad experience?"

"The worst. I thought it'd be an easy way to make a little money." Pam eyed Mia cautiously, as if realizing she might've revealed too much. "And we had an extra room, so, you know? Why not help the kid out? But you couldn't pay me a million bucks to do it again." She laughed. "Well, maybe a *million*."

"It's hard enough dealing with a child that's your own flesh and blood." Mia coated her words in sympathy. "I can't imagine how difficult it must be to raise someone else's."

Pam nodded. "My husband and I tried to set the girl on the right path. In return we got a few measly bucks and a whole lot of backtalk."

When the store manager started casually making his way toward them, Pam quickly added, "But y'all aren't here to talk about that." She stopped alongside an olive-green suede couch.

"So what happened to her?" Mia asked.

"The girl?" Pam cut a wary look at the manager, who had paused across the aisle to watch them. "She stole money and my husband's coat and took off." She kept her voice low. "This time, when they catch her, she'll get what's coming to her. I kept warning her about what happens to kids if they don't act right." Turning, Pam showed Aggie the couch and asked, "What do you think?"

Aggie crossed her arms, her face tight, her body trembling. "I've changed my mind." Her words sliced the air with rebuke. "I don't want a new couch."

"But—" Blinking bewilderment, Pam stepped toward her. "I have others."

"You didn't care one wit about that girl, did you?"

"Excuse me?"

"All you wanted was the money."

Mia reached for Aggie's arm. "Don't, Ag. Let's go."

As they started for the door, the manager rushed toward them. "Is there a problem?"

"No, everything's fine." Mia gestured toward Pam. "She was very helpful." Which was true.

The woman had answered all their questions.

Leanne pulled a short, fitted, denim safari jacket from a clothes rack and held it up for Rachel to see. It was dark green, trendy and definitely on her color chart. "What do you think about this?"

"That's so cute! I *love* it!" Rachel took it from her, slipped it off the hanger and put it on.

Maneuvering around other shoppers and tables stacked with jeans, they walked to a nearby full-length wall mirror. Leanne stood behind Rachel, studying her image in the mirror. "It'll look great with the jeans you picked out. You could wear it with skirts, too."

Rachel tugged the jacket together in front, turned left then right. "I look older in this, don't I?"

"Don't be in such a rush to grow up, Packrat. You look fantastic in it."

"Would *you* wear it?" She glanced at Leanne.

"If it were my size, I'd definitely want to borrow it from you."

Grinning, Rachel looked back into the mirror and, at once, her smile fell away. She stepped aside, shrugging out of the jacket. "You don't need to get me anything else. You've already bought me hiking boots and a coat."

Confused by her sudden change of demeanor, Leanne took the jacket from Rachel and said, "I don't mind buying you things. This is fun for me. You're the only person I know who enjoys shopping as much as I do."

Rachel nibbled the cuticle on her index finger and glanced over her shoulder toward the cash register where a security guard spoke with the sales clerk.

So that was it. Leanne draped the jacket over the hanger and said quietly, "He's not looking for you."

Lowering her hand from her mouth, Rachel tilted

her head to one side and squinted at Leanne. "How do you know? He was watching us a second ago."

"It's his job to watch customers. Besides, don't you think that would be too much of a coincidence? A guard staking out the juniors department of the store we just happened to wander into, hoping to find you?"

"Maybe Mia and Aggie told him I'd be here."

"They wouldn't do that to you. Neither would I."

She blinked back tears. "But, last night you said—"

Leanne placed a hand on Rachel's shoulder, silencing her. "We said we wouldn't do anything."

"For how long?"

"I don't know, Rachel. We're trying to work all that out."

Still obviously worried, Rachel crossed her arms and looked down at the floor.

Leanne glanced at her watch. "It's almost time for my haircut appointment." She nodded at the register. The security guard had left. "Come on. I'm buying you this jacket then we'll head to Reynaldo's."

Fifteen minutes later, a tattooed hairstylist secured a cape at the back of her neck before settling Leanne into the chair.

The young woman nodded up front at Rachel. "Would your daughter like to watch?"

Leanne didn't bother to correct her. Instead, she called out to Rachel to join them.

Rachel carried a chair to the back of the shop and set it down where she could observe without being in the way.

While the stylist sprayed Leanne's hair with water and started combing out tangles, Leanne watched Rachel in the mirror. The girl's uneasiness exposed itself in the way she popped the knuckles of one hand then the other, in the restless, constant movement of her body, in the flick of her gaze across everything and everyone in the room, except Leanne. Obviously, she hadn't eased the girl's mind about the security guard. Rachel didn't trust her any more than Eddie did.

"You okay, Packrat?"

The stylist lifted a pair of scissors and snipped the first strand of Leanne's hair.

Drawing a sharp, noisy breath, Rachel stood. She met Leanne's gaze in the mirror. "I—" Tears erupted. She darted for the door.

"Rachel!" Leanne jumped up and started after her.

"Ma'am?" the stylist called out.

Ignoring her, as well as stares from everyone in the salon, Leanne ran through air pungent with perm solution, past humming blow dryers and women with foil-laced hair.

Outside the door, the mall swarmed with faces, one blurring into the next. Dark, pale, young, old. None belonged to Rachel.

Leanne's heart raced as she pushed through the crowd. She looked over her shoulder, then across the center kiosks to the mall's other side.

A middle-aged man in a ballcap touched her arm as she passed him. "You need help?"

Continuing to walk, she glanced back at him. "I've lost someone."

He caught up to her, his expression alarmed. "A child?"

She nodded. "A girl."

He looked left then right, his eyes alert. "How old?"

"Fourteen."

The man slowed his pace, and Leanne glanced back at him. "Check the food court," he said with a smirk. Shaking his head, he turned and resumed his prior course.

When Leanne turned around, she bumped into the person in front of her, jarring a startled cry from the woman. "Excuse me," Leanne said, but didn't stop.

Ahead, ducking into a shoe store, she glimpsed the back of a kid's head covered in spiky chestnut-colored hair. "Rachel!" She reached out, her arm tangling in the cape she still wore from the salon. She hurried her step, entering the store only moments later.

Peering down rack after rack of shoes, she finally spotted the back of Rachel's head again. Afraid to call out and scare her off, she quickly weaved a pathway around shoppers until she reached the end of the aisle. Coming up from behind, she grabbed Rachel's wrist.

"Hey!" A boy no more than eleven or twelve years old glared up at her with startled eyes. He was Rachel's size, his hair the same color and a similar style. He jerked his arm free of her grasp. "What are you doing?"

"Sorry." Leanne fought to control her breathing. "I thought you were someone else."

Leanne left the store and waded upstream through

a river of teenagers, wishing that they hadn't darkened Rachel's hair. Worrying about her. Frantic. Why? Why did the girl matter so much? Rachel wasn't her responsibility. This time last week, she didn't even know Rachel Nye.

Because she's so lost, came the answer, unbidden. Lost in the world. Lost in her worries. In yearnings and fears. *Because I know that feeling*.

Rounding the corner into the food court, Leanne moved quickly from table to table, searching every face. She scanned the lines of people at the fast food joints, ignoring their amused glances at her wet hair and cape. She didn't care what anyone thought of her. All she could think about was what might happen to Rachel if she didn't find her.

When she didn't see her at any of the restaurants, Leanne hurried back to the main hall and worked her way down the opposite side. She reached an exit and left the building.

Running along the sidewalk that circled the mall, Leanne scanned the parking lot, the outside entrances of every store she passed, shouting Rachel's name all the while. The cold breeze whipped the cape behind her as she dodged occasional icy patches that hadn't yet been cleared from the concrete.

Rachel could be anywhere, Leanne thought, startled by the sting of tears in her eyes as a panicked sense of helplessness swept through her. How would she ever find her with so many vehicles in the parking lot? With all the people inside the mall?

After crossing a long stretch of sidewalk, she

reached the first corner of the mall and rounded it, her lungs aching from exertion and from breathing the brisk winter air. A cement bench sat in a snow-covered patch of lawn beside the next store's entrance. Leanne made her way to it and sank down to rest, her chest heaving. Shivering, she looked across a segment of parking lot she had yet to search. She cupped her hands around her mouth, shouted, "Rachel!" then sighed and closed her eyes.

At first, she thought she imagined the faint voice calling back to her. But the second time she heard it, Leanne opened her eyes and stood. Her gaze scanned over cars and minivans, trucks and SUVs. Then she spotted Mia's Tahoe. Rachel leaned against it, hugging herself. As Leanne started toward her, Rachel pushed away from the vehicle and met her halfway.

When they were face to face, Rachel stared at the ground, her lower lip tucked between her teeth. After a moment, she lifted her gaze to Leanne. "I'm sorry," she whispered, ending with a squeak.

"Don't you *ever*—" Unable to finish, Leanne turned her head, her body trembling from tense relief and exposure to the cold. "I should turn you in right this minute, Rachel. You know that? Give me one good reason why I shouldn't."

"I was scared." A sob shook the girl's shoulders. "I still am. I should've left Mia's a long time ago. Maybe y'all won't tell the sheriff about me now, but one of these days you will. You said so yourself."

"We can't get around that, Rachel. Sooner or later,

we'll have to talk to your caseworker and straighten this mess out."

Rachel crossed her arms. "I won't go back to the Underhills. I won't let them put me in jail, either. If they try, I'll run away again; I mean it."

"Running away from problems never works. You have to face them and try to find a solution." Leanne instantly realized the irony of those words. It was easy to *give* advice, but so difficult to follow it. Wasn't she running from her own problems? Avoiding telling Eddie her feelings? Hoping their problems would all go away?

The look of frightened confusion in Rachel's eyes softened Leanne. "We'll figure something out, Packrat." She touched the girl's arm. "We won't do anything until we're sure you'll be okay with the outcome. And we won't trick you; when the time comes to go to Cade, we'll tell you first." She wiped a tear from Rachel's cheek. "That's a promise. And when I make a promise, I keep it."

Swiping at her eyes, Rachel stepped closer to Leanne. Another tear slipped down her cheek. "I'm *sorry.*"

"Where did you plan to go?"

"I don't know. I just ran. But when I saw Mia's car . . . I couldn't leave you."

Leanne wanted to grab her, to hug her, to offer more reassurances. At the same time, she wanted to shake her senseless. "I care about you, Rachel. If you disappeared I'd worry about you. I couldn't stand it."

She looked into the girl's eyes and felt something

pass between them, one to the other, like an electrical current. Understanding. Recognition. Maybe they'd only met two days ago, but they knew each other. "Let's find Mia and Aggie and go home," Leanne murmured.

Rachel's eyes swept over her, head to toe. "We can't go home, yet. You have to go back to the salon."

"I'm not in the mood for a cut anymore."

"But your hair's, like, really lopsided." Rachel laughed through her tears. "One side's shorter than the other."

Leanne brushed her damp bangs aside. "You're right. I guess I don't have much choice." The emotional roller coaster ride of the past half hour had drained her. The thought of walking back through the mall seemed as much a feat as climbing Mount Everest. She sighed. "I forgot to grab my purse and our shopping bags when I ran out of the salon. I hope they're still there."

Rachel giggled. "You forgot something else, too. "You're *wearing* a *cape*."

Leanne glanced down at herself and winced, then laughed, too. "You should've seen how everyone was gawking at me, running through the mall in this thing. I must've looked like Wonder Woman on speed."

As they started back into the mall, Leanne left her tension and doubts outside. Right or wrong, rational or insane, she was in this thing with Rachel for the long haul. The fear she'd felt when she couldn't find her made it clear to Leanne that, for whatever reason, the girl was important to her. Tomorrow, she'd call Jay, her attorney friend, and make an appointment.

She would do whatever she could for Rachel. Like Aggie had done for her a long time ago.

Relief rushed through Aggie when Leanne and Rachel walked into the salon. The stylist had recounted their quick exit and, for the past fifteen minutes, Aggie and Mia had paced while waiting for the two to return.

"What's wrong?" Aggie asked Leanne, taking note of their disheveled appearances. Rachel's eyes were red from crying and Leanne's hair had dried in ten different directions.

"Nothing. Everything's fine now."

Neither Aggie nor Mia pressed for more information. Leanne's expression indicated that they should drop the subject.

The tattooed hairstylist was nice enough to work Leanne back into her schedule. While the haircut proceeded, Aggie, Mia and Rachel window-shopped in the mall. Mia bought the girl some underthings she needed, and some she didn't. Apparently over whatever had made her so upset, Rachel finagled Mia into buying her a pair of frivolous thong panties. Aggie expressed dismay at the price of three inches of satin and lace held together by dental floss. But at another store, when she saw Rachel eyeing a small radio with earphones, she couldn't resist her own little splurge.

Now, Rachel lay in the back of the Tahoe with her

new earphones on, listening to music, occasionally singing along with a chorus, oblivious to anything else.

Aggie sat in the middle seat behind Mia, who drove, and Leanne, who sat on the front passenger side. Before leaving Amarillo, they had visited an ATM where Leanne and Mia withdrew enough funds from their accounts to pay back everyone from whom Rachel had stolen. Rachel would mail the money to her victims, along with a brief note of apology. She could work off her debt to the women by helping with baking for the coffee shop, laundering tablecloths and cup towels, and any other chores the women could concoct.

Leanne came up with the idea to pay back Rachel's victims. Aggie was all for it, but she took issue that the girl owed the Underhills anything. Still, she admired Leanne's attempt to teach Rachel valuable lessons. Especially since Leanne had learned her own life lessons the hard way.

While Rachel was preoccupied with her music, Leanne explained what had taken place at the salon. Aggie voiced her disappointment that the girl was so slow to trust them.

"Why should she?" Leanne looked over the seat at Aggie. "Why should Rachel trust *any* adult? Every foster parent who discarded her sent her the message that grownups can't be counted on for anything."

"That's so sad," Aggie said, and Mia agreed.

"It is sad." Leanne huffed a humorless laugh. "But I would've done exactly what she did at fourteen in her situation. I would've tried to escape my fears by running from them. And no reassurances would've swayed me, either. Especially after overhearing something like she heard last night."

Mia tapped the steering wheel. "You mean that we were planning to tell Cade about her?"

Leanne nodded. "Rachel couldn't risk the chance that we really hadn't changed our minds about that."

Halfway to Muddy Creek, Aggie's cell phone rang. "I wonder who that could be?" She fished through her purse for the trilling phone.

"Hmmm," Leanne scratched her head. "If I had Bill Gates' money, I'd bet it all on Roy being at the other end of that line."

Aggie located the phone and looked at the caller I.D. *Sure enough.* "How'd you know?"

Mia laughed. "I wonder? He probably can't find something. And he'll ask when you're coming home. Again."

Ignoring them, Aggie pushed the "ON" button. "Hi, sugar."

"Where's the blasted mayo?" Roy barked. "Didn't I tell you to pick some up at the store?"

"Second shelf of the refrigerator. Right hand side." Aggie pursed her lips and turned to the window when Mia and Leanne snickered. "Are you just now eating lunch, Roy? For heaven's sake, it's almost suppertime."

"Maybe if you hadn't spent all last night and the better part of today gallivanting around the country doing who knows what I'd be on schedule. When you gonna be home, anyhow?"

"Around six, like I told you before." More snickers from up front. Aggie lifted her chin, smiling despite herself.

"Here it—*fat free*? This mayo isn't—"

"Goodbye, Roy." Aggie hung up on him mid-sentence. He'd use up all her phone minutes blustering about anything and everything except what was important.

Leanne glanced across the seat. "You have that man so spoiled he stinks. And now you're spoiling Rachel." She nodded at the rear of the vehicle where Rachel lay on her back, knees bent, one leg crossed over the other, her foot tapping the air. "Clothes are one thing, but you didn't need to buy her that radio."

"Be glad she did," Mia said, checking the rearview mirror before changing lanes. "It has allowed us to talk."

Leanne huffed. "You're just trying to avoid me starting in on you about those ridiculous panties you bought her."

Disregarding the comment, Mia relayed the details of hers and Aggie's experience with Pam Underhill at the furniture store. "You can be sure that woman hasn't lost any sleep worrying about Rachel."

"So was it worth it?" Leanne asked.

"Meeting her foster mother?" Mia sighed. "Any concerns I might've had about Rachel's honesty are out the window now. Pam pretty much backed up everything Rachel's told us."

Aggie agreed. "If I have to break a hundred laws to keep that child out of a facility, so be it." She meant it, too. Even though if Roy found out, he would explode like a faulty Roman candle on the Fourth of July.

Leanne crossed her arms. "We still can't let her call the shots. Believe me, I know all the tricks a kid can pull to get attention. I invented most of them. She needs love and nurturing, but she needs discipline, too. Indulging all her whims won't do her any favors."

"It was one pair of frivolous panties, Leanne," Mia scoffed. "Big deal."

When Aggie felt Leanne's gaze boring into her, she said, "I'm not planning on indulging all her whims, either, Leanne. I didn't overindulge *you*, did I?"

"Sometimes." Leanne smiled at her.

"Well, you turned out just fine, if I do say so."

Mia shrugged and said with mock seriousness, "She turned out okay, I guess."

"Aggie?" Leanne said after several silent moments.

"Yes, sugar?"

"I'm not sure I've ever thanked you."

"For what?"

"For everything." Leanne's brow wrinkled like she might cry. "For caring about me when I was a messed-up kid."

Touched and stunned, Aggie said, "Why, that didn't take any effort at all. You're you. Of course I cared. I still do." Blinking, she muttered quietly, "I swear . . . these contacts. Now I remember why I quit wearing them. They make my eyes water."

But it wasn't the contacts at all, and she knew it. She glanced from Leanne to Mia, realization dawning inside her like the morning sun. Yes, she missed Jimmy and the girls, but she didn't have to go all the way to Massachusetts to be near family.

She didn't even have to leave Muddy Creek.

Chapter 10

$\mathcal{M}$ia opened her eyes the next morning, looked at the clock, then pulled the pillow over her head. For once, she had a morning to sleep late, and what did she do? Awoke at her usual time, even without an alarm. And she was *wide* awake; there'd be no drifting back to sleep.

Yesterday, she, Leanne, and Aggie had decided to change their schedules for the week ahead. They would not leave Rachel alone, not even for a minute. Not after what happened at the mall. But sneaking her to the Brewed Awakening every day was a risk they wanted to avoid, if at all possible. So Mia and Leanne agreed to alternate mornings at the shop with mornings at Mia's house, where Rachel would be.

Leanne would tell Eddie she was spending *every* morning at work to take some pressure off Aggie. He knew that Aggie had been out of sorts and wouldn't question her needing some extra help.

They all agreed that, for Rachel's sake, they should

continue to keep the secret between the three of them. Mia sensed that lying to Eddie weighed on Leanne's mind, but Aggie didn't blink about keeping Roy in the dark. Surprisingly, she had no qualms about spending her afternoons at Mia's house rather than going home, whether her husband liked it or not. For as long as Mia could remember, Aggie had catered to Roy's demands. But that was something else she saw changing in her friend—the way Aggie handled her husband. Hanging up on him in the car yesterday, for instance. Sweet, eager-to-please, nurturing Aggie would never have done such a thing a year ago. Or even last month.

After staring into the darkness for ten minutes, Mia gave up and dragged herself from the bed with a groan. She slipped on her robe and a pair of wool socks then went to the kitchen to start the coffee.

The prospect of an idle morning alone while Rachel slept should have pleased her. Instead, she felt restless and unmoored. It occurred to her now why she'd never complained when Leanne, after the opening of their business, all but refused to take turns working the earliest morning shift.

Mia had wanted to escape from home as soon as possible every day.

Mornings were hardest since Dan died. Facing an entire day ahead without him in it often seemed over-whelming. And the silence . . . The house at dawn had never been so quiet while her husband was alive. He'd start whistling the minute his feet hit the floor.

Turning away from the coffee maker, she switched the radio on low. Maybe Dan had the right idea. Maybe music would drown out the whispered concerns and questions in her mind about her daughter. Was Christy still in New York City? Was she healthy? Happy? In love? Did she still sketch and paint?

Mia sat at the table, waiting for the pot to fill. Two minutes ticked by. Three. The music didn't work. She left the table and went to the bedroom where Rachel slept soundly, her breathing steady. The closet door creaked annoyance when Mia opened it, but the tiny lump beneath a bundle of blankets on the bed didn't stir.

A cardboard portfolio sat on a low shelf. Mia took it out, left the closet door open, crept from the room again.

She spread the pages of her daughter's artwork across the kitchen table. Long ago, she'd discovered that if she looked long enough, images she'd never noticed before jumped off the pages, as if they'd been waiting for her to open her eyes, her mind. Christy's work was like that . . . surprising and subtle. Nothing plain, easy or mindless about it. It didn't reveal itself until the viewer invested more than a second glance.

Like Christy herself.

Mia sipped her coffee, her gaze slowly moving from page to page. Christy had talent—a gift. In the beginning, the artwork had seemed amateurish and strange. She and Dan had believed Christy wasted her time dreaming about an art career. But what had they known about such things?

"Wow . . . did you do those?"

Mia looked up from the table. Rachel stood in the

doorway, a blanket pulled around her shoulders and dragging on the floor. She crossed the room and sat in the chair beside Mia. Rubbing sleep from her eyes, she scanned the paintings and sketches.

"They're my daughter's."

Bleary-eyed, Rachel asked, "Can I touch them?"

"Sure."

She chose one. "This is, like, really good. I mean . . ." Rachel blushed. "I *feel* something when I look at it." Rachel stroked fingers across another page. "This one is sad."

Staring deeply into the swirls of red and dark purple and black, Mia saw it, too.

"What do you think it is?"

The girl's brows drew together. "A heart that's hurting." Her fingers slid across it. "Like it's bruised."

Mia's throat ached. "You have a good eye." So much better than hers. So much quicker to see.

Rachel laughed as she moved to the next painting. "This one's funny." Shifting to a sketch, she frowned and said, "Oh, man . . . *this* is *freaky*."

Taking it from her hands, Mia looked at it. A corridor swarming with people on the move, their faces clear, distinct. And in the middle of the chaos, one girl stood still, stared out from the page, her features blurred at the edges, fading. Only her eyes were distinct. *I'm here*, they seemed to scream. *Look at me. Accept me.*

"Is she famous?"

Rachel's voice startled Mia back from her thoughts.

"Christy?" When Rachel nodded, she answered, "No, I'm not even sure she does this sort of thing anymore. But a long time ago, she had hoped to go to art school in New York after she graduated high school."

"Why didn't she?"

Swallowing a knot of shame, Mia answered, "Her father and I wouldn't pay the tuition. We wanted her to go to Tech, like her brothers."

"So she studied art at Tech?"

"Christy didn't go to college." *She didn't even graduate from high school.*

"I hope she's still an artist," Rachel said, her focus on the sketch. "If I could paint and draw like this, I'd never stop. Not ever."

Mia gathered the paintings and sketches and placed them back into the portfolio. "Why are you up at this hour? Did I make too much noise?"

"No." Rachel lifted a shoulder. "Sometimes I just wake up early."

Pushing away from the table, Mia said, "I'll make you some herbal tea. You want cinnamon flavor or peach?"

"Cinnamon." Yawning, Rachel followed her to the stove. "Where does Christy live?"

"In New York City."

"*Shut up!*" Rachel's eyes widened. "That's where I want to go. Does she live by Rockefeller Center? They do *Saturday Night Live* there. A bunch of other shows, too."

Mia drew a steadying breath as she took a plastic honey bottle from the cabinet then reached for the kettle. "I don't know where Christy lives. I've never been to see her."

"How come? Is she still mad at you about the art school?"

"I'm not sure. Maybe." Mia held the kettle under the running faucet. "After Christy left home, she never really found her place. She wouldn't let me help her and we grew apart. She's never invited me out to visit."

Rachel picked up the honey bottle, squeezed a sticky amber dot onto her fingertip, touched the finger to her tongue. "If my mom was alive, I'd want to see her. Even if I pretended I didn't."

Setting the kettle on the stove, Mia flipped on the burner beneath it.

Outside the kitchen window, the moon still gleamed like a polished pearl against a black velvet sky. How many times had she stared at such a moon, thinking of Christy, wondering if her daughter saw it, too? And wondering if Christy ever thought of her.

Rachel squeezed more honey onto her fingertip. "Does Leanne have kids?"

"No, she doesn't."

"How come? Doesn't she like them?"

Mia took two teacups from the cabinet. "Leanne loves children. That's one reason she used to be a teacher. I think she wanted a family, it just didn't happen."

"She's married, though, right?"

"Yes, her husband's named Eddie. They were high school sweethearts."

"I bet she was popular in school."

"She did have a lot of friends." Wondering about Rachel's preoccupation with Leanne, Mia asked, "What makes you think she would've been popular?"

"She's really cool. And pretty." She met Mia's gaze and said quickly, "You're pretty, too, but Leanne wears totally young clothes and stuff."

Mia smiled. "I guess Aggie's not the only one who needs to work on her wardrobe, huh?"

Rachel blushed. "I didn't mean—"

"Don't worry about it, honey. I've never been much of a fashion plate. And you're right, Leanne does have great clothes." The kettle started to whistle. Mia lifted it from the stove and turned off the burner. "You really like Leanne, don't you?"

Rachel shrugged. "She's okay. I hope she'll teach me to sew."

Mia caught her eye and winked. "Then I'll have another friend with snazzy clothes to make me jealous."

They ate French toast for breakfast. Rachel spread hers with peanut butter and smothered it in syrup. She claimed her dad had liked it that way, leaving Mia to wonder which of her foster families had taught her the habit. One thing she knew for sure, many more breakfasts like this one, instead of her usual yogurt, fruit and coffee, and she would soon gain back the weight she had lost in the last year and a half.

In an effort to put Rachel to "work" to repay her debt, Mia had her wash the the dishes. Then they looked through cookbooks for new ideas for the bakery case at the coffee shop. Some variety couldn't hurt; the customers might like a change of pace. Once they chose a few recipes, Mia would call Aggie and have her pick up any ingredients they needed on her way over later. Rachel could work off some more of her financial obligation by helping Aggie bake during the afternoon while Mia joined Leanne at the coffee shop.

Rachel giggled. "Let's do Bourbon Balls."

Mia glanced at the recipe Rachel indicated. "Three jiggers of bourbon? That's all the Coots need. They're loud and rowdy enough when they're just eating plain cherry pie with their coffee."

"Who're the Coots?"

"A group of retired men who meet at the shop for coffee and conversation most mornings and again in the afternoon." Mia flipped the page. "Cream Cheese Pound Cake. That sounds good."

"More like boring." Rachel made a sour face that sweetened quickly when she turned another page. "I know! Rocky Road Brownies. Look. Marshmallows and chocolate chips. Yum."

"Those *do* sound good. I think I have all the ingredients. What do you say we go ahead and bake them this morning? You can choose another one for you and Aggie to do this afternoon. Maybe a pastry or a sweet roll."

Mia turned to that section of the cookbook, handed it back to Rachel then stood. Light filtered in through the curtains covering the window over the kitchen sink. She looked at the clock. 7:43. She walked to the small window that overlooked the front yard. No one could see in from the street during the day. It would be nice to let the sunshine stream in. Leaning over the sink, she pushed the curtain aside . . . and screamed.

"Ohmygod!" Rachel stood up so fast the chair fell over behind her. "*What?*"

Aubrey Ricketts squinted back at Mia through the window, his face scrunched into a thousand wrinkles. She closed the curtain and hissed, "Turn off the light, Rachel."

Rachel moved to the switch on the wall, flipped it and whispered, "Is someone out there?"

"Just a busybody with too much time on his hands," Mia whispered back.

"One of the Coots?"

"Not officially. Aubrey's too preoccupied with nosing around to drink coffee." She'd never pegged him as a voyeur, though.

"So, what do we do?"

"Wait a minute." Mia heard a sputter and a pop followed by the revving of an engine. "Hear that?"

"That rumbling noise?"

"It's his truck. He's leaving." She sighed her relief. "We need to be extra careful."

"You don't think he saw me, do you?" Panic tinged the girl's voice.

"No, it was too quick." Mia smiled. "Turn the light back on. Let's get busy."

It didn't take long to realize that no one had ever bothered to teach Rachel how to cook. Mia showed her how to melt the chocolate and butter, how to measure the sugar and blend it in, too. They had just finished beating the fourth egg when the doorbell rang.

Rachel bit her lower lip. "You think it's that man again?"

Mia turned off the mixer. "Go to the bedroom and close the door. I'll see." As she moved through the kitchen and into the dining room, she checked for any signs that might indicate she had a houseguest. Just in case whoever was outside came in, for whatever reason.

She didn't know why she was at all surprised to find Cade standing on the other side of the door. Still, her heart skipped at the sight of the steady gray eyes staring back at her from beneath the brim of his Stetson. "Hi," she said.

"Morning." His warm breath hit the cold air in feathery white puffs. He handed her a newspaper. "Aubrey Ricketts said he was taking this out of your front flowerbed a few minutes ago when he heard you scream. He's worried about you."

She made a frustrated sound. "I *screamed* because he was staring in my window. What was he doing picking up my paper, anyway?"

Cade smiled. "You know Aubrey." When Mia didn't smile back, he continued, "Aubrey said he sees you every morning on your way to work. When he didn't today, he made a spin by here to make sure—"

"*What?*" Mia interrupted. "That the paperboy wasn't holding me hostage?"

"Just to see if you were okay, I guess." His eyes gleamed. "He means well, Mia. And why wouldn't he be worried?" Reaching into the pocket of his coat, Cade pulled out a pair of tiny, hot pink thong panties, brand new, the tag still on them. "He found these in the flowerbed, too."

"Oh . . . um . . ." She stared, mortified, at the lace-trimmed satin strip dangling from his fingers. The new panties Rachel coerced her into buying with claims that she had been "the *only girl* in the *whole stupid school*" who didn't own a pair.

Mia remembered Aggie dropping a sack in the driveway yesterday when she'd been transferring her new purchases from the Tahoe to the Blazer. Rachel's panties must have been in with Aggie's things. It was dark at the time, and she could have easily missed them if they'd fallen out.

Cade cleared his throat. "These yours, by chance?"

"Um . . . yes." She snatched them from his hand, glanced up at him just long enough to see his brows lift.

"Guess you were right when you said I don't know everything there is to know about you." He cleared his throat again, and she had the distinct impression he stifled a laugh. "I see you used that purple polish."

Mia's face burned. "I bought the panties for my niece, Cade. It's her birthday next week. Not that it's any of your business."

"You have a niece? I thought you were an only child? Dan, too."

Damn him. He might not know *everything* about her, but he knew too much. "Well, thanks for checking on me," she said, dodging his question. "Tell Aubrey not to worry." She backed up and started to close the door. "I'm going in. I'm cold."

"Really? *I'm* a little warm, myself." His teasing eyes slid to the panties she held. "Why aren't you at work? If you don't mind my asking."

"I'm going in later. I woke up with a headache."

"Those seem to be going around." He tipped his hat and grinned. "Later, Mia. Hope you enjoy your new clothes."

Still grinning, Cade sat in his truck out in front of Mia's house. If his mama hadn't raised him to be a gentleman, he would have asked Mia to model those panties for him.

His grin fell away. Damn, he hated this. The games. He and Mia dancing around one another. Getting nowhere. What did she plan to do? Hide that runaway girl until she turned eighteen? He always thought Mia had more sense. What she and the other women were doing could only end one way. In trouble.

Mia could be stubborn. She'd proven that over the past few months of him asking her out and her turning him down. Maybe he should just give up on that. The timing had never been right for them.

Back in junior high, he'd had a thing for her, but had been too young and too nervous to do anything about it. By the time they reached high school, they wanted different things. Mia was the type of girl who went steady; he played the field. Oh, they'd flirted and teased, but she had a boyfriend and he had his eye on various members of the cheerleading squad. Then they went away to different colleges and she fell in love with Dan, while he fell for Jill. Now, he was a lawman, and she'd become a lawbreaker.

Maybe friends were all they were ever meant to be.

Cade put the truck in gear and pulled away from the curb. Sooner or later, Mia would slip up. Or Aggie or Leanne would. Then what? He'd arrest them? It wasn't his place to give preferential treatment or bend the rules if he thought them too harsh. But could he really arrest Mia?

Back at his office, Cade finished up some paperwork, answered a few calls, tended to business in general. At ten, he stopped by the Brewed Awakening to have a cup of coffee with the group of old geezers who gathered there every day to chew the fat and pass the time.

"Well, what do we have here? Who's your new employee, Leanne?" he asked, appraising Aggie head to toe when she came up front. Her hair was no longer gray and she wore blue jeans and a tiny pair of red glasses. "I like the new look, Aggie."

She blushed and smiled shyly. "Why, thank you, Cade."

From the corner table, Tom Pellinger said, "She looks ten years younger, doesn't she, Sheriff?"

Cade nodded. "At least."

Beaming, Aggie waved away the compliment. "Oh, go on, you two."

"No joke, Aggie," Henry Kroger piped in. He hooted a laugh. "I bet Roy's wearing himself plumb out chasing you around the house."

Cade paid for his coffee then joined the chuckling old men at their table. Over the top of his raised cup, he watched Aggie and Leanne behind the counter. They had their heads together and were talking quietly. Leanne glanced his way, tension radiating from her eyes. He was the cause of it. No doubt about that.

The bell over the door jingled, and Roy Cobb walked in. He didn't bother to say hello to Cade or the other men in the corner. With a sour expression on his face, he headed straight for the counter, his gaze on his wife.

"Hi, Roy," Leanne said.

Aggie glanced up. "Roy . . . what are you doing here?"

"Had to come into town for some supplies. Why aren't you answering your cell phone?"

"The battery's dead. I forgot to charge it last night."

Leanne frowned at him. "You could have called the shop phone."

"The damn line was busy."

Aggie polished a spot on the counter with a paper towel. "What do you need?"

Roy jerked off his John Deere hat and barked, "Do I *need* a reason to talk to my wife all the sudden?"

Beside Cade, Tom Pellinger winked at the rest of the Coots and called out, "Can't blame ya for keepin' an eye on her, Roy. Aggie's turnin' heads today, that's for sure."

George Humphrey, the baldest of the group, added, "People'll be thinkin' she's your daughter, old man."

Roy scowled over his shoulder at them, his face flushed cherry red. He returned his attention to Aggie. "What time you plannin' to be home?"

"I don't know. I'll probably work a little late, and then I have some things to take care of in town. Why?"

Roy's eye twitched. He cast a look back at the Coots, faced Aggie again, then muttered something that Cade couldn't hear.

Her chin lifted. She narrowed her eyes. Roy turned and stomped out of the shop.

Ten minutes later, Aggie left out the back way.

Cade waited a minute before leaving, too. He drove a back way to Mia's and broke the speed limit getting there. Parking the truck around the corner at the far end of the block, he walked the alley then stood at the side of a house three doors down. He watched the front of Mia's place and waited. Sometime after he'd left her porch this morning, she had pulled her Tahoe out of the garage. It sat in the driveway now.

Moments later, Aggie eased her Blazer into the driveway beside Mia's Tahoe. As if someone had been watching for her, the garage door went up then closed behind her after she pulled the Blazer inside.

Cade counted to twenty. Mia came out the front door, climbed into her vehicle and left. He waited until she was out of sight before walking down the block to the house. Stepping onto the front porch, he rang the doorbell, waited a full minute then rang it again.

Nobody answered.

It was time to pay Roy Cobb a little visit, Cade decided. Drop a few hints. Ask a few questions. Make certain the man caught another whiff of suspicion. Cade knew Roy; the man would sniff that scent to its source, no matter how much trouble it might cause with Aggie.

Chapter 11

$\mathscr{A}$ggie couldn't sleep. She turned on the light over the stove, illuminating the dark kitchen. Lifting the cordless phone from its cradle, she sat at the table facing the window and dialed Mia's number.

Outside, West Texas wind-blown snow sifted down from the roof. Sometimes she hated the Panhandle's harsh weather, the brutal winters, the scorching droughts of summer. The extremes didn't make a farmer's life easy.

But she loved the windswept land, the velvet darkness of a snowy night. The vast landscape made her all the more aware of her little place on earth, her moment in time. It passed too fast; she knew that now. And she was through sitting idly by while it did.

When Mia picked up, Aggie glanced over her shoulder toward the kitchen doorway to make sure Roy hadn't heard her slip from bed. "What are y'all doing?"

"Rachel and me?" Mia sounded baffled. "Getting

ready for bed, Aggie. What are you doing? It's after ten. You'll never get up in the morning if you don't go to sleep."

"I can't. All that baking with Rachel this afternoon was more fun than I've had in years. Did she decide on any more recipes to try out tomorrow?"

"After today, we have enough brownies and bourbon balls to last through next week." Mia laughed. "Rachel's really getting into this, though, and I hate to stop her. After she washed and folded the tablecloths and cup towels I brought home from the shop, she spent the rest of the evening with her nose in a cookbook. She's still up. Let me put her on."

While waiting for Rachel, Aggie crossed one leg over the other and swung her foot back and forth. She needed new house shoes. Some less dowdy than her terrycloth slip-ons. Preferably something with a pointed toe so she could give Roy a swift kick in the backside. This morning before he left the Brewed Awakening, he accused her of flirting with the Coots. At least he'd kept his voice down so they couldn't hear. Still, she had refused to speak to him since then.

"Hey, Aggie," came Rachel's voice over the phone, followed by a yawn. "What's up?"

"Have you decided what we're cooking tomorrow?"

"Dirt cups." Rachel giggled. "It's pudding with gummy worms on top."

"That ought to make the Coots sit up and take notice." Aggie chuckled. "Or give them the urge to go fishing."

"Yeah, they probably get tired of the same stuff everyday."

"Sugar, old men love their comfortable ruts. But worms are good. We'll shake the geezers up a little. What else?"

"How about Black Forest Torte and Snickerdoodles? My mom always made snickerdoodles. And the Black Forest Torte? It just sounds dark and mysterious."

Forgetting the hour and that Roy snored in their bedroom down a short hallway, Aggie hooted and fanned her face. "It does at that, sugar pie."

"Bring your sewing machine tomorrow. Leanne called a while ago. She said she bought patterns and material. We're going to make me some halter tops for the summer."

"Oh, what fun! I'll be sure to bring it." When a floorboard squeaked, Aggie swiveled around. Roy stood in the doorway wearing only his tighty whities, an undershirt, his snakeskin boots, and a scowl.

Blinking and adjusting her glasses, Aggie turned back to the window and said, "Well, I'd better go, sugar. I'll see you in the morning." She punched off the phone and faced him.

"Who in the sam hill are you talking to at this hour?"

"Mia. And it's not that late, Roy. You're just an old fogey." She glanced down at his boots. "Where are your house shoes?"

"I couldn't find 'em."

A giggle slipped past her lips. "Well, you look silly wearing boots with your underwear."

Roy flinched. His eyes widened then narrowed. His nostrils flared. "So that's how it is, huh? I'm not good enough for you now that you have your fancy new look."

"I never said that." She stood.

He eyed her up and down. "Act your age, Aggie. People think you're pathetic trying to be something you're not."

Her stomach dropped. "And what's that, Roy?"

"Young, namely."

"So I'm old and pathetic?" He might as well have slapped her. "*People* think that, Roy? Or *you* do? I've heard nothing but compliments all day." Lifting her chin, she patted her hair into place. "I happen to like what everyone's saying."

A thin strand of hair fell across his forehead. "Who are you trying to impress with that Jezebel red hair and those silly glasses you bought?" He made a huffing sound and scowled. "And what's up with those skintight jeans you had on today?"

Tears stung Aggie's eyes, but she refused to let them fall. She wouldn't give him the satisfaction of making her cry. "I'm not trying to *impress* anyone. Maybe I'm just tired of looking like an old woman." She started around him and headed for the bedroom.

Roy followed. "I liked the way you looked before."

"Why didn't you ever tell me that? Do you know how much I've needed a compliment from you? Do you?" Aggie tugged at the sash of her robe until it untied. She slipped free of the garment and tossed it across the chair by the window. "Would that be so hard, Roy? To say something nice about me for a change?"

"I shouldn't have to. You know what I think about you."

She climbed into bed, turned her back to him, pulled the blanket over her head. "That's the nice thing about a compliment, Roy. It's a gift. It doesn't *have* to be given."

She sensed his presence beside the bed, felt him staring down at her, heard his staggered breathing. Seconds ticked into a minute. Pressure built in Aggie's chest. She squeezed her eyes shut.

"Who is he, Aggie?" Roy finally asked, his voice a low rumble.

Aggie pulled the blanket down to her nose and opened one eye. "Who is who?"

"The sorry son-of-a-bitch you're steppin' out with behind my back."

"*What?*" Slinging the blanket aside, Aggie sat up.

With his shoulders hunched, his face twisted and red, his eyes bulging, Roy looked like a snorting bull about to charge. He clenched and unclenched his fists. "You heard me." Stomping across the room to the closet, he flung the door wide. "I'll kill him."

"First you accuse me of flirting, now this?" Aggie's feet hit the carpet. She crossed to him in three strides. "How dare you—"

"I may look silly, but I'm not stupid." Roy jerked a work shirt free of a hanger, stuffed one arm in then the other. "Giggling into the phone like a school girl.

Coming home late from work. Sneaking over to Mia's."

Heat singed her cheeks. "I—"

"Did you think I wouldn't put two and two together?" He pulled a pair of clean jeans from the pile on his closet shelf. "People are talking. You go over to Mia's house while she's at the shop. You park in her garage. Who are you meeting? Buck Miller?"

"*Buck*—?" Flabbergasted, Aggie followed him to the bed where he started to tug on his jeans, then stopped to take his boots off first. "He's the one who told you about me being at Mia's in the first place. Besides, if I was going to cheat on you, it wouldn't be with Buck Miller."

"Oh, I get it. Now that you're all fancy and prissy you want some young stud, is that it?"

She punched his shoulder. "Would you listen to yourself? You're talking nonsense."

"Is it that Bailey kid?"

"Aaron Bailey?" Stunned, Aggie barked a laugh and stepped backward away from the bed. "Stop it, Roy. Aaron's not even thirty years old."

"He lives on Mia's block. Damn pantywaist stays home all day with the kids while the wife brings home the bacon." He stood, tucked his shirt into his jeans, zipped his zipper and snapped the snap beneath his belly.

Grabbing for his arm, Aggie ran after him as he started from the bedroom. "Where are you going?"

"Out." He jerked free of her grasp.

Aggie stopped in the living room and crossed her

arms. "Roy Cobb, don't you do anything we'll both regret."

The front door slammed.

Aggie went to bed alone but didn't doze off until Roy tiptoed into the room three hours later, reeking of root beer.

The next morning, Leanne told Eddie she had a doctor's appointment in Amarillo and that Mia and Aggie had agreed to cover for her at work. Only her yearly physical, she assured him, when he asked what was wrong. She felt so guilty lying to him. Ever since she'd begged off from going to his football reunion, the questions in his eyes had intensified. More than once, he had asked why she was so quiet, why she suddenly spent so much time away from the house.

Eddie gathered some loose change from the bedroom dresser and dropped it into his pocket. "How long are you going to be gone?"

"I'll be home long before supper." She buttoned her coat. "Will you?"

He raked his fingers through his wavy dark hair and said defensively, "I'd planned on it, why do you ask?"

"I'm not the only one spending a lot of time away from the house these days."

His eyes narrowed. "Maybe that's because, even when you're here, this is a lonely place, Lea. I can't stand the quiet."

Leanne pushed her purse strap up to her shoulder. Now was her chance. She should just say the words, tell him she felt incomplete. But she couldn't do it. He thought that was all behind them. She had, too, until recently. More than once, Eddie had made it clear to her that she was enough to make him happy; he didn't need anything else. How could she tell him that she didn't feel the same? "Let's not get into that again, Eddie."

"Okay." He grabbed his coat from the back of a chair and walked across the bedroom without putting it on. Pausing beneath the doorway, he looked back at her, and she glimpsed the wounded look in his eyes before he cloaked it with anger. "Didn't you have your yearly physical a couple of months ago, Lea?" Before she could answer, he left the room.

Leanne closed her eyes. She heard the front door slam.

An hour and a half later, she sat across the desk from her old friend Jay, partner in the Amarillo law firm of Roanoke and Wilde. Back in college, he had dated Leanne's roommate, and they'd become friends in the process. In fact, their friendship had endured though she and her old roommate had stopped corresponding more than a decade ago.

"Given the foster mother's abuse," Jay said, "I think a judge might be more inclined toward leniency."

Leanne looked up from the spiral notebook where she scribbled. "Even though it's the girl's third strike?"

"Yeah. That is, if she can back up the abuse claim with evidence. Maybe a witness or two." He leaned back, his expression curious. "So, you're researching a novel? I never knew you were so creative."

She tilted her head and smiled. "A woman can't tell all her secrets. Gotta keep a man guessing."

Jay chuckled. "You sure know how to do that."

"I've always been a closet writer." Leanne shrugged, amazed and a little concerned that the lies slipped from her mouth so easily. "Maybe the book will never get published. It's just something I want to try." She laughed and closed the spiral. "You know . . . before the vision goes."

They both stood and Jay smiled across at her. "If only we could go back to the good old days, right?"

"I don't know." She cocked a brow. "You look pretty suave with silver in your hair, Jay."

He blushed. "Suave, huh?"

"Yeah." She laughed. "Besides, I'm not sure I'd want to go back. I hit a lot of bumps getting to where I am now. I was too stupid to dodge them, you know?"

He rounded the desk. "The parties were fun, though."

Not for her, but Leanne guessed she'd kept her feelings well hidden back then. She had hated all the excessive drinking in college. Not that she'd joined in on that part of the action.

After leaving the office, Leanne headed for a coffee shop where she purchased an iced mocha and borrowed a phone book. She sat and searched the listings of every "Oberman" in Amarillo, hoping to find the number and address of Rachel's classmate, the girl who, along with her mother, had witnessed Pam Underhill's abuse. She wanted to call and set up a meeting. The directory listed only five "Obermans" and, when she studied the enclosed city map, Leanne narrowed her search to two addresses in the district close to Rachel's school.

Using her cell phone, she dialed the first number. The elderly man who answered said he was Lacy Oberman's grandfather. "Paula's my daughter," he told her.

Thinking that was easy enough, Leanne apologized for dialing the wrong number and hung up. The man had unwittingly provided Lacy's mother's first name. She scanned the listings again and found P. Oberman.

No one answered when she called so Leanne left the coffee shop and made a trip by a school supply store to pick up some things for Rachel. Books, paper and pencils, items to keep the girl's mind occupied by more than MTV while she was still out of school.

Before leaving town, Leanne made a swing by the address listed in the phone directory for Paula Oberman, an apartment building within walking distance of Rachel's school. Since nobody had picked up when she called, she didn't expect an answer when she knocked at the door. And didn't get one. Still, Leanne felt she'd made headway. Tonight, if Eddie wasn't around, she'd call again.

Halfway back to Muddy Creek, Leanne began to suspect someone followed her. Slowing her speed, she realized the blue Mazda sports car tailing her belonged to Eddie. She pulled into a rest stop twenty miles from home. A couple of minutes later, Eddie parked behind her. They climbed from their vehicles at the same time.

Wind whipped hair into her eyes. Cars zipped by on the two-lane highway beside her. "What's going on?" Leanne yelled. "Is something wrong?" She followed him to the nearest picnic table, ducking beneath the metal awning to escape the wind.

"You tell *me*, Lea." He jerked off his sunglasses. "*Is* something wrong?"

"What do you mean?"

"You didn't go to the doctor's office."

Her stomach dipped. Not because she'd been caught, but because her husband had followed her. It struck her as ironic that she was upset at his lack of trust. After all, she *was* deceiving him. Just not in the way he suspected. "You followed me, Eddie?"

A guilty look flashed across his face, but he quickly masked it with an accusatory frown. "Are you leaving me, Lea?"

Her pulse throbbed so loud in her ears, she didn't hear the wind anymore, the rush of passing vehicles. Leanne shook her head and stepped closer to him. "Why would you think that?"

"You went by Jay's office. Why? To ask about a divorce?"

"*Eddie*—"

"Then you stopped by the school supply store and an apartment building."

"And that says *what* to you?"

He jammed his hands into his front pockets, shifted to stare at a windmill in a field across the road. "That maybe you got a job teaching again. In Amarillo. That you're looking for a place to live."

"For God's sake, Eddie. I'm your wife, for crying out loud. Couldn't you have asked me if I'm planning to leave you?"

"I've wanted to, but you won't talk to me."

Leanne drew her lower lip between her teeth. What he said was true. "We're okay, Eddie," she said softly.

"You don't act like we're okay."

She crossed her arms. "I don't appreciate being stalked. By anyone, but most of all you."

"I'm not stalking you."

"What do you call it? If after twenty-eight years together, you feel like you have to keep tabs on me, maybe we *aren't* okay." She turned toward her car.

Eddie grabbed her arm from behind, spun her around to face him again. "What am I supposed to think? It wouldn't be the first time you walked out."

"Is that what this is about?"

"You're drawing inside yourself, just like before when you left me."

"I didn't leave *you*. My leaving . . ."

She turned to stare at the road, tried to steady her breathing. That one incident in their past had shaken Eddie to the core. Years ago, after she had decided she couldn't take in a foster child, she had needed some space to get her head right. She hadn't ever really dealt with losing their baby, so she took some time to do that.

Leanne looked up into the sullen gray sky. "That was twenty years ago, Eddie. We've been over it and over it. I thought you understood."

"I thought I did, too, Lea. I thought we were both past it. But this feels like the same thing happening all over again. So apparently I *don't* understand. I feel shut out. Why won't you talk to me anymore?"

Tears stung Leanne's eyes. "I want to, Eddie, but you take everything so personally."

He shook his head. "What are you talking about?"

"Something's missing, Eddie. In our lives." There, she'd said it. Leanne held her breath.

"In our marriage, you mean. Why wouldn't I take that personally?" He looked away. "It doesn't get more personal than that."

"You're twisting my words." She touched his arm. "I knew you'd misunderstand and be hurt."

Eddie pulled back. "Why did you lie and say we're okay?"

"I'm not unhappy with *you*. I love you. But something's not right. Don't you feel it, too?"

He wouldn't look at her.

"You still think I was making arrangements to leave you today, don't you?" When he didn't respond. Leanne turned and started for the car.

He followed her. "Where are you going?"

"I think we could use some time apart." When she reached the car, she swallowed past the lump in her throat and climbed in. "I'll be staying at Mia's."

He caught the door before she closed it. "What do you want? An explanation for my behavior today? Why should I explain anything? You're the one sneaking around."

"What I did in Amarillo had nothing to do with you."

Shoving his sunglasses on, Eddie stepped away from the car and crossed his arms.

"Fine, then." Leanne closed the door and reached for the key in the ignition. When the engine turned over, she took off, spraying gravel on his running shoes.

Chapter 12

$\mathcal{M}$ia closed the cash register drawer then counted out a handful of change to her customer. "There you go, Betty. Enjoy the latte."

"I'm sure I will, Mia. You *are* coming to the Red Hat birthday luncheon for Mary Jane on Friday, aren't you?"

"I'll try. To be honest, though, I've been so busy I forgot all about it. I haven't been a very good member lately."

The hairdresser's expression oozed with sympathy and encouragement. "You've had things on your mind the past year or so. I understand. But some socializing would do you good."

Mia felt smothered by Betty's compassion. She reminded herself that the woman meant well. They all did. Everyone who, for the past year and a half, had murmured, *how are you doing? You need anything? I'm here for you, honey.*

Betty sipped from her cup and asked in a half-whisper, "How's Aggie?"

"I'm fine," Aggie said as she came through the swinging kitchen doors wearing her new flare-legged khakis, trim-fitting V-neck sweater and butter-soft leather boots. She carried a tray of Rachel's dirt cups, which she took over to the table where the Coots sat. "On the house," she said, setting the cups of pudding in front of them.

The old men eyed the gummy worm topping with wary expressions.

"Well, I've just been so worried about you," Betty said.

Aggie lifted her chin and asked, "For heaven's sake, why? I couldn't be better."

"Well, you certainly *look* fabulous. Why you've been hiding that drop-dead figure underneath baggy clothes all these years is a mystery to me. And your *hair* . . ." Betty pouted. "My feelings are a little hurt you didn't come to me, but I have to admit that whoever colored it knew what they were doing. That shade of auburn is perfect for your complexion."

"That's so nice of you to say." Aggie bloomed with happiness beneath Betty's shower of compliments. She touched a hand to her shimmering locks and said, "I have Leanne and Mia to thank for that."

And Rachel most of all, Mia thought, biting back a smile. Amazing what a healthy dose of admiration could do for a woman's self-esteem. Mia loved the light that sparked in Aggie's green eyes each time someone complimented her youthful new look. And every single person who had walked through the coffee shop door the past two days had done just that—

praised Aggie's appearance. The town was abuzz with talk of her makeover.

Betty leaned in closer to the counter when Aggie walked behind it and said to her quietly, "Girl, your transformation is incredible, but that's also what has me worried for you. There's talk in town that Roy's been . . ." When the shop fell silent, Betty did, too.

Mia looked to the corner table where, only a moment before, the Coots had been guffawing and carrying on like a schoolyard full of adolescent boys. Now every eager eye peered in Aggie's direction. Throats cleared. Coughs sounded. Tom Pellinger jabbed Henry Kroger with an elbow. Henry jabbed back.

Two explosions of pink appeared high on Aggie's cheekbones. She took her apron off the wall hook and put it on. "Roy's been what, Betty?"

The hairstylist glanced over her shoulder at George Humphrey, her father. No doubt the source of her gossip, considering how his bald head was as red as Aggie's cheeks. Betty sipped her coffee and faced Aggie again. "You know I don't pay attention to rumors." When the bell over the door jingled and Eddie walked in, she added, "Speaking of which . . ."

"Hey there, Ed," Henry called out from the corner.

Eddie nodded at the table of old men. "Mornin'."

"See you over at Joe Pat's again tonight?" George asked as he slid a wry look at Tom Pellinger.

"Maybe." Eddie walked to the counter and looked from Aggie to Mia then back again. "Ladies." He gave a low whistle as he took in Aggie's appearance.

"You're looking spiffy, Ag. I almost didn't recognize you." He held up a hand. "Not that you didn't look good before."

Aggie fluttered her lashes at him. "So you approve?"

He smiled. "I sure do."

When he shifted his attention to Mia, she inwardly winced at the sight of his bloodshot eyes. Still, even exhaustion and worry didn't detract from the high school quarterback machismo Eddie Chilton had never lost. At one time or another, every female in Muddy Creek had swooned over his swagger and moody James Dean eyes. And had cursed Leanne for taking him off the market.

"Lea in back?" he asked, running a hand through his wavy dark hair.

"She hasn't come in yet," Mia told him.

"I expect she's sleeping late this morning," Aggie said. "Crying yourself to sleep at night will wear a person out."

"*Aggie*." Mia frowned. If Leanne had shed a tear the night before, Mia hadn't seen it.

"Well, it will." Aggie dipped her chin and peered over the top of her red glasses at Leanne's husband. "You two kids have no business spending the night apart, mad at each other."

"That was her doing, not mine, Ag." Eddie sounded like a little boy responding to a scolding from his mother. "She thinks we need time apart."

Aggie tsked. "Just apologize and put an end to this foolishness. It's as simple as that."

"Apologize?" Eddie slapped a palm against the counter. "Shoot, if I will. For what?" He took the cup of coffee Mia handed him. "Lea's the one acting crazy. I didn't do anything."

Mia crossed her arms, pressed her lips together, and stared at him. He looked from her to Aggie, and found identical expressions on their faces.

Chuckles drifted from the corner table. "You look to be outnumbered, son," Tom said.

Eddie glanced over at the group of men. "Whose side are y'all on, anyway?"

"When you get to be our age, you'll figure out it's no use trying to stand your ground against a pack of females."

Shifting to look at Aggie, Eddie said, "Even if I wanted to apologize, I couldn't. I stopped by Mia's. Lea didn't answer the door. She won't answer the phone, either."

The bell jingled again and Cade walked in. Mia met his gaze as Eddie asked, "What's she up to? And don't say 'nothing.' I know better."

Betty slid into a table by the door and pretended not to listen. The Coots didn't try to hide anything. They stared openly, as if watching the best show in town.

Grabbing a damp towel, Mia wiped down the counter. "What's wrong with everybody? I swear the whole town's paranoid all the sudden."

Henry's spoon clinked against his cup as he dipped into his pudding. He took a bite, his gaze never leaving the group at the counter. Choking, he reached for his coffee, took a drink, then sputtered, "What *is* this concoction?"

"A dirt cup," Aggie informed him. "With gummy worms on top."

"Do I look like a fish to you?" He wrinkled his nose. "What ever happened to the days when you only served pie and sweet rolls around here?"

"A little variety's a positive thing." Aggie looked coy as she tilted her head and smiled at the men. "Don't you know? It's the spice of life."

Tom returned her smile with a flirtatious one of his own, and George muttered, "Maybe Roy's right about his wife, after all."

"What's that?" Aggie blushed to the roots of her hair.

The men drowned their snickering with coffee, avoiding Aggie's humiliated eyes.

Mia wanted to pop the fools with the tip of her wet towel. What were they talking about, anyway? And why on earth would they want to embarrass Aggie? So what if she was feeling the effects of her makeover, trying a few of Leanne's flirty moves? That didn't mean she was making a pass. Aggie remained the same innocent soul she had always been. Mia glared at the men. All it took was a woman jazzing up her appearance for people in town to start talking scandal.

She shifted to Cade. "Coffee?"

"Please." He took his hat off and sat it on the counter. "While you're pouring it, I'd like a word with Aggie."

"With me?" Aggie frowned.

He nodded toward the kitchen. "In private, if you don't mind."

Wringing her hands, Aggie started for the swinging doors, motioning for Cade to follow. "Is anything wrong?"

He winked. "Nothing you can't put a stop to pretty darn quick, I'm betting."

Cade leaned against the kitchen sink and cleared his throat. He admired Aggie Cobb and always had. He hated having to tell her something he knew would humiliate her. And he felt guilty. He was partly to blame for Roy's recent bad behavior. They'd had their little talk a couple of days ago, and Cade had dropped plenty of hints that Aggie might be brewing up something other than coffee. Cade never guessed that Roy would take that to mean his wife was cheating on him.

"For heaven's sake, Cade, spit it out." Aggie fidgeted with her apron tie. "Has something happened to Roy?"

"No, Roy's fine. I didn't mean to scare you."

"Then what?"

Cade sighed. "I hate to be the one to tell you, but Roy's been all over town the past couple of days accusing men of . . ." He cleared his throat. "Of having an affair with you."

"What?" She touched her neck, staggered back against the stainless steel workstation. "That man . . . I didn't think he'd go this far."

"So he mentioned his suspicions to you?"

She nodded. "Crazy fool. As if anybody'd be interested in messing around with me."

Cade smiled. "Don't be so sure about that." He scanned her hair, her new glasses, her clothes. Aggie looked like she'd been on one of those TV makeover shows.

For a moment, Aggie looked flattered before worry crept back into her expression. "I'll talk to him, Cade. I'm sorry if his silly notions upset anybody."

"I'm afraid there's more to it than that, Aggie. Buck Miller called a couple of hours ago to file a complaint. Apparently Roy almost banged his door down late Monday night and again last night."

"Oh, good grief."

"Roy made threats that if Buck so much as glances in your direction, he'll have his hide." Cade bit back another smile. "Or something to that effect."

Aggie pursed her lips and blinked eyes that, to Cade's horror, shimmered with tears. "That man," she said again.

"I'd no more than hung up the phone from Buck when Marcus McCoy dropped by the office. And not to deliver the mail, I'm afraid."

"Mr. McCoy's such a nice young man. I've talked to him a time or two at Mia's when he brought her mail. Don't tell me—"

"Roy stopped him this morning on his route and asked if he delivered to Mia's house. When Marcus said he did, Roy started asking some pretty strange questions about whether or not Marcus had ever run into you over there. Things like that. Before long, the questions started sounding like accusations."

"Oh, that poor boy."

"Marcus said the last thing he wanted to do was get into a tussle with a man twice his age, but he had to defend himself."

Aggie looked startled. "Defend himself?"

"Roy punched him."

Her expression shifted from mortification to anger.

"I convinced both Buck and Marcus not to press charges, Aggie. I told them I'd have a talk with Roy, and I did. He knows if he crosses either one of those men again, they're not likely to be so easy on him."

"What did Roy say?"

"He said he'd back off." Cade winked at her. "But that husband of yours has a head as hard as marble. He didn't convince me, which is why I'm here. Maybe you can get through to him."

Aggie tugged off her apron. "Oh, I'll get through to him, all right." She hung the apron on a hook beside the freezer and went for her purse. "Don't you worry about a thing, Cade. Just leave it to me."

Cade followed her up front where, without going into any detail, she told Mia she needed an hour or so to tend to some personal business.

"While I'm out," she added, "I'll run that box of sweet rolls the Rotary Club ordered over to the Cactus Hotel for their meeting later this morning." Aggie took the back way out.

Cade sat on a stool at the counter and shot the breeze about nothing in particular with Eddie Chilton while Mia finished serving a customer. He'd heard that Leanne had left Eddie yesterday. Something about a mysterious trip and a shouting match at the rest stop outside of town. Kay Lynn Ryan had passed them on her way to Amarillo. She said they looked ready to murder each other.

When Mia's customer left the shop, Eddie stood. "I'd better get back to the paper," he told Cade, then nodded at Mia. "Would you ask Leanne to call me?"

"Sure, Eddie. But I wouldn't count on her doing it. You know Leanne. You're going to have to make the first move."

"I just did, by asking her to call."

Mia crossed her arms, tilted her head, scowled at the ex-football stud. "You know what she wants."

"Maybe she needs to give some thought as to who owes who what." He glanced at the Coots, who watched him, talking quietly. Eddie lowered his voice. "When Leanne gives *me* an explanation, *I'll* think about returning the favor. Tell her that, too." He headed out the door.

Mia shook her head. "Stubborn."

Cade narrowed his gaze on her. "Like someone else I know."

She escaped his scrutiny by turning to refill containers on the coffee bar. "What's going on with Aggie? Can you say?"

"Probably be best if she told you since it's personal. But don't worry. Nobody's hurt or anything like that." He chuckled. "I take that back. Marcus McCoy's probably not going to be doing any winking with his left eye for a while."

Mia's frown brimmed with speculation. "What does Marcus McCoy have to do with Aggie?"

"According to Marcus, not a thing. But ask Roy and you're likely to hear a different story."

Mia blurted a laugh. "Poor Aggie. She told me Roy's all worked up about her new look. You'd think the man would enjoy being married to a knockout."

"He'd rather knock out anyone who notices." Cade handed her his cup for a re-heat then asked, "So I hear you have a houseguest."

The muscle beneath her right eye jumped as she turned to top off his coffee. "You mean Leanne?"

He waited until she faced him again, took the cup from her hand and said, "Who else would I mean?"

Mia busied herself behind the counter pouring coffee beans into a grinder. "She and Eddie had a fight so she spent the night with me."

"She do that a lot?"

"No, this is the first time."

"Seems we have an outbreak of marital discord in town. Must be something in the coffee." He shifted on the stool. "I always thought Leanne and Eddie's marriage was solid."

"It is." At least, she hoped that was true. Ever since Christmas, she'd sensed unhappiness in Leanne. "The thing with those two is that, whatever they do together, they do it with gusto. Even fight." She smiled. "This'll pass."

Cade sipped then said, "Rumor is, Eddie's not too

happy about all the extra hours Leanne's putting in here at the shop." He shrugged. "Funny, I haven't noticed her being here any more than usual. If anything, seems like I see less of her."

"We've changed up our hours some. I guess you keep missing her." Mia seemed determined not to look at him. She kept her gaze on the bag of beans as she closed it and put it away beneath the counter. Then she turned on the grinder and wiped up the coffee she'd spilled while refilling his cup.

Another customer came in. A young woman whose name Cade couldn't recall. She'd married the Richardson boy a couple of months ago. They'd met at college, but she was from somewhere south of Abilene.

He watched Mia fill the woman's order. She was quick and efficient while making leisurely conversation with the customer. Cade liked that about her. Her relaxed way with people. The smile as quick as her hands. The slow, fluid cadence of her voice.

Once, just once, he'd like her all to himself. To have that smile directed at him alone, her sweet words spoken only to him. But he knew once wouldn't be enough. It wasn't likely to happen, anyway, now that she'd taken the law into her own hands. Eventually, he'd be forced to call her on it. He'd taken too long already, dragging out the inevitable, biding his time before really pursuing some hard evidence she couldn't deny. If Mia had Rachel Nye, and Cade was certain she did, he knew the girl was safe, at least. Maybe he used that as an excuse to go slow. Which bothered him.

Excuses weren't his style. But he'd never dealt with a situation like this one. Until now, he'd never had his personal feelings tangled up in his work.

The young woman paid Mia, took her coffee and left the shop. Cade set down his cup. "I heard you made a trip to Amarillo on Sunday with Aggie and Leanne."

Mia straightened the bills in the register then closed the drawer. "That's right. We did some shopping."

"That when you bought those panties?"

He heard a choking noise behind him and turned to see Henry spewing coffee out his nose.

"Shhh." Mia paled. "Now you've done it," she whispered. "By supper time, everyone in town will think we've got something going on between us."

"In that case, maybe we should give them something to talk about, like the song says." He grinned. "So did you?"

"Did I what?"

"Buy those panties in Amarillo?"

Mia glanced at the chuckling table of old men then propped a hand on her hip. "Is this another interrogation, Cade? If so, quit. I don't see what my purchases have to do with anything law-related."

He caught her hand when she reached for the sugar container. "Tell you what . . . I'll make you a deal. I'll stop interrogating you if you'll have supper with me."

She flinched, drew back as if he'd burned her. "Cade—"

"One date, that's all."

Glancing across at the Coots, she said in a lowered voice, "And you'll stop stalking me, too?"

"Done," he said to her. She might not know it, but there was a big difference between stalking and investigating.

She drew her lower lip between her teeth then slowly met his gaze. "Okay. But not in Muddy Creek."

Cade felt as giddy as a teenaged boy. "We can drive over to Brody for Mexican food at Paco's. You ask me, they make the best homemade tortillas in Texas. Best hot sauce, too. I'll pick you up at six-thirty."

"Make it seven. And I'll pick *you* up." When he started to protest, she added, "We women have been liberated. I'm allowed."

Shrugging, he steadied his gaze on hers. He wasn't fooled. He knew good and well why she didn't want him coming to her house. It had to do with liberation, all right. But not the sort of which she spoke. It had to do with liberating a young girl from the long arm of the law. Guilty or not.

Fine time to finally get his chance with Mia, Cade thought. Thanks to Rachel Nye, what could become of it now?

Chapter 13

*I*nching over the speed limit, Aggie neared Muddy Creek Methodist Church at the edge of town where she and Roy had attended services their entire marriage. In the parking lot, close to the building, she spotted Roy's truck pulled up alongside the choir director's faded LTD.

"What in the world?" Tapping the brake, Aggie pulled in.

Wayne Muncy and Roy stood between the vehicles. Roy towered over the gangly, bespeckled, fiftysomething man. He jabbed a finger toward the choir director's startled face.

When Aggie stopped and opened her window, the choir director's voice drifted in on a rush of cold air.

"Mr. Cobb, I assure you I'm completely innocent."

"You think I'm blind?" Roy bellowed, red-faced and spitting rage. He didn't appear to notice Aggie's Blazer idling close by. "I see how you single out my wife every Sunday, giving her solos even though she sounds like a sick warbler."

Insulted now as well as angry, Aggie didn't bother to turn off the ignition. She unbuckled her seat belt, threw open the door and stepped out, not bothering to close it behind her.

Wayne peered at her with pleading eyes. "Agatha . . . thank goodness you're here." His Adam's apple quivered. "Your husband has the misguided idea that we're . . ." The skinny man coughed and blushed.

Grabbing Roy by the arm, Aggie tugged until he looked at her. "You should be ashamed of yourself. I've never been so humiliated in my life. You've pulled a lot of stupid stunts in the past, Roy Dean Cobb, but this takes the cake."

"Don't you deny it, Aggie." Roy jerked his arm from her grasp. "You didn't give two hoots about joining the church choir until *he* took it over."

"That was thirty years ago! We didn't even have a director before Wayne volunteered. Just a bunch of members who couldn't get along."

Wayne's head bobbed and his body shook like a wet dog in a blizzard. "That's right," he said timidly. "And Agatha has a lovely voice. She's my only soprano." He cringed, as if expecting Roy to slug him.

"*Agatha*." The veins in Roy's neck bulged. "That's your special name for her, isn't it, Muncy? Do ya think I don't hear you talking to her? '*Can you stay a little late after the sermon to work on that solo, Agatha?*'" he mimicked. "'*Bravo, Agatha.*'" Roy clapped his hands. "'*Your voice sent chills up my spine.*'" He feigned a shiver.

"That does it." Aggie dug her fingertips into her

palms. She'd never hit anyone in her life. Not ever. But right now, it took all her control not to beat her husband black and blue. "You tell Wayne you're sorry or you can find someplace else to sleep tonight."

Roy opened his mouth. Closed it. His nostrils flared. "You wouldn't kick me out of my own house."

"Oh no?"

His eyes narrowed and his mouth curled into a sneer. "Joe Bob Jenkins is the only one in town who could change the locks on such short notice."

Her muscles tensed. "What are you saying?"

He crossed his arms, propped them atop his belly. "If I tell Joe Bob not to change the locks, he won't do it. His boy works for me, Ag. Besides, I bought and paid for that house. It's mine, not yours."

"So I'm just the housekeeper and cook? Is that what you're saying?" His silence stung, but Aggie wouldn't shed one more tear over Roy's terrible behavior. "Fine then. If forty-five years of cleaning that house and decorating it and tending to the yard doesn't make it mine, too . . ." She drew a shaky breath. "If turning it into a home instead of just a place to hang your hat at night doesn't count, then you can have it. *I'll* leave."

She saw his confidence slip, watched a hint of doubt seep in. "You'd leave me? After all we've been through?"

"If you don't apologize to Wayne and everyone else in town you've offended with this nonsense, including me, then don't expect me home tonight." She crossed her arms. "Or any other night until you've done what's right."

The corner of his mouth jerked. One eye. His cheek. "Where would you go?"

"Mia won't think twice about letting me stay with her. She knows what an ass you can be."

Roy's dark eyes clouded over, his stony face crumbled bit by bit. Lord, she hoped this didn't throw him into another episode of chest pains. Short of that happening, she wouldn't back down. One thing she knew about her husband; he'd have a hard time choking out the words "I'm sorry." If he had ever once uttered them during their marriage, she couldn't recall when.

Just as she thought he might surprise her and give in, the stubborn glint returned to Roy's eyes.

"So, that's the way it's going to be, is it?" She pursed her lips and squinted at him.

Beside her, Wayne pointed and shrieked, "Your car!"

From the corner of her eye, Aggie saw the Blazer rolling slowly across the parking lot toward the children's wing playground.

"Dang it, Ag." Roy's head jerked around. "Go get it before you mow down the swingset."

Fuming, Aggie arched a brow. "If you're so worried about it, you go get it."

He squared his shoulders and didn't budge.

Wayne looked frantically from one to the other then took off after the vehicle.

Roy grumbled inaudibly.

"Did you say something?" She blinked at him.

Turning, Roy stomped over to his truck and climbed behind the wheel.

As Wayne caught up to the Blazer and jumped in, Roy drove his truck away. The Blazer came to a halt two feet shy of the jungle gym. Wayne backed up to where Aggie stood, then climbed out and returned to her side.

"Thank you, Wayne."

"Everything's okay, Agatha," he said in a small voice.

"No. No it isn't." She stared down at her shoes. "You didn't deserve that."

Wayne opened his car door. "It wasn't your fault."

"You're right, but he's my husband." And she loved the ornery hothead. Though, at times like now, she didn't know why. "He owes you an apology. He owes a lot of people one." Her included.

Until he paid up, he'd get nothing from her. No clean laundry. No hot meals. No fresh sheets on his bed.

And no her in that bed, either.

At close to noon, the shop emptied for the first time all morning. In the kitchen, Mia took a break and tried calling the number Leanne had given her for Rachel's classmate's mother. After talking to her attorney friend, Leanne seemed certain that the Oberman woman's testimony about the abuse she'd witnessed was the only chance they had of saving Rachel from a detention center. If only they could get her to answer her phone, or at least call them back. So far, that wasn't happening.

The phone rang and rang without answer, so Mia hung up and prepared for the next rush. When she heard the back door open, she looked up. Aggie blew in like a tornado.

Mia rushed over, alarmed by the dark look on her friend's face and eager to hear what news had spurred Aggie to leave the shop earlier in such a hurry.

"He did *what*?" Mia shrieked, when Aggie told her.

"He woke your neighbor the past couple of nights to harass him, gave the mailman a bloody nose this morning, and accused the choir director of teaching me more than hymns." Aggie dragged a stool to the island workstation and sat. "Plus he insulted my singing."

Mia covered her mouth to muffle a laugh. "Sorry, Aggie. I know it isn't funny, but skinny little *Wayne Muncy*? Has he ever even *had* a girlfriend?"

"I doubt it. The thought of asking someone out on a date would probably make the poor man's teeth chatter so hard he wouldn't be able to get out the words."

"So, what now?"

"Well, sugar." Aggie blinked hurt eyes at her. "I'm afraid you have yourself another roommate."

Mia nibbled her lip. Her house was fast becoming a home for runaway females. "I have plenty of room."

"I hope you don't mind."

She hugged Aggie's slumped shoulders. "Of course I don't. You're always welcome at my house, you know that. But I do hate that you and Leanne are at odds with Roy and Eddie. I feel like it's my fault. Hiding Rachel was my idea."

"We made up our own minds. Don't blame yourself." Aggie stood. "Guess I better take over at the house with Rachel so Leanne can come to work. I just wanted to let you know what's going on. Oh, and I delivered those sweet rolls to the Cactus Hotel for the Rotary Club meeting."

"Thanks. You want to go to the farm and pack a suitcase before you take over for Leanne?"

Aggie shook her head. "I'm not setting foot back in that house until he apologizes. I'll buy whatever I need and charge it to Roy's MasterCard. He made it clear I've been nothing but a housekeeper and a cook to him all these years. The way I see it, he owes me a truckload of past wages."

"You're more to him than that, Ag. That man's crazy about you, and you know it."

Aggie's face twitched with emotion. "I'd say he has a funny way of showing it, but I'm not laughing. Now everyone in town knows just how little he trusts me."

"I don't think it's you, Aggie. I think Roy's suffering from a bad case of insecurity. You're looking pretty sexy these days. He doesn't know what to think about that. And he probably senses you're hiding something."

"That doesn't excuse his behavior."

"No, it doesn't. I'm not taking his side. I just don't want you doing something rash in the heat of the moment. Leanne, either."

"Well, I'm not planning on visiting any lawyer if that's what you mean. Not yet, anyway."

"Aggie—" The phone rang and Mia picked it up,

only to hear Cade's voice on the other end of the line. She talked to him a moment then extended the receiver to Aggie. Something she'd detected in Cade's tone bothered her. Stepping aside, Mia crossed her arms and waited for Aggie to hang up.

Aggie looked like a limp balloon when she finally returned the phone to its cradle.

"You okay?"

"Cade put Roy in jail to cool off."

"In jail? What happened?"

Aggie sighed. "Apparently when I was at the Cactus Hotel delivering those rolls, Roy saw my Blazer in the parking lot. He heard a man and woman laughing behind the door to room ten so he busted in thinking he'd find me inside with Roland since he didn't see Roland up front at the desk."

"Roland Wade?" Mia screeched, referring to the hotel proprietor. "He's eighty years old if he's a day."

"I swear Roy's lost his mind. The couple he burst in on were just passing through town last night on their way to Dallas. They're young enough to find the whole thing funny, so they're not pressing charges. But Roland was fit to be tied, so he called Cade, anyway."

"Oh, Aggie . . ."

"Cade asked if I wanted to bail him out, but I'm not about to. Let him sit there all night and stew over what he did."

Mia couldn't decide whether to laugh or cry. Rachel's arrival in all of their lives had set something in motion, kicked up a dust cloud of uncertainties and hopes, fears and desires that had lain dormant too many years.

She wondered if that was good or bad.

At six-thirty that evening, Mia mentally kicked herself for at least the tenth time for accepting Cade's dinner invitation. Insecurities she hadn't felt since before marrying Dan taunted her. Was she overdressed? Underdressed? What if they couldn't think of anything to talk about? What if he tried to kiss her?

Worst of all, was she betraying Dan?

She stepped away from the full-length mirror, but Rachel grasped her arm, pulled her back, then held a black dress up in front of her.

"This is better," the girl said. "Tell her, Leanne."

Leanne hung up the phone on the nightstand after attempting to reach Paula Oberman again without success. She and Aggie sat at the edge of Mia's bed. For the past forty-five minutes they'd observed, even participated in, Rachel's primping session. Their expressions said *we knew this night would come*.

"Rachel's right." Leanne winked. "You definitely want Cade to get a good look at those legs of yours. He probably hasn't seen them since high school. That's the last time I recall you wearing anything that showed them off."

Mia pushed away the dress. "I'm sticking with slacks. They're more comfortable."

"Sugar, when a woman's trying to snag a man's eye, comfort should go right out the window," Aggie said, to which Rachel replied, "*Duh.*"

An afternoon spent with the girl had perked Aggie up. They'd painted each other's fingernails and had plans to do toenails at a later date. Rachel's nails were orange; Aggie's were pale pink with sparkles. Aggie claimed to be at least fifty years too old for glittery nail polish, but Rachel had chosen it, and so she'd gone along. Mia thought Aggie secretly liked the touch of glamour.

"I'm not trying to snag Cade's eye," Mia insisted, heading for her boots in the closet.

"You don't have to." Leanne leaned on one elbow and grinned. "It's already snagged. Watch out, girl. That man has ideas."

In Mia's opinion, they were making too much of one measly dinner. It wasn't as if Cade was taking her somewhere swanky and romantic. Mexican food at Brody was a casual, low-key affair. Lots of Muddy Creek residents made the drive to eat at Paco's, since the only Tex-Mex in Muddy Creek was the taco basket at Dairy Queen.

"He just wants to pump me for information," Mia said over her shoulder. When Leanne snorted, she realized the implication and felt her cheeks heat. "You know what I mean. He just wants to feel me out."

Leanne snorted again.

Aggie started humming.

Rachel snickered and said, "*Duh.*"

Boots in hand, Mia left the closet and sat at the opposite side of the bed from them. "Okay, you three," she said, shoving her foot into a boot. "Quit it. You're making me tongue-tied. He's just hoping I'll slip up about you, Rachel. That's what tonight's all about. Not romance."

Rachel popped her knuckles. "What*ever*. You are *so* in denial. If it's about me, why'd you say you'd go?"

Good question, Mia thought. Leave it to a fourteen-year-old girl to cut to the quick of things.

"Yes, why *did* you agree?" Leanne grinned at her.

Mia shoved on her other boot and stood. She took her coat from the back of the chair. "He promised to stop asking so many questions and following me around all the time if I'd go."

"And you believed him?" Aggie pulled off her red glasses and blinked puffy eyes. "You can't trust a man. It's taken me a whole lot of years to figure that out." She glanced at her watch. "Roy'll be wanting his dinner about now. I hope they don't feed him anything fried at the jail. His cholesterol's—" She cut off the sentence. "I'm not going to worry about it."

Leanne patted her arm. "Good girl."

Mia didn't buy Leanne's tough act for a minute. True, she'd turned off her cell phone, but she checked for missed calls about every fifteen minutes. Eddie had come by the coffee shop again this afternoon, and the two of them had gone another round in the back room. Mia didn't know which one was more stubborn.

"Men." Aggie sighed. "Don't they understand it's not their suspicions so much as the way they handle them?"

"Exactly," Leanne agreed. "If Eddie hadn't tailed me like some sleazy private eye I wouldn't be so upset with him." She lifted a brow at Rachel. "Listen up, Packrat. You can learn a thing or two from the three of us. We've had a lot of years to figure out what makes a man tick."

"I'm not so sure we've accomplished that feat." Buttoning her coat, Mia started out the bedroom door.

"We won't wait up for you," Leanne called out. "After we eat, Rachel and I are going to lay out the patterns for her halter tops and cut the fabric, then I'm going to bed."

"It may have been years since you went out, sugar," Aggie yelled. "But don't worry. Some things don't change. It's good to make a man wait. No kissing on the first date."

Rachel made a sputtering sound and said, "More like, no *doing* it."

"*Young lady.*" Aggie sounded shocked. "The very idea. Nobody decent would even consider such a thing."

"Oh, Ag, come on now," Leanne scoffed, laughing, "you can't tell me you and Roy didn't get frisky from time to time back when you dated."

Silence, then Aggie said in a small voice, "Do they allow aspirin in jail? Roy always gets a headache and a sore back when he sleeps on a strange bed."

Mia smiled and kept walking. As she opened the front door to leave, Leanne yelled, "Wake me up if I'm asleep when you get home. I want to know if the rumors I heard back in high school were true."

"What was that?" Aggie asked.

"That Cade's one heck of a kisser."

Chapter 14

$\mathcal{S}$o much for no romance.

Cade surprised Mia with equal measures of old-fashioned manners and new-age respect for a woman's independence. He met her at the door of his small ranch-style house with a single red and pink stargazer lily. No clichéd rose. And lilies were her favorites; she wondered how he knew.

He offered to drive, rather than insisting. Gallant, but not chauvinistic. She admitted to herself that she liked the gesture and put away her keys.

It had been a long time since she'd sat on the passenger side of a vehicle. Mia leaned back, tried to relax and watched the night slide by.

"You look nice." Cade smiled across at her.

"Thanks." Twirling the lily between her fingertips, she glanced down at her simple black slacks and white sweater. "The fashion police who've taken up residence in my home seemed to think I'm too casual."

Cade looked at his jeans and dark blue button-down

shirt. "No more casual than me." He shrugged. "I don't like fussy clothes."

"Me, either."

His cheek twitched. "Except for lacy pink under-things, you mean."

Tilting her head, Mia scowled at him. "Not that again. You promised."

"I promised not to *interrogate* you. That wasn't a question, it was a comment."

"Whatever you say." She looked out the window and smiled despite herself.

"I like your hair down like that."

Her hand automatically lifted to her shoulder. She pushed back a strand. "Thanks," she said again, embarrassed.

"Not that I don't like it pulled back," he quickly interjected. "It looks great however you wear it."

Nice save, Mia thought, her smile returning. Jill had taught him well.

Only a few lights twinkled in the distance. Mia guessed most people would consider this the middle of nowhere. Sometimes she did, too. Sometimes she longed for water, the sparkle of an ocean, a winding river. The town's namesake wasn't even muddy anymore, only a jagged, dusty fracture in the landscape. At least the endless horizon had its merits. She usually knew what to expect down the road, since it was almost possible to see into the next county and the one beyond that.

"You're quiet," Cade said, coaxing her out of her thoughts.

She placed the lily across her lap. "I was thinking what a wide open place we live in."

"It is, at that. Can't beat the sunsets. Sometime I'll show you my land out by the canyon and we'll watch one together."

"I didn't know you had land."

"I bought it just after Jill and I split up." He glanced across at her. "Anyway, I like our wide open scenery."

"Me, too. Most of the time."

"What do you like about it?"

"That I can see what's ahead." She sighed. "Too bad life can't be the same."

"What?" His brows drew together. "And never have any surprises? What fun would that be?"

"Not all surprises are good." Mia's chest tightened. She wished they hadn't stumbled onto this subject.

"But I'm not sure I'd want to give up the good ones in order to avoid the bad," Cade said.

"I guess I have a hard time remembering the good ones sometimes." Mia smiled, hoping to lighten the mood. "Sorry to be such a downer tonight. I'm not the best company lately. Nor the best conversationalist." Which was exactly why she had no business going on a date with Cade or anyone else.

"We don't have to talk. I just like being with you."

Cade checked the rearview mirror, eased into the left lane to pass a slow-moving flatbed truck. His hands rested on the steering wheel in a relaxed, easy way. And he drove slowly, as if in no hurry to reach their destination. He was a man who took his time. Mia liked that about him.

She wondered if he'd be as slow and thorough a lover.

The second after the question crossed her mind, guilt crept in behind it. Since marrying Dan, she'd never wondered such a thing about any other man. Mia tried to push awareness of Cade from her head, but considering his nearness, it kept wandering back. His broad shoulders. How she felt so small and feminine around him. The laugh lines beside his twinkling eyes and the rich laughter that etched them there. The deliberate, patient way he handled matters.

Even when trying to persuade her to go out with him, he hadn't pushed *too* hard. Not that he'd given up the pursuit. Just as he hadn't given up on finding Rachel behind her door. Mia was well aware he wasn't fooled. Cade knew she hid Rachel. But he was taking his time proving it. She wondered why.

For the remainder of the drive, they talked about their kids and the high school basketball team's winning season this year. They laughed about the rival town's bungled attempt to kidnap the Muddy Creek Cowboy's mascot—a four-foot-tall statue of a wrangler on horseback that sat in the school courtyard.

After pulling into Brody and parking at Paco's, they grabbed their coats from the backseat then went inside. The scents of sizzling beef, onions and peppers wafted over Mia, making her mouth water. She scanned the darkened interior of the restaurant for familiar faces from home. Relieved not to see any, she followed the hostess to a table and sat in the chair Cade pulled out for her.

Mexican guitar music played quietly on the sound system. Sombreros and multicolored fringed blankets decorated the walls. Over tacos, enchiladas, and carne asada, they commiserated for Aggie over Roy's antics. Cade mentioned Aggie's sudden change of appearance but, to his credit, didn't speculate as to what might've spurred it. Mia wondered if he even suspected. Would a man be baffled that a young girl could come into the lives of three grown women and remind them of their own youth? That she could shake them up? Make them want to grasp hold of the years ahead, and not let another day slip by unenjoyed or underappreciated?

At once, Mia realized why she'd agreed to see Cade tonight. Because of Rachel. The girl had brought back memories of Mia's own days of homework and friends and popularity contests. Of crushes, stolen glances, and the brushing of fingertips. To a time in her life when taking chances had been fun rather than frightening. Rachel had made her remember that all those feelings were well worth the risk of a broken heart.

On the way home, they talked about old times; junior high, high school, the early years of raising kids. They laughed about the Coots, about Aubrey Ricketts assigning himself Mia's watchdog.

Cade recounted some of the more unusual incidents he'd dealt with during his stint as sheriff.

"Probably the best one was the time on graduation night three years ago," he said. "Some of the high school seniors dumped twenty or so gallons of bubble bath into the Cactus Hotel's outside pool during the middle of the night."

Mia laughed. "I read about that in the paper."

He shook his head. "What a mess. They jumped in and stirred up the water and bubbles went everywhere. Roland Wade was in such a tizzy when he called me he could hardly breathe."

"At least your job's not boring."

He grinned. "It has its moments." Tapping the steering wheel, he squinted at her and asked quietly, "Can I trust you with a little secret? One that *didn't* make the papers?"

Curious and amused, Mia leaned closer to him. "Sure. My lips are sealed."

"Last year, at the Chamber of Commerce Christmas party, Mayor Higby drank one too many spiked eggnogs."

She lifted a brow. "That's no secret."

"Yeah, but afterward? Mrs. Higby called at two A.M. and reported him missing. I found him staggering down Main."

Mia widened her eyes. "You're kidding!"

Cade's cheek twitched. "All he was wearing was a cowboy hat, boots, and a pair of chaps. His backside was bare as a newborn baby's."

By the time they pulled into Cade's driveway, Mia was wiping tears of laughter from her eyes, and she felt a lightness of spirit she hadn't known in a long time.

Cade walked her to her Tahoe and opened the door for her.

She placed the lily inside on the seat then faced him. "Thank you for dinner. I enjoyed it. Next time, the margaritas are on me."

One corner of his mouth curved up. "I'm glad to hear there'll be a next time."

The look in his eyes made her heart beat too fast. Mia hesitated a moment before returning his smile. She hadn't meant to imply that she expected to see him again socially. That she wanted to. But she realized that's exactly what she'd done. And exactly what she wanted.

"How about we take a drive tomorrow night? I'll show you my land I told you about."

It wouldn't exactly be a date, Mia thought. Just a drive. No pressure in that. Nodding, she said, "I'd like that." She turned to climb behind the wheel. "Well, goodnight."

"Mia?"

Pausing, she looked back at him.

"What you said about surprises? About not remembering any good ones?"

Mia nodded, so aware of him she could barely move. She ached for him to touch her, but the thought of that happening scared her, too.

"I hope you think this one is good."

"This one?" She searched his face, her stomach a flurry of nerves.

"You and me." He stepped around the door and gently grasped her shoulders. "It's the best surprise I've had in years." His hands swept slowly down her arms.

Mia almost stopped breathing as she stared into his eyes. For one heartbeat, maybe two, she thought to stop what she knew was about to happen before every ounce of rationality rushed right out of her mind. But he smelled like menthol shaving cream and, oh, how she'd missed that scent on a man. And his hands on her arms felt too warm, too right.

Cade bent his head, kissed the corner of her mouth, lifted one hand and grazed his knuckles across her cheek.

Closing her eyes, Mia felt her muscles relax, one by one. When he murmured her name, his voice flowed through her, thick and rich and sweet as honey, slowing everything down. She kissed him back, small quick brushes of skin against skin, her lips and his . . . coming together . . . apart . . . together again. Reaching up, she traced his jaw with her fingertips and drank in his taste—the coffee he'd had after dinner, the cinnamon breath mint.

As he drew her closer and deepened the kiss, one thought crossed Mia's mind. Leanne would be pleased to hear that all the old rumors were true.

Then she didn't think anything at all. Instead, she lost herself in each sensation.

Less than an hour later, Cade unlocked the door of the jailhouse. Reaching inside, he flipped on the light. He made his way across the office, through a doorway and down a short hall, flipping more light switches as he went.

He and Mia had made an early night of it. He would've eagerly gone on kissing her until the wee hours of the morning and beyond, but she'd ended that unexpected, passionate episode after about ten minutes.

And Cade wasn't about to press his luck by trying to entice her into staying longer.

Mia hadn't wanted to stop any more than he had, Cade thought, pleased by that fact. He smiled. She was something. He still felt her body's warmth, smelled her soft scent, tasted her. Not a hint of girly bubblegum lip gloss on her perfect lips. Mia tasted like a woman. And he'd been dead-on right when he thought that once would not be enough. He wanted to kiss her again. And again.

When he reached the block of cells, Roy Cobb, his only prisoner, blinked bloodshot eyes at him from behind the steel bars. "You awake?"

Roy scowled. "Who could sleep on this rotten piece of plywood you call a bed?"

Cade took a set of keys from his pocket and unlocked the cell door. "I'm taking pity on you, buddy. Don't ask me why. Any more running around town acting like a one-man lynch mob and I won't be so soft-hearted again."

Roy tugged on his boots as if he couldn't do it fast enough. Standing, he stuffed the tail of his wrinkled work shirt into the waistband of his pants. "Yeah? Well you're who got me started, Sloan. Talking about all the extra hours Aggie's puttin' in all the sudden at that dadgum frou-frou coffee shop. How people are gossiping about the migraines she's been sleeping off every afternoon at Mia's when nobody's home."

Cade closed the door after Roy stepped from the cell. "I was afraid you'd say that." They walked down the hallway side by side.

"So, you riled me up on purpose?"

Bingo. But Cade wasn't about to admit it. He glanced at his watch. "It's still early. How about I buy you a beer, Roy?" He placed a friendly hand on the older man's shoulder.

"I don't drink, but considerin' the past few days, I'm beginning to think I might start."

Cade chuckled. "Wouldn't be the first time woman troubles turned a man down a crooked path."

Roy patted his bowling-ball belly. "Could use a root beer float, though. Joe Pat over at the pool hall makes a good one."

"Root beer, huh?" They stepped out the office door then Cade turned off the light and locked up. Leave it to Roy Cobb to drown his sorrows in ice cream and root beer instead of alcohol. Too bad all that sugar didn't sweeten his sour attitude. Cade gestured toward the truck. "I'll spring for a double float, how's that? We have some things to talk over. It might take a while."

Joe Pat packed in a crowd on weekends, but on work nights like tonight, the parking lot was less than half full. Cade and Roy entered the dimly-lit bar to the sound of Tim McGraw on the corner speakers. Glass balls clacked together atop the pool tables lining one half of the smoky room. Two players looked up when the door opened. Nodding, they said, "Hey, Sheriff."

Echoing their greeting, Cade scanned the faces of the few other customers at the scattered tables that filled the room's remaining space. Only two men sat at the long narrow bar across the way.

Roy nodded toward one dark head bent over it. "Well, look who's here again."

"Appears you're not the only man in town dreading an empty house tonight," Cade said as they walked over and pulled up stools on either side of Eddie Chilton. "What's up, Eddie?" Leanne's husband, he noticed, had opted for something stronger than root beer to wash away his troubles.

"Not a whole hell of a lot."

"You staying a while?" Cade hoped so. He could save some time by talking to both of the men at once.

"'Til closing, most likely." Eddie shrugged. "Beats another long night alone in a cold bed."

"Hey, now." Cade chuckled. "That's my life you're talking about."

Roy ordered his float then settled his forearms on the bar top. "When you gonna get that high-strung wife of yours under control, Eddie? She's puttin' ideas in Aggie's head."

"Shoot." Eddie twirled a toothpick between his teeth. He didn't appear offended by the older man's bluntness. "Lea spent a lot of time at your place growing up. You should know as well as anybody that nobody convinces the woman to do anything until she's good and ready."

Roy grunted. "They oughta be ashamed. Married women their age carrying on like that. Gettin' all dolled up and prancin' around town like a couple of cheerleaders. What are they tryin' to do? Catch the eye of every Tom, Dick, and Harry in town?"

"What are you getting so worked up about?" Eddie

sipped his whiskey. "So Aggie dyed her hair red. Big deal. Your wife's true blue, you know that. She'd never fool around with another man while she's married to you."

Roy grunted again.

"And the only thing different about Leanne is her hairdo," Eddie continued. "Which I happen to like. She's always been a flirt. I'm used to it. Hell, it's one of the things I love best about her."

When the bartender set Roy's float and Cade's beer down in front of them, Roy said, "If it's not that, then what are they up to?"

Eddie stared down at the amber liquid in his glass. "I don't know about Aggie." He shrugged. "As for Lea? My guess is, she's thinking about leaving me. Not for some other dude, necessarily. I think she's bored."

Roy scratched his head. "With what?" He licked the froth from the top of his mug.

"With this town." Eddie glanced up at his own image in the mirror behind the bar, caught Cade's glance and averted his eyes again.

He didn't say that Leanne might be bored with him, too, but Cade saw that worry in him, anyway. In the way he sat hunched over his drink, in the lines around his eyes.

"She's sick of the same routine every day and night," Eddie said.

Roy frowned at himself in the mirror and muttered, "Not Aggie. She loves the same ol' same ol'." He spooned a bite of ice cream from his float.

Cade bit back a smile. Roy sounded like a man

trying to convince himself of something. "You're both on the wrong track."

Eddie shifted to study Cade. "You know something we don't?"

"What's going on with your wives . . . Mia, too . . . doesn't have a single thing to do with secret flings or plans to leave town. It has everything to do with a girl named Rachel Nye."

Even Roy managed to keep quiet as Cade told the two men about Rachel. About purple nail polish and bubble-gum lip gloss. About pink thong panties in Mia's flowerbed and MTV blaring from her television set.

"When Buck Miller filed his complaint on you, Roy, he also said he glimpsed into Mia's bedroom last night before she pulled the window shade."

Roy bristled. "That perverted son of a—"

"He swore it wasn't on purpose," Cade interrupted, with a laugh. "He just happened to look out his window in that direction."

Eddie's cheek twitched. "Did he just happen to have on a pair of binoculars at the time, too?"

"He said Mia, Aggie, Leanne, and someone else he didn't recognize, thanks to his failing vision, were having a pillow fight."

"So that's where Aggie took off to last night." Roy snorted again. "She said she had to run to the store and she got cornered by Reba Bodine on the produce aisle. You know Reba. The woman's gabbier than all get-out."

"The thing is," Cade continued, "the judge won't grant another warrant to search her place unless I can show him proof she's harboring a fugitive."

Eddie shifted. "And he doesn't consider lace panties and the word of a Peeping Tom proof? Is that what you're saying?"

"That's it." Cade asked himself the same question he'd gone over time and again. Even if he had proof, could he really arrest Mia? Mia, who he'd been trying to get close to for months before this whole mess landed in his lap. Who had finally agreed to go out with him for the first time today. Who, less than two hours ago, had kissed him back like she meant it.

Mia . . . Cade lifted his hat and ran a hand through his hair. He hadn't been able to get her off his mind the past few months. Now, after that kiss, she was in his blood, too. And he was in a predicament.

"So what we need is evidence." Eddie tapped his fingers against his whiskey glass. "I may only run a small town newspaper, but I know a thing or two about investigative reporting. This shouldn't be too hard."

"It shouldn't?" Roy frowned.

"Not if the Sheriff here's willing to give us a little leeway."

Cade didn't like the sound of that, but right now he was willing to listen to any and all ideas. "That depends. What do you have in mind?"

"Tell you what, Sheriff." Eddie slapped Roy on the back. "Maybe you're better off not knowing. Roy and I can take care of things, can't we, Roy?"

"We can?" When Eddie nudged him, Roy jumped and said, "Sure we can."

Cade narrowed his gaze. "Whatever you do, it's got to be on the up-and-up."

"Don't you worry about that. Just leave it to us." Eddie nodded toward the pool tables. "Roy, let's you and me play a game or two and have ourselves a talk. I'll drive you to your truck when we're through. That's you parked over at the Cactus Hotel, isn't it?"

Roy cast a sheepish glance in Cade's direction then nodded.

"Thought so." Eddie pushed away from the bar. " 'Night, Cade. Talk to you soon."

"Don't go too far, Eddie," Cade warned again.

"Just far enough to get you your evidence without hurting anything or anybody. And maybe get our women back in the process."

Cade watched the two men as they ambled over to a pool table. He blew out a noisy breath. What in the hell was he doing? Had he really let himself sink to this? Allowing a couple of civilian yahoos help him do his job? And by what methods?

But, the truth was, Cade had run out of ideas. All he knew for certain was that, for the first time in his career as sheriff, he'd reached a dead end.

Cade realized that Eddie and Roy didn't seem aware that if their wives were involved in hiding Rachel, a runaway foster kid, a ward of the State, they could be accused of a crime right along with Mia. He decided not to mention that fact. He'd gone this far, why not take it to the end? Once he had his proof and the girl safely in custody, he'd worry about how to protect the women.

Chapter 15

*A*cross town, Mia sat on her bed, her nightgown-covered knees drawn to her chest, the stargazer lily Cade had gaven her in a vase on the nightstand. Aggie, Leanne, and Rachel, all in pajamas, had gathered in her room. Aggie sat beside Mia, working on a needlepoint canvas Mia had started years ago and never finished. Leanne sat at the foot of the bed with Rachel standing in front of her. Rachel wore the halter top they'd cut out earlier, and Leanne was using straight pins to fit the garment to her tiny body.

"Trent called," Aggie said.

"Oh, shoot." Mia winced. "I forgot to call him with an excuse about why I can't fly to Dallas on Saturday. What did you tell him?"

Leanne took a pin out from between her teeth. "I answered the phone. I told him Aggie and I ran away from home and that you were out on a date with Cade."

Mia's stomach flip-flopped. "Thanks a lot."

Leanne smiled and tucked the pin into the seam beneath Rachel's left arm. "Well, it was the truth. Oh, and by the way, Brent called, too. He wanted to know if you could drive over and babysit on Sunday."

"All the sudden I'm in demand." Mia wasn't complaining. She'd love to spend Saturday with Trey and Sunday with her grandkids if not for the fact that her life was in chaos at the moment. "I guess you told Brent I went out to dinner with Cade, too?"

"Nope. I said y'all went parking out at Cooper Lake."

Mia pressed a foot against Leanne's back and tried to push her off the bed.

Laughing, Leanne glanced over her shoulder and said, "Watch it."

"Yeah." Rachel made a face at Mia. "You're *going* to make her *stick* me."

Leanne held out one bare leg and wiggled her toes. "So, is he?"

"Is who what?" Mia asked, widening her eyes and trying to look innocent.

"You know who and what," she scoffed. "Is Cade a good kisser?"

Rachel made a gagging sound.

Aggie dipped her needle into the canvas and looked at Mia over her reading glasses. "I, for one, hope you don't know the answer to that question. Make the man wait, I'm telling you. You won't be sorry."

"I seem to recall hearing," Leanne said in an exaggerated sultry tone, "that even at sixteen, Cade had a certain finesse in the way—"

Covering her ears, Rachel groaned, "He's *old*."

Mia scowled at the girl. "That's a matter of opinion.

But I'm still not going to compare notes with Leanne's high school friends."

"Hmmm." Winking at Rachel, Leanne cupped a hand to her mouth and whispered, "So, something happened that she *could* compare if she wanted to. That's a good sign."

"What's the big deal about kissing, anyway?" Rachel lifted her gaze to the ceiling.

"After your first time, we'll talk, sugar," Aggie said with a smile.

Leanne slid Aggie a look of disbelief. "She's fourteen. This isn't 1950. Even in my day, fourteen-year-old girls kissed."

Rachel blushed three shades of red.

"Speak for yourself, Leanne." Compassion for the girl squeezed Mia's heart. She wished Leanne would notice Rachel's humiliated expression. "I was two months short of sixteen before my first kiss. Steven Fargo. Backseat of the band bus after the football game over in White Deer." Her lips felt bruised just thinking about it.

"Fat Lips Fargo?" Now Leanne gagged instead of Rachel. "The tuba player?" When Mia nodded, she said, "You've got to be kidding. I'm surprised that didn't scare you into never kissing anyone ever again. What were you doing on the band bus, anyway? You weren't a member."

"Steven was sweet," Mia protested, trying but failing to keep a straight face. "His lips *were* a bit large, now that you mention it. And moist. Which was why he was so great on the tuba, I suppose."

Aggie kept her gaze on the movements of her needle. "I remember that boy. He hit the low notes so loud during halftime the stadium bleachers vibrated."

"What about you, Mia?" Leanne's eyes glinted with mischief. "Did Fat Lips vibrate your bleachers?"

"*Leanne*, hush." Aggie's head jerked in Rachel's direction as she paused to give Leanne a playful stab with her toe.

With a dismissive laugh, Leanne asked, "How about it, Packrat? Have you been kissed yet, or are you following Mia's example? Which wouldn't be a bad thing, by the way," she quickly interjected. "In fact, it beats the path I took by a long shot. When I was your age, I spent way too much time worried about what *guys* wanted, when I should've been worrying about what *I* wanted."

"I kissed somebody." Rachel blinked down at her hands. "I suck at it."

The women fell silent. Finally Mia said, "Everyone does the first time, Rach."

"I remember when Roy and I first kissed." Aggie sounded wistful. "We were in the swing on my parents' front porch. I was scared to death and stiff as beef jerky. I think Roy was nervous, too. He pressed his mouth against mine so hard, I leaned my head way back and the swing tipped until we almost fell over."

After the laughter died down, Leanne had Rachel step back, sized up the halter on her then said, "Please tell me Roy wasn't your first kiss, Aggie."

"No, he was my second. And my last."

Leanne looked as shocked as she might've if Aggie

had just admitted to an affair. "That's like buying shoes after trying on only two pairs in a whole store full of Jimmy Choos."

"I think you should be real worried, Aggie," Mia said. "Especially since the marriage has only lasted, what . . . forty-seven years?" She glanced at Rachel. The girl watched them, her attention shifting from one woman to the other. "You're sure quiet."

"I *so* can't picture y'all young."

Mia laughed. "Believe it or not, I once wore a halter top that looked a lot like that."

Rachel turned to the mirror over the dresser and studied her reflection. "I *totally* love this material you picked out, Leanne."

"It looks good on you, Packrat." Leanne glanced at the other two women. "Rachel laid out the pattern and cut the fabric herself. Didn't she do a good job?"

They agreed, and Rachel looked proud of herself.

Mia swung her feet over the side of the bed. "I have an idea. Meet me in the living room, girls. I'll be right back."

In the upstairs attic, Mia searched the shelves for the old movie projector and screen she'd inherited from her parents. While she did, she thought of Cade and their evening together. She could've told Leanne that he was a natural when it came to kissing. That he kissed like a man who'd had plenty of experience at it. Yet at the same time, he made her feel as if, out of all the kisses he'd ever had, hers was the only one that mattered.

Mia thought of her own first kiss and smiled. In all

the best ways, Cade's kiss had been like that one. The feelings he stirred in Mia both frightened and thrilled her. Made her think maybe, just maybe, she might recapture the joy in her life that had all but disappeared after losing both Christy and Dan. For far too long, she had not been able to recall how spontaneity felt. Letting go. The anticipation of good things ahead. Tonight, Cade had brought that all back to her.

She finally located the projector and screen and, twenty minutes later, had everything set up in the living room downstairs. Digging through a box of film reels in round metal canisters, she found one labeled "1972."

Several minutes passed before she figured out how to thread the film through the projector. Mia wasn't sure she'd ever operated the thing by herself. In the early years of her marriage, before video cameras came into being and the projector was packed away to gather dust, Dan took charge of their old home movie viewings.

Aggie flicked off the lights then headed for the couch.

Mia hit the projector switch. The machine *click-click-clicked* like fingernails on a computer keyboard as the reels began turning and static filled the screen. She settled at the opposite end of the couch from Leanne, with Aggie between them. Rachel sprawled on the floor at their feet.

The static gave way to a jerky off-color image, then it was senior year all over again. Young men and women in caps and gowns filled the high school gymnasium. A girl with straight, dark hair to the center of her back walked across stage, accepted a diploma from a middle-aged man, then turned and smiled into the camera.

"Is that you, Mia?" Disbelief rang in Rachel's voice.

"Lord, what a sweet face." Aggie shook her head.

Mia laughed. "Underneath that gown, I wore a mini skirt that barely covered my butt."

Rachel sat up straighter. "You're, like, really pretty." She glanced back at Mia, studied her, as if trying to find the girl on the screen.

"I was almost eighteen."

The scene shifted, the screen went black a second then flickered bright again. The picture panned wide to encompass the entire gym. A hundred or so black caps soared toward the ceiling like ravens in flight.

Another shift. The picture narrowed in, focusing on specific faces.

"Oh, look . . . is that Cade on the left?" Mia pointed, but the camera moved. "Shoot. He's gone now."

Leanne sat forward. "Look at Eddie. He's so handsome it hurts." Mia heard a hitch in her friend's voice before Leanne laughed and added, "And he's grinning like a fool."

A bleached blonde girl ran up to Eddie. The two hugged before she turned to the camera and waved.

Laughter erupted in Mia's living room. "Leanne, look at you!" Aggie and Mia shrieked at the same time.

Rachel giggled. "Oh, man. It looks like black widow spiders are attacking your eyeballs."

"Those are false eyelashes, goofball. They were *the thing*, for your information." Leanne burst out laughing, too. "Why didn't somebody tell me how horrible they looked?"

Aggie wiped away tears of laughter. "You think you would've listened? More than half the girls in school had spider eyes, too."

"Your hair's almost the same color mine was before we covered the blonde," Rachel murmured, turning to Leanne. "I sort of look like you did in high school, don't I? You could be my mother."

When Leanne locked eyes with Rachel, Mia saw her friend's startled, yet pleased, expression. "Maybe we look a little alike, Packrat," Leanne said softly. "But you're a lot prettier than I was."

The scene moved outside the building to the courtyard. Mia recalled that warm Saturday afternoon in May. Watching the captured memory, she almost felt the heat of the sunshine on her face, the charge of anticipation in the air. She almost smelled the rosebushes that had lined the courtyard flowerbeds, and heard the excited chatter of young voices.

"Oh . . ." Aggie pointed at the screen. "There's Jimmy. And Roy."

Aggie's husband looked robust, healthy, and as full of bluster as ever. He sauntered up beside his son and slapped Jimmy on the back.

"He's so thin," Mia murmured.

"And look at all that hair," Leanne added.

Suddenly, Aggie appeared on screen. Tiny, pink-cheeked and bright-eyed, she joined her family.

"Oh, my heavens," she said, pressing a hand to her chest. "Look at that beehive."

Overcome by a sudden swell of tenderness, Mia squeezed Aggie's arm. "You're gorgeous. How old were you? Thirty-four?"

Aggie nodded. "Something like that."

On the screen, Leanne and Eddie joined the Cobbs. Leanne waved at someone beyond the camera, motioned them over. Seconds later, Mia and her mother entered the group. Mia recalled that her father held the camera.

She remembered, too, that her friendship with Leanne had taken root that year. The accident had occurred the summer before, and Leanne didn't spend much time with her old crowd anymore.

The group on screen smiled, waved and laughed, their arms around one another's shoulders.

Watching from the couch, Mia's breath caught when young Leanne and Eddie exchanged a lingering glance. It was quick and subtle, but filled with such tender sadness her heart ached. All those years before, she'd noticed that look between them, too. And understood. So had Aggie.

In 1972, standing in the high school courtyard, seventeen-year-old Mia took hold of Leanne's hand while Aggie placed a palm on her shoulder. The three of them connected, just like now.

On the couch, they touched again, linked hands and hearts. Mia glanced at the women beside her, their faces older, their souls wiser. They didn't speak; words weren't necessary.

Maybe, over time, they had begun to take their friendship for granted. But the connection that started in another time had never broken.

Leanne dressed for bed that night with a change of heart about the situation with Eddie. No, he shouldn't have followed her. Yes, she was irritated that he had. But watching the old graduation movie had reminded her of more than the fact that she'd worn too much makeup in high school. She remembered what was most important to her. Her friendships.

And her husband.

More than once, she and Eddie had been to hell and back, side by side. Even when at odds, they'd survived every time because they'd at least *tried* to stay honest with one another. Sometimes they had to set each other straight, but not like this. The battle of wills between them now was silly and senseless. Maybe Mia was justified in not trusting Cade with the truth about Rachel, but Leanne couldn't justify deceiving her husband. Not anymore. Not about anything. She owed it to Eddie to give him the benefit of the doubt. To trust that he would not try to overrun their decisions.

She loved Mia and Aggie, the strength she drew from them, the richness they added to her life. She wished she could uphold her promise to them about the secret without betraying her husband, but she couldn't. They would have to understand. They had to allow Eddie into their circle. Leanne should have insisted on that from the start.

She wouldn't deceive Eddie another day. About

Rachel . . . or about her need to bring a child into their home. It was a need she'd always possessed, but had put aside due to an insecure fear that she wouldn't be a fit mother. Her realization at Christmas that she and Eddie would grow old alone had brought the need back. Then Rachel showed up, and it grew even stronger.

Stretching and yawning, she climbed into one of the twin beds in the room that had once belonged to Mia's two sons.

In the matching bed across the way, Aggie tossed and turned.

"Goodnight, Ag."

" 'Night, sugar. You ever reach that Oberman woman?"

"No. She's either out of town or she doesn't want to talk to us. Mia and I together must've left at least ten messages on her machine. She's starting to feel like a lost cause."

Aggie sighed. "What now? You have any more ideas on what we can do to save that poor girl?"

"I'm working on it, Aggie. Don't give up yet." Leanne switched off the lamp on the table between the beds.

"Leanne?"

"Yes?"

"I'm sorry we laughed at you in that film. I think you were pretty in high school."

Leanne smiled into the darkness. "Pretty what, Ag?"

"Pretty wonderful. I may not have given birth to you, but you're my daughter. You know that, don't you?"

"I know," Leanne answered, touched and thankful. "And you're like a mother to me."

Knowing what she had to do tomorrow, Leanne closed her eyes. As she succumbed to sleep, Rachel's words drifted like a velvet whisper through her mind.

"You could be my mother . . ."

Chapter 16

$\mathcal{W}$hen Leanne awoke the next morning, Aggie's bed was made, the spread smoothed and tucked, the pillow plumped and in the sham.

Leanne looked at the clock. Eight forty-five A.M. She had not heard Mia and Aggie leave for the coffee shop. She guessed Rachel still slept, since the house was quiet.

Padding barefoot across the hall, she peeked into Christy's room. As expected, Rachel's eyes were shut, her breathing soft and even in the sun-dappled room.

Leanne tucked the blanket around her and smiled. If she didn't know better, she'd think the kid was an angel.

Hope swept through Leanne. Maybe it would be possible to have her and Eddie's foster parenting credentials reinstated without repeating the long process of approval. That could take months. She didn't want to wait so long. Already, she cared too much for Rachel to give her up.

But how should she broach the issue with Eddie?

Just telling him that she'd been helping Mia hide Rachel would be difficult enough. Would he balk at the idea of parenting a teenager? Even if she explained how much Rachel meant to her? Twenty years ago, they'd talked about fostering a baby, not an older child.

She wished there was more time to talk to the proper authorities and find out the possibility of reinstatement before she brought up the subject. But time was running out. Today was the day she had to come clean with Eddie.

After a final look at the tiny girl snuggled beneath the blankets, Leanne turned away from the bed. She decided to go out front for the paper and start the coffee before waking Rachel.

Before she stepped from the room, she spotted the pink suede boots on the floor beside the closet door. She'd admired those spiked heel, pointy-toed beauties in Jesse's display window more times than she could count. Leanne tiptoed over, picked them up and fell in love.

Taking the boots with her, Leanne headed for the kitchen where she sat and slipped them on. They didn't exactly go with the black "Property of Muddy Creek Cowboys" jersey she had worn to bed, which had belonged to one of Mia's boys. Still, Leanne was crazy about them.

Humming an off-key rendition of "These Boots Are Made For Walking," Leanne strutted to the front door and unlocked it. She poked her head out. The newspaper boy had actually managed to land the paper close to the porch. She'd have to tell Eddie to give the kid a raise. The plastic-covered morning edition lay just three or four steps down the walkway.

Leanne scanned the neighborhood left to right. No neighbors in sight. Not even nosy Buck Miller from next door. Shivering, she stepped out, ventured another step, then another. Crisp morning air raised goose bumps on her bare arms and legs. The snow, a constant presence on the ground since before Christmas, lay in patches now, adorning the shadiest yards like shrinking meringue on a pie.

Stooping, Leanne grabbed the paper. When she stood again, she noticed the bushes rustle in front of the house across the street. She paused and frowned. Someone hid in the narrow space between the Thurmans' two tall evergreens.

Pretending not to notice, Leanne turned and walked back to Mia's porch. At the front door, she swung around in time to see Eddie step from the Thurmans' bushes and into their yard, a camera in his hand.

Leanne didn't care that she wore only a jersey that stopped mid-thigh. Or that the temperature was no more than forty-five degrees and she wasn't wearing a coat. She didn't care that Buck Miller had ventured out front of his house. Let the whole neighborhood, the entire *town,* gawk.

"What do you think you're doing?" she yelled at her husband. Eddie met her at the Thurmans' curb, and she poked a finger against his chest. "You're spying on me."

"Baby, please." His brow wrinkled. "Give this up and come on home."

"You took my photo, didn't you?" She grabbed for the camera.

Eddie held it out of her reach. "This is nuts, Lea. I've talked to Cade. You're in over your head here." He nodded at the house. "All of you."

"*You're* calling *me* nuts?"

He backed up a step. "I didn't say that."

She poked him again. "*I'm* not the one hiding in the bushes like some lowlife paparazzi."

He took another backward step. "I know what you women have up your sleeve. Cade and Roy do, too. Come clean, Lea. Talk to Cade."

"Don't tell me what to do."

Behind Eddie, the Thurmans' door opened and Bobby Thurman came out carrying a lunch box. He looked Leanne up and down, his grin spreading slowly.

"Dang it, Lea. Cover yourself up." Eddie took off his jacket and tugged it around her shoulders. He glared at Bobby and barked, "What are you looking at?"

Across the way, Buck Miller blurted a laugh that turned into a wheezing cough when Eddie glared at him, too.

Leanne jerked off the coat, threw it at Eddie, then turned and wobbled on the spiked heels back toward the house.

"Y'all are busted," Eddie yelled after her.

She glanced over her shoulder, saw him lift the camera above his head, as if in explanation. "What does that prove?"

"I know those boots came from Jesse's. And I know who took 'em."

Leanne's heart tripped. Pausing, she glanced down at her feet. "Jesse's not the only place that carries boots like these. I bought them in Amarillo the other day."

"You could've, but you didn't."

Leanne stared at her husband. For once, she didn't know what to say. How could she have been so stupid as to come outside wearing Rachel's stolen goods? Now Eddie had a photograph. Evidence for Cade.

Would it be enough for the judge to grant another warrant?

As predicted, the weather warmed to an almost spring-like low sixties that afternoon. All the snow that had hidden in shaded areas, stubbornly refusing to leave, took off for parts unknown.

Aggie showed up at Mia's close to noon and, when Leanne left for work, Rachel pleaded to go out to the backyard patio.

"After Leanne's run-in with Eddie this morning, I'm not sure it's a good idea for you to leave the house, sugar."

"*Please*? As if anybody will see us in the back yard." Rachel kicked a toe against the couch. "I'm *going* totally *crazy* stuck in here."

Aggie gave in. The patio sat close to the house, and a six-foot fence encased the yard. She couldn't imagine that they'd even be noticed by anyone passing down the alley. And fresh air and sunshine would do them both good.

She was right; birdsong and the earthy scent of

damp soil bolstered Aggie's attitude. The temperature was perfect for their light jackets and jeans.

"Okay," Rachel said, unscrewing the cap on a bottle of nail polish. "Roll up your jeans."

Aggie pulled her chair around to face Rachel's, then did as instructed. She stretched out one leg, propped her left foot in Rachel's lap. "Lord." Aggie shook her head as Rachel made the first stroke across her big toe. "A sixty-eight-year-old woman with pink glitter on her toenails. This stuff's made for teenagers."

Rachel rolled her eyes. "*Duh.*"

"So, you agree I look silly?"

Rachel shrugged. "Who cares? Do *you* like it?"

Aggie studied her foot and smiled. "I do. Just for fun, though." Yes, it made her feel silly, but good, too. Happy and alive. So what if she was sixty-eight? She had a right to feel all of those things, didn't she? Now should be one of the best times of her life, and she'd decided to turn it into just that. Roy could either enjoy it with her, or grow moldy sitting alone at home every night, week after week, with his TV remote and constant complaints. She'd leave that decision to him.

This morning at the shop, she'd heard through the Coots that Cade let Roy out of jail late last night. The stubborn ol' mule still hadn't called to apologize. Maybe he never would. It wouldn't surprise her one bit if Roy chose living without her over admitting he'd done anything wrong.

Aggie gave a blissful sigh as a cool breeze tickled her bare toes. "This is pure heaven, Rachel. Thank you."

"You're welcome." Rachel finished Aggie's left foot then sat back and admired her work. "I'm good. I used to want to be a makeup artist for horror movies. You know, aliens and vampires and stuff? But I could be a pedicure lady, too."

"You could." Aggie switched feet. "Or you could go to college."

Rachel dipped the tiny brush into the polish. "College costs a buttload of money."

Aggie had about given up on reminding the girl to watch her language. Just like she had with Leanne. "There are all kinds of ways to get money for school. Student loans and scholarships and such."

"You've got to have good grades to get a scholarship. Mine stink."

"How come? Don't you study?"

Shrugging, Rachel kept her gaze focused on Aggie's toes. "School bites."

"Maybe you just haven't found your niche."

"What's a niche?"

"The thing that holds your interest, that you love doing even if it's hard work. Your passion, some people call it."

Rachel glanced up briefly, the brush poised mid-air. "What's yours?"

"Cooking, I suppose."

"That's Mia's passion, too."

"It's something we have in common."

"What about Leanne?"

Aggie thought about that. "Fashion. The woman loves to dress up. Always has."

Rachel smiled. "Me, too."

"Leanne's other passion is kids. Teaching them." Aggie cocked her head to the side. "Maybe you should ask her to help you with your studies. Leanne has a knack for making learning fun."

"Why isn't she still a teacher if she loves it so much and she's good at it?"

"Sometimes a person needs a break, even from things they love. Time to re-evaluate and reconsider."

Her own statement startled her. Was that what was going on with her and Roy? Did she need a break from him in order to figure out what *she* needed for a change? Without him barging in with his opinion, his needs, and pushing hers aside? She loved Roy. That would never change. But maybe her approach to their relationship needed a makeover, too. Just like her appearance.

"What would I do in college?" Rachel blew on Aggie's wet toenails. "I mean, just when I think I know what I want to do, something else comes along and I want to do that too, you know? Like, I saw *Lord of the Rings* and decided to do movie makeup? Then the next week? I thought, *duh*. Why *do* Gollum's makeup when I could *be* Gollum, instead?"

Aggie blinked over the tops of her glasses at the girl. "Who is Gollum?"

"Don't you watch movies?"

Aggie shrugged. "Well, whoever she is, you can be whatever you want to be, Rachel. The sky's the limit."

Rachel shrugged. "Now that I'm learning to cook? I'm thinking maybe that's my passion, too. Like you and Mia. I could be a famous chef with my own restaurant."

"Now, there's an idea."

"Only no green foods in my restaurant." Rachel shuddered. "And no loaves."

Such a sweet girl, Aggie thought. But odder than all get out, sometimes. And indecisive.

Rachel's brows drew together. "But, now I totally love sewing, too. Leanne says I'm a natural. We're alike like that. Maybe I could be a clothes designer." Her head came up, her eyes widening. Smiling broadly, she lifted the polish brush and pointed it at Aggie. "I know! Leanne and I could be designing partners!"

Aggie smiled, too. "I think you're on to something."

Rachel's hand paused halfway down to Aggie's last toe. She glanced toward the fence separating Mia's backyard from Buck Miller's. "Did you hear that?"

"What?"

"A noise in that tree next door. It moved, too." Rachel leaned forward, squinted. "Something's up there."

"Probably a squirrel," Aggie said, then heard a loud sneeze from that direction. She removed her leg from Rachel's lap, jumped up, moved to the patio's edge. Her heart lurched when she peered toward the treetop and spotted the cause of all the commotion. "Get inside," she said quietly to Rachel. "That's no squirrel." It was a two-hundred-forty-pound, gray-haired, pot-bellied weasel.

As Rachel escaped through the back door into the house, Aggie hobbled toward the fence, keeping her wet toes pointed skyward. "Roy Dean Cobb, come down here this minute."

Roy lifted a camera, pointed it at her, snapped.

"Why are you taking my picture? And wearing your hunting cammo? Does Buck Miller know you're in his tree?"

He snapped again.

Aggie reached the fence. She couldn't see over it, so she peeped through a knothole, only to find an eyeball staring at her. She screamed and jumped back, ruining her pedicure. "Is that you, Buck?" Moving away from the fence, Aggie held her hand up to shade her eyes and glared at Roy in the tree again. "Get down!"

Behind her, she heard the back door open. Turning, she saw Rachel running toward her.

"No!" Aggie hissed, flapping her hands. "Go back!" She returned her attention to Roy in time to see him lift the camera again.

"Use this," Rachel said, handing her a sling shot. "I found it in the boys' room."

Aggie's hand shook, half from nerves, half from fury, as she took the slingshot from Rachel then reached down into the dead grass for a pebble. She'd show that man a thing or two. How dare he spy on her? Placing the pebble into the leather sling, she looked up at her husband, closed one eye, and aimed. She took a deep breath. Her hand steadied.

"Now, Aggie girl. You wouldn't shoot me," Roy

called down. Then, in a small voice, "Would you?" When she didn't answer or lower the slingshot, he gave a nervous laugh. "You couldn't hit the broad side of a barn, woman."

"Maybe not, but I bet I can hit the broad side of you. My big brothers taught me a few things when we were kids."

The tree branches trembled as Roy scrambled to get down. Turning his back to her, he wrapped his arms and legs around the trunk and clung like ivy around a lamppost.

Aggie turned loose. The pebble hit Roy sqaure in the butt.

He cried out, let go, and crashed to the ground.

"Roy!" Aggie screamed. Dropping the slingshot, she ran to the fence and climbed up on the lower support bar. "Oh Lord, sugar, are you hurt?"

Roy lay on the ground, the camera and Buck Miller beside him. He pushed up on one elbow, his face twisted and turning from bright red to purple. "I'm coming over there," he roared. Rolling to his hands and knees, he started crawling toward the fence.

Aggie jumped down. She turned and started running. "Oh, no, you're not."

"Oh, yes I am."

Ahead of her, Rachel slipped inside the back door. "You're not invited," she yelled.

Darting into the house behind Rachel, Aggie slammed the door and turned the lock.

Seconds later, the pounding started. "Enough is enough, woman!" Roy boomed.

"Go away. You're trespassing." Aggie tried to catch her breath.

"I got pictures of that girl paintin' your toes, Aggie."

"I don't know what you're talking about!"

Aggie covered her ears and said a silent prayer that the camera had broken when Roy fell from the tree.

Chapter 17

That evening, Cade pulled to a stop at the edge of a rocky, dirt road. "This is it." He turned off the truck. "What do you think?"

Mia studied the grassy section of land. It stretched to a canyon wall layered in shades of clay pink, red, and rusty sienna. The evening sun set the wall ablaze. She imagined the cottonwood trees in spring, their branches filled with dancing green leaves. "It's beautiful, Cade."

"You really think so?"

Glancing across the seat at him, Mia smiled. "I do."

He stared out the window again, a faraway look in his eyes, as if he saw something no one else did. A fishing shack? Mia wondered. During the drive over, he had mentioned a small lake somewhere close by.

"Let's take a look." Cade reached for his door handle.

As they walked to the back of the truck, Mia asked, "Why did you change your mind about building? It's a perfect spot for a house."

He shrugged. "Maybe I will one of these days. Until then, it's a good place just to get away and hike around with Bart."

At the sound of his name, the golden retriever in the truck bed whined. He jumped up, placed his front paws on the edge.

Cade let him out. "Too lazy to jump over now, is that it?" he said to the dog, tossing a stick that Bart ran after.

"How much of this land is yours?" Mia asked.

"Just ten acres."

"What are you waiting for? You should go ahead and build. It's not too far from town. It's so peaceful."

"I don't know. Seems wrong somehow to build a place for just me. Like something's missing." He took off his hat and put it inside the truck. "And I imagine it'd get lonely living out here by myself, peaceful or not."

"I think you should get started." She laughed. "As they say, none of us are getting any younger."

"That's for sure. And I'm tired of waiting."

Bart ran up to Cade, tail wagging, the stick in his mouth. Cade threw it again.

Mia had the impression he wasn't only talking about building a house, that he was also tired of waiting to meet the right person with whom to share it. She knew Jill had been the one to leave their marriage. At least, those were the rumors. Cade had brought a city girl to the country, and she couldn't make it fit her. Trouble was, the city didn't fit Cade. Neither could find a compromise.

"It's hard starting over," she said, watching him as they began to walk. "I never imagined I'd be alone at this stage of my life."

"What did you imagine?"

"Traveling with Dan. Taking our kids and grandkids along sometimes. Having someone to share things with. Little things, you know? The sunset, a good bottle of wine." She looked away, embarrassed. "I didn't mean to go on like that."

"You didn't go on. I understand."

When she faced him again, she could see that he did understand, that Cade had wanted, had *expected*, those things in his life, too.

He smiled. "It's not over, you know. You could marry again."

"Haven't you heard the statistics on women my age remarrying? I have a better chance of winning the lottery."

"I don't put much stock in statistics."

When Bart returned again with the stick, Cade ignored him. Rebuked, the retriever ran ahead to explore.

Cade offered Mia his hand, and she took it. As they walked, he pointed out how the house would sit on the lot, where each room would be. "I don't have it all worked out. When I do build, I plan to take my time and do it right."

"You'll build it yourself?"

He nodded. "Most of it. I learned the ropes working construction during the summers to put myself through college. I'm rusty, but it'll come back to me."

"If you're as thorough and patient with this as you

are with your work, I'm sure the house will be a show-place."

Mia's face heated as she wondered again if he would also be a patient lover. She let go of his hand. Ever since the drive to Paco's, she'd had no luck banning such thoughts about Cade from her mind. A change of subject; that's what she needed.

They stopped beside a cottonwood, and she leaned against it. "Speaking of being thorough, did you sign Eddie and Roy on to do some investigative work for you?"

"Roy and Eddie?" His look of astonishment appeared far from genuine. "Why would I do that?"

Mia smirked at him. "You have an annoying habit of responding to my questions with more questions."

"And you," he said, nodding her away from the tree and leading the way toward the canyon wall, "have a habit of not answering my questions at all." He glanced back at her. "I thought that topic was off limits when we're together after hours. Have you changed your mind about that?"

Mia knew it was pointless to pretend any longer. If Cade didn't already have the proof he needed for another warrant, he soon would, thanks to Eddie's and Roy's photos. She wondered if that was his reason for bringing her out here where they were alone and there'd be no interruptions. Maybe he was affording her one last opportunity to confess. If she did, what would happen? Would he make a beeline for his truck? Drive to the house immediately and pick up Rachel? Take her away tonight?

She wasn't prepared for that possibility. Despite the fact Cade knew the truth, if Mia could give the girl one more night by keeping quiet, she would.

Still, she didn't want to jeopardize what she felt between her and Cade. Last night's kiss made her realize she couldn't grieve forever. She had to let Dan go. Not forget, but move on. Make a new life for herself. She yearned to live each day again, not merely survive it.

When they stopped alongside the rugged canyon wall, Mia looked up at Cade. "I know you're on to us," she said.

Surprise sparked in his eyes. "So you're admitting you have her?"

"I don't like being difficult, Cade." She crossed her arms. "But I'm going to make you come up with your proof. Until then, I'm not admitting anything. I'm not in a rush to cause heartache to someone who has already suffered so much."

"You're not causing it, Mia." He scrubbed a hand over his face. "Believe it or not, I'm not in any hurry, either. Not anymore. This isn't easy for me. I have some tough decisions to make."

"About me, you mean." Mia saw clearly how heavy those decisions weighed on him.

"You. Aggie and Leanne. Even the girl. Don't think I don't care what happens to her. I do. I have a heart. I'm not only a sheriff, I'm a dad, too. I hate seeing *any* kid in trouble."

"I never thought you didn't care. But the law takes priority for you. Right or wrong. I don't blame you for that, it's your job. I guess, this time, I just don't agree."

He blew out a noisy breath and looked away. "I'm not sure what I think anymore. But I don't want to think about this. Not tonight."

When he reached for her, she went to him without hesitation.

Cade wrapped his arms around her, pulled her close. "You feel so good." He nuzzled his face in her hair. "I don't want you to hate me."

Mia leaned back to look at him. "I could never hate you, Cade. No matter what happens." Rising onto her tiptoes, she pressed her lips to his. "You taste like coffee."

One corner of his mouth curved up. "I've been drinking a lot of the stuff, lately. It reminds me of you." When she tilted her head back, he brushed kisses across her eyes, her cheeks, her lips.

"So you think of me?" she murmured, lacing her fingers together behind his neck, feeling the soft prickle of his hair.

"All the time."

"I think about you, too."

They touched noses, smiled at one another.

"Look," Cade said quietly as Bart ran up beside them and sat at their feet. Pulling away, he turned Mia so that her back was to him.

On the western horizon, the sun melted like liquid fire into the earth. Cade encircled her waist with both arms. Mia leaned back against him, feeling grounded, safe, happy for the first time in too many months to count.

Sometimes, she thought as, inch by inch, the ball of

fire slowly disappeared, fate gave back what it took away.

Like someone with whom to share sunsets.

The next day, the women continued the routine that had become their norm. No one spoke of the photos or about the final showdown they expected to occur at any moment. Still, dread radiated from each of them until it almost shimmered.

Aggie jumped at the slightest noise.

Leanne snapped at the other women, at Rachel, at Brewed Awakening customers.

As for Mia, she held her breath each time the bell over the coffee shop door jingled. In some ways, she was ready for all the drama to end. They might never find a solution to Rachel's dilemma on their own. Leanne's visit with the attorney had given them hope. But so far, they had not been able to reach Rachel's classmate Lacy Oberman or her mother. Without their testimony about witnessing Rachel's abuse, Mia feared the girl's chances of staying out of a juvenile placement facility were about zero.

Despite the tension permeating the air, the day passed without so much as a peep from Cade, Eddie, or Roy. Last night before leaving his land, Cade had asked Mia to have dinner with him again tonight. Mia had agreed. She suspected the invitation was Cade's way of ignoring the trouble they both knew would come when those photos were developed.

After returning home last night, she'd stayed awake

for hours thinking about Cade. His playful smile and solid warmth. How the touch of his body against hers made her ache with happiness. She relived his kiss, and the memory of the heat in his eyes the moment before their lips touched consumed her.

Mia tried to convince herself it was too soon after Dan's death to feel so deeply for someone else. Too soon to want Cade after only two dates. But she knew it wasn't true. She had suffered through sixteen lonely months. And she and Cade weren't two people getting to know one another; they'd been friends for most of their lives.

"You're going out with him *again*?" Rachel sat on the edge of the kitchen counter. "Where?"

"To eat pizza."

Rachel turned to Aggie, who stood at the sink washing dishes. "We should have pizza, too."

Dipping her chin, Aggie glanced over the tops of her reading glasses at the girl. "You've eaten so much pepperoni since you've been here, you're going to turn into one."

In her chair at the table, Leanne drummed fingertips on a placemat and looked at her watch, restless over Eddie. "What time is Romeo due, anyway?"

"*Cade* will be here at six-thirty." Mia opened her compact and checked her lipstick for the third time in ten minutes.

"I'll have to give it to the man." Leanne wiggled her brows. "Once he finally talked you into going out with him, he knew what to do to keep you coming back."

Making a face, Mia snapped the compact shut and

slipped it into her purse. "It's only pizza. And my going out with him *has* stopped his questions."

Leanne tilted her head. "It's hard to talk when you're in a liplock."

Mia smirked at them. "Very funny."

Wiping her hands on a clean dishtowel, Aggie said, "Well, I think it's wonderful."

Leanne's face softened. "So do I. But it puts an awkward spin on things, doesn't it?" She glanced at Rachel.

"I'd like to talk to y'all about that." Mia drew a steadying breath as she turned her attention to the girl. "Honey, I feel like we're spinning our wheels and not resolving anything for you. Whether Cade gets his warrant or not, maybe it's time we—"

The doorbell's ring interrupted Mia mid-sentence. Her heart jumped to her throat, and the look of panic on Rachel's face didn't escape her notice. "That must be Cade." Grabbing her coat from the back of a chair, Mia draped it over her arm and started for the entry hall.

Cade stood on the porch, but he wasn't alone. Roy was on his left side and Eddie was on his right. "Hey, you three." She laughed nervously. "Funny that you all showed up at the same time."

Their expressions assured her the simultaneous arrival was no coincidence. *This is it*, Mia thought, preparing for the inevitable and hating it for everyone, Rachel most of all.

She stepped back. "Let me tell Aggie and Leanne you're here."

When she turned toward the kitchen, Cade stopped her by touching her arm. "We need to talk to you first, Mia." He pulled several snapshots from his coat pocket and handed them to her.

Mia glanced at the first one. Leanne in the front yard wearing Brent's old school jersey and the pink boots Rachel stole.

Meeting Cade's gaze, she said quietly, "I could argue that this doesn't prove anything. There are certainly more than one pair of pink boots in the world."

Cade appeared sorry rather than smug. "Take a look at the others."

Mia shuffled through images of Rachel giving Aggie a pedicure on the backyard patio. Rachel darting for the back door while Aggie looked toward the camera. Rachel standing behind Aggie holding a slingshot.

"Can't argue with those," Roy blurted.

Focusing her attention on Cade, Mia sighed and asked, "So did you get another warrant?"

"I was hoping you wouldn't force me to do that. If the judge sees these photos, it'll incriminate you, Aggie, and Leanne."

Mia studied Cade's face. "Cade . . . what you're doing . . . it means a lot."

"Don't be so quick to thank me." He pushed back his hat, looking as if he'd rather have a tooth pulled than go through this. "I'm sorry, Mia. Sooner or later, the girl's going to have to go back to Amarillo and face the consequences. I can't promise you how she'll be treated if somebody else finds her and takes her back.

But I can promise you that if I take her, I'll do everything in my power to see that her case is handled fairly. I can't help thinking that, if we're honest, everything will work out for the best."

Mia couldn't speak. She nodded, stepped back, motioned for him to come in.

"Not you two," came Leanne's voice from behind as the other two men started to follow Cade inside. "After what y'all did yesterday, you can freeze your butts off outside, for all I care."

Roy looked around the others at Aggie. "My bad hip flared up after that fall," he said, sounding pathetic. "The cold aggravates it."

"I'm not over my mad yet, Roy." Aggie crossed her arms. "As for your hip, I guess you got what's comin' to you."

Looking dejected, the two retreated to Cade's truck to wait.

"Can we talk to her first?" Mia asked Cade. "Before she sees you? I don't want to scare her."

"She already knows," Leanne said, her eyes bleak.

"The poor girl." Aggie's voice wavered. "She's been through so much."

"She's going to be mad at us." Leanne turned toward the kitchen. "I'll go get her."

Mia shook her head and looked from Leanne to Aggie. "We'll all go together. The three of us."

Cade nodded. "I'll wait here."

They found the kitchen empty.

"Rachel?" Mia called. "She must've gone to the bathroom."

They didn't find her there. Or anywhere else in the house. No Rachel. No backpack. Not a trace of any of her things. It was almost as if she'd never been there at all.

After searching the back yard and alley, Cade said, "Eddie, Roy, and I will separate and look around town for her. You three stay here in case she shows up."

"Try the Nelson's storm cellar," Aggie suggested, her face creased with worry. "That's where she hid last time."

Mia glimpsed uncertainty in Cade's eyes and knew what put it there. She touched his arm. "If she comes back here, I'll call you. I promise."

Right now, she regretted she hadn't called him after they'd first found Rachel in their storage room. What good had their little undercover operation done for her? The girl was in no better position than she'd been before. She was alone, afraid, and on the run.

Cade handed her a business card he pulled from his pocket. "My cell number," he said.

Dusk shadowed the lawn. Soon darkness would descend. Bitter cold. Mia took the card, her fingers brushing his. "Find her, Cade," she said, her voice cracking.

He squeezed her hand. "I'll be in touch."

Chapter 18

$\mathcal{A}$n hour passed, then two, with no word from Cade. Mia prepared for a sleepless night reminiscent of ones she had spent ten years earlier when Christy had run away.

She relived the sinking dread, the rising panic that followed; a bumpy road she had hoped not to travel again. Would the nightmare repeat itself? Would one frantic day stretch into another then another until, finally, time blurred into a week, and still no news? When would they hear Rachel's voice again? What if they never did?

She, Leanne, and Aggie sat around the kitchen table drinking the same house blend they served at the coffee shop. Aggie had offered to cook supper, but they were all too nervous to eat.

Leanne wrapped both hands around her mug. Steam drifted toward her face. "I've decided to look into the possibility of having mine and Eddie's foster parenting credentials reinstated."

"Reinstated?" Mia said. "I wasn't aware you ever went through the process."

"Twenty years ago we were approved. But when they called and said they had a baby . . ." Her eyes misted. "I couldn't go through with it. The child was a boy. He was only two years old."

"I remember," Aggie said softly. "I was heartsick when it didn't work out. You and that child would've been so good for each other."

Leanne closed her eyes. "I felt I didn't deserve him. Not after what I did to my own baby."

"Leanne." Mia shook her head. "You were a child when that happened. You made a stupid mistake. All kids do in some way or another. Stop beating yourself up. Any kid would be blessed to have you for a mother."

She looked at them. "Most kids' stupid mistakes don't end up killing a baby."

Aching for her, Mia said, "It was a tragedy, but you learned from it and made a better life. Now you have to forgive yourself."

"I think you're doing the right thing." Aggie smiled at Leanne. "These days, lots of folks your age raise babies."

Leanne blinked at her. "I want Rachel."

The moment she heard the words, Mia knew it was the answer. Leanne and Rachel were meant to be together. Like Rachel, Leanne had lived a turbulent childhood. Both had lost parents while young. Both had made poor choices, and paid dearly for them. And, more than once, Mia had noticed something special between the two of them.

"I wanted to have everything lined up before springing the idea on Eddie," Leanne said. "Before, he was reluctant about taking in an older child. He was afraid there would be too many ingrained problems." She sipped her coffee. "He might take some convincing. But there's no time to work all that out now. After Rachel's found, I'll talk to him about it."

"You're sure you want to do this?" Mia asked. "It's a huge step."

"I'm sure."

"It's meant to be," Aggie said, smiling.

"This may sound silly, but I think you're right, Ag." An expression of wonder passed over Leanne's face. "Rachel ended up in our storage room for a reason. She's the child I've prayed for."

Aggie patted Leanne's hand. "That doesn't sound one bit silly."

Mia agreed.

"If it works out for all of us," Leanne said, "if she's happy with us, I hope maybe Eddie and I can adopt her." Her attention drifted toward the window, out into the black night. "They have to find her," she whispered.

"They will," Mia insisted. "Cade doesn't stop until he gets what he's after."

At eleven o'clock, Cade called to say they'd seen no sign of Rachel, but he refused to give up.

Though he'd told Eddie and Roy to go home and

get some sleep, they wouldn't until Aggie and Leanne went with them. They both knew that wasn't about to happen unless they found Rachel.

Mia didn't remind Cade that, as far as Aggie was concerned, Roy had a few more tasks to complete before she'd return to the farm. Mia would bet that the new, more stubborn and confident Aggie would set Roy straight about that soon enough.

The women moved from the kitchen to the living room. Mia stretched out in the recliner, Aggie on the loveseat, and Leanne across the couch.

They dozed fitfully until three-thirty A.M. when Aggie rose to brew fresh coffee. Mia and Leanne joined her in the kitchen. Again, they tossed around ideas of where Rachel might've hidden.

"Maybe she found a way into the coffee shop's back room again," Aggie suggested.

"We locked up, Ag." Leanne yawned. "Unless she broke a window, I don't see how she could get in."

"Cade said they checked there," Mia told them. "Eddie used his shop key."

Leanne leaned back and crossed her arms, her eyes as tired as Aggie's. "Crazy little Packrat. What if she hitched a ride with some trucker again?"

"Lord." Aggie pressed a hand to her chest. "Don't even think that."

Mia breathed in the scent of perking coffee. "Remember that morning we found her? Leanne, you mentioned something about how she should've broken into Betty's."

"That's right." Leanne straightened. "Betty can't

stand the beauty shop to be cold when she arrives in the mornings. She keeps the heater blowing full blast all night. I told Rachel that."

"Sometimes Betty stays to do a cut or a perm after dark," Aggie said, her eyes alert now rather than sleepy. "If she did last night, the back door might not have been locked. Rachel's a wily little thing. I bet she could've slipped right in unnoticed."

Mia thought they might have their answer. Crime was practically nonexistent in Muddy Creek. Residents were relaxed about locking up. Even merchants.

With a trembling hand, Mia reached for the phone to call Cade.

Cade locked Rachel inside his truck then turned to Betty Rigdon. "Thanks for hightailing it over here so fast."

"Thank *you*." She nodded toward Rachel. "How'd you know she was in there? You don't usually roam the streets this early, do you?"

"I had a phone call, an anonymous tip from somebody who said they'd seen movement inside the shop."

"You didn't recognize the voice?"

Cade shook his head. "It was muffled."

Betty frowned. "Had to be Aubrey Ricketts. Who else is up and out this time of the morning? Wonder why he wouldn't identify himself?"

He shrugged. "Can't say. Maybe he didn't want to get involved. In case it was a friend of his inside or something like that."

"Aubrey? Knowing him, he'd be all too happy to be in the thick of things. Maybe he didn't want me knowing he noses around my shop in the middle of the night."

Shrugging again, Cade glanced toward the truck at Rachel. "You want to pursue this, Betty?"

"No way." She tossed tangled hair from her face. At the moment, she looked like anything but a person in charge of other women's grooming. "I looked around. The kid didn't bother anything. I'm just glad she found a warm place to sleep."

Cade smiled at her. "You're a good woman."

"So where're you taking her?" she asked as Cade started around to the driver's side of his truck.

He paused, his hand on the door handle. This was the moment he'd both hoped for and dreaded. What he had to do now would break Mia's heart. Aggie's and Leanne's, too. They would want to say goodbye to the girl. But he was duty-bound to do his job. And his job entailed taking in fugitives. He couldn't risk Rachel Nye slipping away again. But Cade also didn't want to lock her up in *his* jail. "I'm heading straight to Amarillo."

"Now?" Betty squinted at her watch. "It's not even four in the morning."

"No sense wasting time." After telling Betty goodbye, he climbed in beside Rachel and took off.

He'd wait until they were on the road before calling the others to let them know he'd found her. Roy and Eddie. The women, too. Otherwise, they would try to talk him into waiting so they could see Rachel one last time.

When Mia had called him about looking for Rachel at Betty's, she'd said she and the other women would wait for him at the coffee shop, that they were too antsy to stay at the house any longer. He'd asked that they avoid the beauty salon, and they'd respected his request.

Cade didn't tell Mia he would bring Rachel to the coffee shop, though without question, it had been an unspoken understanding between them. But all it would do was make Rachel's leaving harder for everyone. Better to cut the cord sharp and quick rather than drag out the pain.

Cade turned onto Main and, when they passed the coffee shop, he saw lights on inside. He glimpsed the women behind the window.

Beside him, Rachel started sobbing. She stared out at the Brewed Awakening, her body trembling.

"Sweetheart, don't." He'd rather suffer a sharp blow to the solar plexus than deal with a female's tears.

Rachel cried harder.

Something turned over inside him. Reaching across the seat, Cade opened the glove box, where he stashed paper napkins collected from too many fastfood meals. "Here." He handed her one.

She took it, pressed it to her eyes.

Damn it, the girl was getting to him. Cade told himself he was doing the right thing. The only thing he could. He forced his attention to the road, determined to harden his heart. Though he had always loved being Sheriff, right now he hated the job.

Too nervous to talk, Mia, Leanne and Aggie prepared for the day ahead. They all sensed strongly that Cade would find Rachel at Betty's. With that hope in mind, they'd called Roy and Eddie and told them to meet them at the coffee shop. Then they had left both the front and back doors unlocked. Mia guessed Cade might want to slip Rachel in through the storage room so that no passersby might see her.

If he came at all.

She hadn't mentioned to the others her fear that he wouldn't show. Cade's sense of responsibility to his job might push him to take Rachel to Amarillo right away, without stopping to allow them goodbyes.

They were all in the kitchen when the front bell jingled. Everyone went still and looked toward the swinging doors.

Leanne made the first move. Aggie and Mia followed.

Cade stood in the middle of the front room with his hands on Rachel's shoulders. Her face was splotchy red and tear-streaked, her eyes wide and dark.

Mia's gaze locked with Cade's. He smiled and shrugged. "I found her huddled up in Betty's back room. She ate a package of Pepperidge Farm sugar cookies for supper last night but Betty was fine with it."

"I'm sorry," Rachel wailed, bursting into tears as Eddie and Roy rushed through the door behind her. "I'll pay the lady back for the cookies. I promise."

"Don't worry about it, darlin'." Winded from hurrying, Roy leaned forward, hands on his thighs, to catch his breath. "Those gals over at the beauty shop could stand to eat a few less cookies."

Rachel's tears started a chain reaction. First Aggie, then Mia, followed by Leanne. They gathered around the girl.

"You worried us sick, sugar."

"Packrat, I'd wring your neck if I wasn't so happy to see you."

"Rachel . . ." Mia's relief made her feel ten pounds lighter. "I think you managed to gray every hair on my head that Christy missed."

Rachel blinked up at her. "Your hair's not gray."

Mia laughed, then cupped a hand around her mouth and whispered, "That's what you think. Just ask Betty." She introduced Rachel to Eddie and Roy, then broke free of the circle and made her way over to Cade. Taking him aside while the others talked, she asked quietly, "What now?"

"Are you asking me what I *should* do? Or are you asking what I *plan* to do?"

Overwhelmed by the affection she felt for him, Mia answered, "Both."

"I *should* take her straight to Amarillo." He pushed his hat back, scratched the top of his head. "What I plan to do is give you ladies a couple of hours with her first." When the others in the room quieted and turned to look at him, Cade squinted at Rachel and added, "Don't you be getting any ideas, though, young lady. I'm not letting you out of my sight." He shifted to Aggie. "How about some of those special sweet rolls? I don't know about the rest of you, but I'm hungry."

Aggie hustled off to the back as the room filled with conversation again.

Mia took Cade's hand. "Thank you."

He looked down at their joined fingers, then up at her. "I wouldn't do this for anybody else."

She tilted her head, smiled at him. "I know that." And it warmed her heart. Later, she'd let him know just how much that meant to her.

Cade glanced toward Rachel, Aggie, and Leanne, then met Mia's gaze. "Why did y'all hide her? We could've worked all this out a long time ago. Putting it off didn't change anything."

"I know we were foolish, but we were afraid for her. We didn't know how to help her so we just hung on." Biting her lip, she looked at her friends. "And you're wrong; having her with us for a while did change things. It changed us." She nodded toward the women and Rachel. "All of us. Aggie, Leanne, and I had selfish reasons for keeping her, too. Rachel reminds us of things we've lost, *people* we've lost, because of our own mistakes. I guess giving her a taste of happiness seemed like a way to right past wrongs, at least a little."

She saw understanding in Cade's expression. Nodding toward the others, he smiled and said, "Come on. Let's make the most of the time that's left." Holding hands, they joined the group.

"Why did you take off like that?" Leanne was

asking Rachel. "Didn't you know you'd get caught again?"

The girl jerked her head in Cade's direction. "I heard what he said about those pictures and taking me back. So I *had* to leave Mia's." Tears bubbled up in her eyes again. "Not for me, for all of you." She looked at all the women. "I didn't want to get you in trouble."

As Aggie returned to the dining area, Rachel said, "I mean, you're the only ones who ever acted like you really love me, and all I did was cause you problems."

Aggie crossed to her. "You didn't cause us problems."

"Yes, I did. You and Leanne? You left your husbands. And Mia might get arrested, because . . ." she sniffed then cried harder. "Because you stuck out your necks for me."

Leanne blinked back tears of her own as she folded the girl into her arms.

"That's what you do for people you care about, honey," Mia said. "Stick out your neck to help them." She met Cade's warm gaze and held it.

"I made that up about having a real mom and dad," Rachel sobbed. "I don't even remember them. I'm sorry I lied."

Leanne hugged her tighter. "It's okay, Rachel. We all avoid the truth sometimes." She looked across at Eddie. "We all make mistakes."

Rachel held fast to Leanne and murmured, "I'm afraid."

"It'll be okay." Leanne stepped back, lifted Rachel's chin. "Just do what Cade says. He'll take care of you."

She pushed Rachel's hair back from her face. "Why don't you tell him what you told us?"

Over a breakfast of sweet rolls, milk, and coffee, Rachel told Cade about Pam Underhill's abuse, then Leanne relayed what the attorney had said. Taking notes, Cade questioned the girl about her life with the Underhills and took down the names of her witnesses.

While they talked, Mia watched Leanne leave them and lead Eddie across the room to another table. They pulled out two chairs and sat facing one another, their knees touching. As Leanne started to talk, Mia held her breath. Soon, Eddie spoke quietly, too. After several minutes of discussion, he pulled Leanne onto his lap. Over his shoulder, she blinked shining eyes at Mia.

When Mia turned away, she saw that Aggie and Roy had moved to another nearby table. She overheard their conversation.

"Aggie girl, I'm . . ." Roy cleared his throat.

"You're what, Roy?" Aggie's voice didn't waver.

He coughed. "I'm . . ."

Aggie crossed her arms. "Yes?"

"Damn it, woman." Roy's face flamed. "I'm sorry. There. I said it."

"You sure did, sugar." Leaning across the table, Aggie kissed her husband's ruddy, beard-stubbled cheek. "Now maybe it won't be as hard for you to spit out the other six or so apologies you need to make around town so that I can come home."

Puffing up, Roy rumbled, "You mean to tell me—"

"Starting with Buck Miller," Aggie interrupted,

lifting her chin. "And ending with poor Wayne Muncy over at the church."

When the clock struck six, Cade pushed away from the table, stood and cleared his throat. "It's time to go, Rachel."

Rachel stood and faced the women. "Thank you." Tears streamed down her face again. "If you hadn't found me, I don't know what would've happened to me."

Mia smiled. "You did as much for us as we did for you, honey." She glanced at the other two women. "More, really."

Aggie laughed through her tears. "Why, sugar, just look at me!" She swept a hand down her front. "Thanks to you, I'm a whole new woman!"

Rachel hugged each of them and, when she came to Leanne, she didn't let go. "I don't want to leave you," she whispered.

Leanne pressed her lips together tightly, fighting her emotions in an obvious effort to stay strong for Rachel's sake. "You won't go through this alone, Rachel. I'll come see you just as soon as they'll let me. I promise." She looked toward Eddie. Their eyes met. He nodded and smiled. "Eddie and I will both come."

At Cade's gentle urging, Leanne and Rachel stepped apart. Leanne held the girl's gaze. "I love you," she said clearly, as if she wanted to make certain Rachel had no doubts about what she'd heard.

Every ounce of fear drained from the girl's face. She smiled then said in a choked voice, "I love you, too."

Holding Rachel by the arm, Cade led her to the door then paused to look back at Mia. His eyes told her everything she needed to know.

For the first time in a long while, Mia felt certain that everything would turn out fine. Rachel would be okay. So would Leanne and Aggie.

And so would she.

Chapter 19

$\mathcal{R}$achel slept during most of the forty-five minute drive to Amarillo, giving Cade plenty of time to think. Though it was a Saturday morning, he had managed to reach Lynn Fellowes, Rachel's caseworker, by cell phone, and she had agreed to meet him at her office.

He decided the best approach to take with the woman was the one he had always used in the past: honesty. If the caseworker were a reasonable person, Rachel's story about her life with the Underhills would urge her to follow up the girl's claims by tracking down Lacy and Paula Oberman to get their testimony.

Cade would vouch for Mia's character, as well as for Aggie's and Leanne's. He would urge Miss Fellowes to speak with them, too, before deciding how to proceed. He hoped that, after meeting them and hearing what they had to say, the woman would realize they'd had good intentions, that they didn't deserve any legal reprimand, and that Rachel deserved another chance.

Just before they reached the city limits, Rachel

stirred. Cade waited until she seemed fully awake then said, "Mia believes in you, Rachel. So I will, too." He looked from her to the road and cleared his throat. "But I'm not going to lie to Miss Fellowes, and I don't want you to, either. I'd like to see you make a fresh start. If you tell the truth, I'll do whatever I can to help you stay out of a placement facility."

"Thanks," she said, sitting straighter, her eyes wide and vulnerable. "I won't lie to her."

"Good. Because if you mess up this chance, you won't get any more help from me. From here on out, you're going to have to show me and everyone else that you're ready to change your ways."

She nodded enthusiastically. "I will."

"You'll do whatever your caseworker says?"

"Yes, but—"

"No 'buts.' No backtalk, either. No attempts to run away again. And if they do place you with another family, no skipping school or drinking or doing drugs."

"Uh-uh." She shook her head. "I'd *never* take drugs."

"Good girl. And no more stealing. Promise?"

"I promise. I'll be good." When he eyed her long enough to make her squirm, she added, "I mean it. Really."

"Let's hope so. I'm holding you to it. Just toe the line and be honest and everything will eventually work out for the best." He focused on the road.

After a long stretch of silence, Rachel asked, "You think they might let me live with Leanne? She needs me. She and Eddie don't have any kids."

"I'm not sure that's an option." When her lower lip quivered slightly, Cade added, "We'll just have to see."

Lynn Fellowes already waited for them when they arrived at her office. Cade summed her up with a glance. Late thirties. No-nonsense mousy-brown hair, pulled straight back from her face. Stern eyes behind wire-rimmed glasses. Black pantsuit and sensible, low-heeled shoes. This woman was no pushover. He and Rachel might have some tough convincing to do.

Cade told her where Rachel had spent the past week, how she had run off last night when he came for her, about finding her this morning asleep in the back room of Betty's Beauty Shop.

Rachel filled in the rest when the caseworker questioned her. She tied up all the loose ends, explaining that she and the Underhills had fought and they locked her out, how she took money from their car glove compartment, how she'd hitched a ride with a trucker with no particular destination in mind. Rachel admitted to stealing from Jesse's Boutique and Mack's Grocery and told how Leanne, Aggie, and Mia had insisted she reimburse them. She explained that they loaned her the money then put her to work baking for the coffee shop and doing laundry. "It didn't feel like work, though," she admitted. "It was fun, and I learned a lot." Her eyes filled as she added, "Leanne was teaching me to sew, too. I guess we might not ever finish making my halter tops now, though."

The caseworker looked perplexed. "Didn't you and

the women know it was only a matter of time before you were discovered?"

"I guess I was, like, *pretending* I could stay there forever with them. I mean, it felt like home . . . like I belonged." Rachel blinked rapidly. "I never thought I could love somebody so fast, but I love all of them, and I think they all love me, too. They told me they'd have to turn me over to Sheriff Sloan sooner or later, but I think they were as afraid as me, so they just put it off."

She stared down at her hands, popped her knuckles, one by one. "They didn't treat me like everyone else does, you know?" Her voice quivered. "I kept hoping some miracle would happen or you and everybody else would forget about me and I'd get to stay."

Cade watched Miss Fellowes. Her unrelenting façade had slipped and, behind it, he glimpsed compassion. She was touched by Rachel's emotionally raw honesty, by her vulnerability and her obvious hunger to love and be loved.

The caseworker seemed to sense that he studied her. She met his gaze then quickly averted hers, covering her sympathy with professionalism again.

At Cade's request, Rachel told the woman about the Underhills' abuse while she lived with them. When the girl turned away from Cade to expose the few faint bruises still visible on her backside, Lynn Fellowes' eyes lifted to his and, this time, she didn't look away. In that silent exchange, Cade saw that Rachel had gained a fierce ally.

Rachel named Lacy and Paula Oberman as witnesses to Pam Underhill's abuse, and the caseworker jotted down the information.

When they finished, and Miss Fellowes led Rachel from the room, the girl paused at the door and glanced back at Cade. "Tell them all thanks again," she said. "And tell Leanne I'm waiting for her."

Her wide, dark eyes seemed to say *I'm counting on you.* Maybe that shouldn't matter to him, but it did. He felt an enormous responsibility toward her. Now Cade understood why Mia, Leanne, and Aggie had risked so much to protect the child. In the space of only a few hours, the girl had managed to find his soft spot.

On the drive home, Cade couldn't block out that image of Rachel walking away from him. So small and vulnerable. So fearful. So trusting of him.

Back in Muddy Creek, he headed straight to Jesse's Boutique, then to Mack's Grocery. He explained the situation and encouraged them not to press charges. They both agreed. Recently, they had received cash in the mail from her, they said, along with notes of apology for the thefts. They figured that was enough.

It was near closing time when he finally made it to the coffee shop. He found Mia pulling the red-checkered cloths from the tabletops. Aggie had gone home. Leanne rattled around in the kitchen.

Mia's face paled when he walked in. "It's done?"

He nodded. "I'll stay in touch with the people handling her case and give you a daily report."

Leanne pushed through the swinging doors, her eyes tired and concerned. "How was she?"

"A little scared, but okay. She said for me to tell

both of you thanks. Aggie, too. She told her case-worker she loves all of you."

They both teared up and Cade added to Leanne, "She told me to tell you she'd be waiting for you to come see her."

Leanne swiped at her eyes with her fingertips. "Eddie and I will go right now if you think they'll let us in."

"Why don't you wait until morning and give her caseworker a call? She looks and acts like a hard case, but after seeing those bruises, I think she's on our side one hundred percent."

Mia lowered herself into the nearest chair, a table-cloth bunched up in her lap. "What about us? Leanne, Aggie, and me."

Cade settled across the table from her and took off his hat. "What about you?"

"Are we in trouble?"

"I put in a good word for you. I'm sure Lynn Fel-lowes will want to talk to all of you. The police might, too. But, like I said, now that they know Rachel was abused, I think they'll focus most of their attention on the Underhills, not you three."

Mia tilted her head to one side and smiled. "Thanks for all you've done, Cade."

"It's all good. Don't worry about it. Like I told Rachel, if we all tell the truth, everything will eventu-ally work out for the best. I really believe that." He took her hand. "Have supper with me tonight."

"Aren't you tired of my company?"

He hoped his lingering look set her straight about that.

Mia blushed. "Sure. I'd love to."

Behind the counter, Leanne fanned her face and headed toward the back. "My, my. It's getting awful hot in here."

"Aggie still staying at your place?" Cade asked when Leanne stepped out of earshot.

"Nope. Roy spent the afternoon making rounds and eating crow."

"I would've paid good money to see that." With a laugh, he nodded toward the back room. "What about Leanne and Eddie?"

"They made up, too. They want to see about becoming Rachel's foster parents."

Cade knew how happy that would make Rachel. He was a little surprised at how happy it made him, too. "In that case, I'll go with them tomorrow to see Lynn Fellowes and make introductions," he said.

"Great idea."

He thumped his hat. "Where do you want to eat tonight?"

The light in her eyes warmed him all the way to his toes. "How about my place? I make the best chicken fried steak in town."

Sometimes wishes came true, Cade thought. This one had taken its sweet time.

He decided it had been well worth the wait.

Chapter 20

Two Months Later

March brought the usual topsy-turvy Texas Panhandle Spring to Muddy Creek. Warm, windy and sunny one day, overcast with snow flurries the next, rain the day after that. Life in the little town returned to normal in other ways, too.

With a few changes.

After the state renewed their foster parent credentials, Leanne and Eddie brought Rachel home. She started school and the threesome settled in together, eager to become a family. They spent their first few weekends decorating Rachel's bedroom. At Rachel's request, Eddie painted each wall a different color—purple, pink, blue, and yellow—while Leanne and Rachel sewed a bedspread and dust ruffle, as well as curtains for the windows. They squeezed in shopping trips for a new school wardrobe, during which Leanne couldn't resist buying herself a few new funky items of clothing, as well.

When the room was finished and Rachel's closet stuffed with clothes, she started working a couple of hours after school every day and on Saturday mornings at the Brewed Awakening.

Meanwhile, Aggie informed Roy that, come May, she'd be flying to Massachusetts to attend their twin granddaughters' high school graduation, whether he liked it or not. Money saved from her coffee shop wages would buy two plane tickets. Roy was welcome to join her, Aggie said, but with or without him, she would be boarding a plane.

Roy gruffly owned up to a white-knuckle terror of flying that, before, he had been too embarrassed to admit. Still, he agreed to face his fear and go along for the ride. He wasn't about to let her travel alone. Aggie's new red hair and recent loss of ten pounds made her resemble Shirley MacLaine. Men would be "hittin'" on her "left and right," Roy insisted.

As for Mia, she spent more and more time with Cade, and less time involved in mental conversations with Dan. Her husband had embraced life. He would not have wanted her to stop living because he died; she knew that.

But, though Dan was gone, Christy still lived.

Mia also knew that her life would never be truly complete until her daughter was part of it again. So she made calls that were never returned and wrote letters that didn't garner responses.

Mia persisted, prayed, and learned to be patient.

• • •

When the ten o'clock news ended, Cade turned off the television and Mia snuggled closer to him. They lay stretched out, side by side on the couch, Cade's front against her back, his arms around her. "I hate to break this up, but if I'm going to get up at the crack of dawn and go to work, I'd better head home for some shut-eye."

"Stay over tonight, okay?" Mia sounded half asleep already. "It's supposed to get cold again." Her bare toes wiggled against his ankle.

"So I'm only a bed warmer to you now, is that it?"

The throaty texture of her laughter made him forget about sleep. "I can think of worse things to be," she said.

"You've got that right." Cade nuzzled her neck. *Like alone in bed without you.* "If I stay, the whole town will be abuzz about us tomorrow. You okay with that?"

"Your truck's in the garage."

"That's never fooled Buck Miller before. Or Aubrey Ricketts. I'd have to leave your house before four-thirty in the morning to slip past him."

Mia yawned. "Let them talk. I don't care anymore."

Cade smiled. Without suspicions and secrets between them, their relationship had quickly blossomed into something they'd both hoped for, but hadn't dared to expect—love. A second chance at happiness. They had been cautious at first. But when life handed you a gift, you took it and held on tight.

Mia told him, time and again, his love was enough, all she needed to be content the rest of her life.

Cade knew better.

Though she never mentioned it, he knew she had tried every night for the past month to reach Christy by phone. Christy never answered or returned the calls. Mia wrote countless letters to her daughter's last known address in New York City. Since the letters didn't come back in the mail, Cade assumed the girl received them, but she didn't write back.

So Cade had taken it upon himself to do a little investigative work on the side. He found out the name of the restaurant in New York where Christy waited tables. He didn't tell Mia, though. He hoped to give her one more gift.

"Twist my arm," Cade said. "Maybe I'll stay."

Mia shifted to face him, snuggled so close that an ant couldn't squeeze between them, pressed a slow, sultry kiss against his lips. She teased and taunted him, promising more to come with a whisper and a sigh.

"Okay," he murmured against her mouth. "If you insist. I'll stay."

She laughed. "I never had a doubt."

"I need something to remember you by since I'm leaving town in a couple of days," he joked.

"You're leaving?" She leaned away from him, looked up into his face.

"That law enforcement conference in Austin, remember?"

"That's right." Mia brushed her lips across his again. "I'll miss you."

"I'll miss you, too. How about I bring you back a surprise?"

Her eyes sparkled. "I love surprises."

On the Saturday Cade was in Austin, Mia drove to Brister to spend the day with Brent, Sherry and the grandkids. She took presents. Spoiling her son's children was one of the very best things about being a grandparent. Mia loved their laughter, loved seeing how much they'd grown.

When she and Brent had a moment alone, he asked her about her relationship with Cade. Brent was her direct child. He saw no point in subtlety. If he wanted to know something, he asked, and always had.

"What's up with you and the sheriff, Mom?" Brent handed her an iced tea then sat in the lawn chair beside hers, where she watched the children jump on the backyard trampoline. "I called your house the other day and he answered. You weren't even home."

Mia studied her oldest son. Six foot three inches, two hundred pounds of solid muscle. And still her baby. He didn't know that, though. When Dan died, Brent took on the role of protector in her life. She loved him for it, though he sometimes drove her crazy with his worries.

"Cade didn't tell me you called. I guess he forgot."

"So?" Brent prodded.

"I told you and your brother that Cade and I are dating."

"The man hangs out at your house while you're at

work. He answers your phone." Brent frowned. "You ask me, that indicates you've moved past the dating stage."

"Cade doesn't *hang out* at my house." Mia's stomach fluttered. "He was fixing the toilet."

Brent scowled. "A man doesn't volunteer to fix a woman's toilet without ulterior motives."

Mia sipped her tea and avoided his eyes. She didn't want her sons to resent Cade, to view him as a threat to Dan's memory. She wanted them to accept him. The thought of anything tarnishing this unexpected bright spot in her life was unacceptable. Mia loved her kids, but she would not allow them to force her to choose between them and Cade.

She took a deep breath. "We're serious."

Brent lowered his glass. "Marriage serious?"

"For the moment we're happy to take one day at a time."

Behind her son's solemn expression, she glimpsed the rambunctious little boy who had given her so much joy while running her ragged. "You're happy?" he asked.

"Very."

Nothing could have surprised Mia more than the tears she saw glistening in his eyes. Setting his tea glass down on the bricked patio beside his chair, Brent leaned over and hugged her.

Her entire body exhaled, leaving behind the gentlest sense of peace. "I hope Trey is as accepting of this as you are," she said, pulling back.

"He is. We've talked."

Mia nodded, looked down at her lap. "You haven't heard from Christy, have you?"

"No, Mom. Sorry. If she contacted anyone, it would be Trey, and he hasn't talked to her in months. We've both tried, though."

Sherry stuck her head out the back door. "Lunch is ready," she called.

Mia smiled at her daughter-in-law. "Sorry I didn't help. Sign me up for dishwashing duty after we eat."

"You just relax and enjoy the kids," Sherry said.

At the sound of her mother's voice, five-year-old Lindsey climbed off the trampoline, ran over and grabbed Mia in a bear hug. "Whoa there, sweetie!" Mia scooped the girl up. "You've gotten so big you almost knocked your poor grandmother over." When six-year-old Alex joined them, Mia took both kids' hands and stood. "Come on. Let's see what your mother cooked up for us."

On the way back to Muddy Creek later that afternoon, Mia stopped at a shop in Amarillo where, a week ago, she'd left four pieces of Christy's artwork to be matted and framed. She stacked the two sketches and two paintings on the seat beside her, resisting the urge to tear off the brown paper wrappers and peek.

Once home, she ate a bowl of soup for supper then poured a glass of wine. She carried it into the living room, put the Carole King *Tapestry* CD Cade had given her into the player, then sat on the couch. The frames lay on the coffee table. One by one, Mia un-wrapped them.

Lovely. Incredible. Unique.

No word seemed adequate to describe what she saw. The matting and frames she had chosen only added to the beauty of Christy's work. The "bruised heart," as Rachel had called it. The haunted eyes of the disappearing girl, lost in a swarm of people.

Hope and pride brought a familiar ache to Mia's throat. She held on to what her heart told her: Some day, she and Christy would reunite. She would win back her daughter's love. It was only a matter of time.

Aggie finally had a second chance to be a grand-mother.

Leanne had a second chance to be a mother.

Surely, Mia thought, God would grant her a second chance with Christy.

As she had done so many times before, Mia studied each painting, each sketch, memorizing every detail, every stroke.

Soon, Christy would come home again. When that day arrived, she would find her artwork on the living room wall alongside her brothers' photographs in their sports uniforms and graduation gowns.

Mia held the sketch of the vanishing girl to her chest and whispered, "I see you, honey. And I'm so proud of you."

In her mind, she heard Rachel's voice saying, *If my*

mom was alive, I'd want to see her. Even if I pretended I didn't. Mia hoped Christy felt the same.

She would find her daughter and ask for forgiveness. Maybe, like Mia, Christy yearned for a new beginning.

Chapter 21

$\mathcal{T}$he early morning rush subsided, leaving behind echoes of gossip, the scents of sweet roll crumbs and leftover coffee. As customers headed for work and school, the shop quieted. The Coots parted ways, off to their various daily activities.

Mia straightened the tables, and Aggie wiped down the counter and workstation while humming along with Patsy Cline.

"Did I tell you the twins called last night?"

Mia loved the perkiness in Aggie's voice. "Really? What're they up to these days?"

"They said they're excited their grandpa and I are coming for their graduation. Jimmy and Sheila are having a dinner party after the ceremony to celebrate. They wanted to know if we like Italian. I lied and said yes."

"You don't?"

"I do," Aggie said. "Roy says the pasta served at fancy Italian cafes is nothin' but dressed-up spaghetti."

Mia laughed. "I'm happy for you, Ag. You're going to have so much fun."

One of Aggie's brows arched over the top of her red reading glasses. " 'Course Jimmy or Sheila probably told the girls to call, but it's a start."

The front door opened and Leanne walked in. "Sorry I'm late. Had to run the packrat's books up to the school again. Second time this week. If that kid's head wasn't attached, I swear she'd forget it, too."

Leanne's smile stayed firmly in place as she strolled across the dining room then through the swinging doors to the kitchen. It did Mia's heart good to see her friend so happy. Eddie, too.

After a few weeks of adjustment, Rachel hit her stride at Muddy Creek High. The smaller atmosphere suited her. The girl had told Leanne that she felt like a "somebody" there.

Duh, Mia thought with a smile. Muddy Creek's schools didn't often see a new student. Rachel was a novelty, and all the kids were anxious to get to know her better. Of course, the fact that she was a "city kid" didn't hurt, either. Rachel knew every trendy clothing style, and Leanne made sure they hung in the girl's closet.

Again, the doorbell jingled. Mia glanced up.

Cade stood on the welcome mat, wearing an ear-to-ear smile beneath his Stetson.

"You're home!" Mia met him halfway and threw her arms around his neck. Snatching off his hat, she tossed it atop the nearest table. She didn't care that

Aggie watched them, or that the squeak of the swinging door hinges meant Leanne was up front again, too. "I thought you weren't due back until tonight."

When she stepped away from him, Cade said, "I finished up sooner than I expected and caught an earlier flight."

The curious light in his eyes accelerated the pace of Mia's heartbeat. Something was up. "How was Austin?"

"I didn't go to Austin, Mia. I went to New York City."

"New York? But the conference—"

"There wasn't a conference."

"Then what?" Her heart dipped. Mia looked into his eyes and knew the truth.

Cade pulled an envelope from his pocket, handed it to her and said quietly, "Here's that surprise I promised you."

Gripping the table's edge, Mia sat. She couldn't speak; she could barely breathe. Dizzy with anticipation, she glanced across the room to where Aggie and Leanne stood behind the counter, side by side. In their faces, she saw the same hope and nervousness she felt.

The envelope shook in Mia's hand. She looked at it, opened the flap, pulled a card from inside it: an engraved invitation to an art exhibit in New York City next month.

As she scanned the featured artists' names, Mia's breath caught. "Christine MacAfee," she whispered. "Oh, Cade."

Tears welled in her eyes as she read the words scrawled across the bottom in her daughter's handwriting.

Mom, I'd love for you to come.
I love you,
Christy.

*When love is just around the corner,
you can't be over the hill!*

The Red Hat Society brings together
women across the world for friendship, fun,
and laughs. Now, there's a new treat—
official Red Hat Society novels about
companionship, adventure,
and love over 50.

THE RED HAT SOCIETY'S
ACTING THEIR AGE
(0-446-61674-5)

THE RED HAT SOCIETY'S
QUEENS OF WOODLAWN AVENUE
(0-446-61675-3)

THE RED HAT SOCIETY'S
DOMESTIC GODDESS
(0-446-61676-1)

Don't miss out on these red-hot romances!

Available from Warner Books
wherever books are sold.

FOR PASSIONATE ROMANCE
AND HEART-TUGGING EMOTION,
NOBODY DOES IT LIKE

SUSAN CRANDALL

ON BLUE FALLS POND
(0-446-61639-7)
"An up-and-coming star."
—KAREN ROBARDS

PROMISES TO KEEP
(0-446-61411-4)
"FOUR STARS!"
—*Romantic Times BOOKclub Magazine*

MAGNOLIA SKY
(0-446-61410-6)
"Emotionally charged . . . engrossing."
—*BookPage*

THE ROAD HOME
(0-446-61226-X)
"A terrific story."
—RomRevToday.com

BACK ROADS
(0-446-61225-1)
"A wonderful read, don't miss it!"
—SUSAN WIGGS, national bestselling author

At a bookstore near you, from Warner Books.